# After the Wind

## A LOVE STORY

By Jaclyn M. Hawkes

# After the Wind

## A LOVE STORY

Spirit
Dance
Books

After The Wind A love story
By Jaclyn M. Hawkes
Copyright © September 2014  Jaclyn M. Hawkes
All rights reserved.
Published and distributed by Spirit Dance Books.  Spiritdancebooks.com
855-648-5559
Cover design by Roland Ali Pantin

Printed in USA
First Printing September 2014
LOC
ISBN: 0-9851648-8-1
ISBN-13: 978-0-9851648-8-1

# Acknowledgements

Thanks to all the people who either helped me get this book together, or helped me keep the rest of my life together while I got this book together.

Mostly, thanks to my family for their patience while I try to juggle all the balls. Especially, thanks to my nearly perfect husband. He is absolutely the wind beneath my wings.

# Dedication

This book is dedicated to all the teenagers of the world—particularly the ones I call my own. They are the most marvelous creatures and I truly believe they are those strongest-and-best-saved-for-last spoken of in the scriptures. (Don't tell anyone, but they are definitely the secret weapon that is going to save the world from the idiot politicians in these troubled times. Just wait and see.)

This book is also dedicated to my husband, who sometimes thinks he is still a teenager. Like the hero in this book, he has perfected the fine balance between being nice and being powerful. That is an incredibly attractive thing!

# Prologue: Eastern Kansas

Kristin Kelsey drove the straight, flat road toward home and her husband's nursery without consciously thinking about it. Her mind was occupied with checking the errands she'd just accomplished off her list and thinking about what else she had to do this morning.

She finally saw the house in the distance and was mentally planning the rest of her day as she pulled up the road, past the rows and rows of Ryan's greenhouses, to her own perfectly landscaped house and yard. As an award winning landscape architect, Ryan made sure the yard was a showplace of color and design and always groomed to perfection.

Kristin glanced at the propane truck that was delivering a load of propane to the tank behind the house as she pulled around the drive, but her attention was drawn to her husband and three tiny daughters who were apparently getting ready to grill their lunch on the outdoor barbecue on the back deck.

The girls' shiny blonde heads glistened in the sun, their curls bouncing as they walked her direction in their matching sundresses. She smiled at four year old Enika struggling to cross the lawn carrying her baby sister Anna in her best careful, responsible way, as two year old Amy toddled at her heels. The three of them were Kristin's pride and joy. After Enika's birth, Kristin had put her career as a physical therapist on hold and her girls had become her very life. She'd never dreamed motherhood would be so incredibly satisfying to her. Getting out of the car, she walked toward them, marveling one more time at how beautiful they were.

That thought suddenly shattered as the very earth beneath her feet detonated into a shocking hell of violent, excruciating sound and pain and horror, and her entire universe disintegrated in an unbelievably huge explosion. The picture of peace and beauty and harmony she'd been marveling at erupted into a maelstrom of flames, smoke, and flying debris, the splintering kaleidoscope of color a nightmarish contrast to the searing, soul-deep horror that swallowed her as she saw her three girls violently thrown by the ferocious blast.

The force of it knocked Kristin across the yard as well, and in the ensuing cataclysm of smoke and falling pieces of debris, it took several seconds before she had enough air to scream out her horror and shock at watching her little girls be so suddenly and brutally taken from sweet, happy, innocent life into tragic, mutilated death. In the space of an instant her world as she knew it was blown into ragged, smoking, bloody pieces, and what had been her three small, energetic children were now silent, lifeless bodies.

Then within only several seconds, as the last of the flying bits rained down in a final deluge of complete and utter destruction, the light breeze began to blow the cloud of smoke and dust off to the east. It was as if Mother Nature didn't understand the absolute devastation that had just overturned the axis of Kristin's world.

In the eerie silence that followed, broken only by her own cries, she tried to get to her daughters, not entirely realizing that the reason she was having trouble reaching them was because she herself had been all but fatally wounded in the blast, the pain in her heart and mind far overpowering the excruciating pain from her injuries. It wasn't until later that she realized Ryan, too, had been instantly and permanently taken from her life.

Literally dragging herself across the lawn, she fought to where the broken and bloody little bodies lay in the midst of the burning rubble and she tried to tenderly hold them to her.

She knew they were dead. Had known it instantly when everything exploded. She had no idea what had just happened, but she knew her daughters were dead.

Her screams subsided into sobs as she got near them. The innate motherly instinct in her stifled the screams that she knew would have frightened her sweet babies. She reached to straighten the tatters of their little sundresses and brush back the fine, soft hair, trying to ignore the ghastly, mortal wounds the two older girls had sustained. Baby Anna had somehow been spared of much obvious devastation. Except for one tiny arm and some black smudges, she looked like she had simply closed her eyes and gone to sleep.

Kristin pulled them toward her as gently as she could and held them desperately, sobbing uncontrollably. Her mind didn't register anything else except the three little bodies in her arms. Her grief and horror had somehow shut her psyche away in a dark and silent place and there was only a desperate, choking, blinding pain that slowly drained away into unconsciousness.

Jaclyn M. Hawkes

# Chapter 1

## Six month's after the explosion:

Post traumatic stress disorder was what they kept telling her. And that eventually, she would be okay. Often, they even shortened it to an acronym that seemed to almost mock what had happened to her universe. PTSD was a politically correct, but utterly frustrating term they all seemed to think would miraculously fix the complete devastation of her life. She'd begun to believe that all psychologists were somewhat delusional. Even the surgeons seemed to think she should be over it all by now and that if no one said anything, it was all neatly handled and behind them.

And what did okay mean? Time had gone by, but her whole family was still just as gone. The nightmares hadn't gotten one iota better and her days had gotten marginally better only because she was learning to channel her thoughts by sheer force of will. Even her leg where it had been ripped apart by flying metal was still horribly sore and weak when she was tired, in spite of the past months of intensive physical therapy. At least she believed it would eventually regain its strength because of her background as a physical therapist herself.

That part of her life had changed as well. After these last months of struggling through two surgeries and both physical and emotional therapy, she didn't want to work in a hospital anymore. There was too much death and heartache there. It was strange that she hadn't ever noticed that before. Before . . . before all the people she loved most dearly had been killed.

At least she could finally try to face that brutal fact in her head when she was awake. Awake she could purposefully make her mind only slightly touch on that reality and then think of something else. But the nights were still unbearable.

# Chapter 2

Two years after the explosion:  In the mountains near the Idaho-Wyoming line.

Joe Faciano listened to his sons trying to yodel and it made him laugh.  They were trying to mimic an old fashioned cowboy song as they rode horses along the ridgeline, but they sounded more like adolescent donkeys with laryngitis.

He looked all around him and breathed deeply of the cool mountain air.  He was glad they had come on this vacation together.  He knew he had a better relationship with his boys than most dads did, simply because he spent more time with them than a lot of dads could, but it was good to get away into the wilds as a family from time to time.  There was something about the mountains that felt right.  It almost felt more like coming home than actually going home did.  Phoenix, their real home, was a world away from these pristine peaks and lush valleys.

He looked ahead to their trail guide.  Even from the back she was beautiful.  Her long, blonde hair glistened in the mountain sunshine like it was made of spun corn silk.  Watching her ride ahead of them made him feel like a young man again, instead of a thirty-seven year old, father of three, business man.

It had been twelve years since his wife had walked out when his youngest son Gabriel was only two weeks old. Since then, he'd admitted that part of her leaving had been his fault because he'd failed to understand either post-partum depression or how alone she'd felt. He'd tried to make it up to her by sending her a check every month. And for all these years, he had been content to focus on the boys and let his own social life go. But there was something about Kristin that had him riding horses with her for the third day in a row.

He was finally seriously considering getting an official divorce and moving on romantically. When he was away from her next week, that thought would fade and he would be content again. At least he hoped so. It was hard to tell. She was the only woman in twelve years who had made him feel that way.

In the back of his mind, he knew he would never do it. It was bad enough that the boys had only one parent. He wasn't going to mess them up even more by focusing on his own selfish needs. Thank goodness for Gram, the nanny/grandmother he'd had the marvelous good fortune to find shortly after his wife left. Not only had she helped him raise his sons, she had also helped him to understand that his wife had been sick. Gram had helped Joe find himself as well. Without her, they would never have survived.

Still, Kristin was incredibly intriguing. She was beautiful, and fun, and dynamic, and had the most musical laugh he had ever heard as she joked around with his boys. She had a way of having a great time, but yet knowing when to be still and let the quiet of the wilderness seep into their very souls.

She had an absolutely engaging personality, but there was something about her. Something in her eyes that made him wonder if somewhere in the past she hadn't faced the deepest of sadness, and had never truly gotten past it. It was an impression that made him want to find out more about her and somehow wipe that shadow away.

****

The next week when he was away from her, he talked himself out of the whole divorce idea, but he couldn't get Kristin out of his mind for long. There was something almost haunting about her that lingered with him.

Jaclyn M. Hawkes

# Chapter 3

## Three and a half years after the explosion: Grand Targhee ski resort, Wyoming

Joe watched the ski instructor in the lift line in front of him handle her rebellious student with a style that was admirable. She turned to the youth. "Either the helmet stays on, Jeremy, or I'm going to kick you out of class and you'll have to tell your dad he paid all that money for you to sit in the lodge and watch the rest of us ski."

The spoiled Jeremy snapped back, "You can't kick me out of class! My lesson is already paid for, and there's no way you can make me wear this stupid helmet!" With that, the out-of-control youth tossed his helmet aside and skied forward in the ski school lift line. The rest of the skiers in the line were watching with interest as well, wondering just what the instructor with the long, blonde braid hanging out of the back of her own helmet would do.

With no hesitation, she skied forward to the lift attendant and said, "Chuck, don't let this kid on. Take his pass. If he gives you any static have security handle him and then call me and I'll phone his dad's cell. He can go pick him up in the security office." With that the instructor loaded onto the lift with her three other students and for a minute didn't even look back.

Finally, she turned around and shouted, "If you change your mind about the helmet, Jeremy, I'll pick you up on the next run. If not, it was nice to meet you." She turned back around and rode the lift without another glance at the grouching youth. Joe made a mental note then and there to request her for the duration of his boys' lessons. She was just the kind of person he wanted teaching his kids.

For the rest of that day, he kept his eyes open for her, which wasn't hard because she had a distinctive, bright purple helmet cover that had spikes like a jester's hat, and the resort was relatively small. He could hear her clear across the runs sometimes, shouting encouragement and laughing with her students. It was impossible to see her face in her helmet and goggles and uniform, but she obviously had a great personality!

As the lifts closed for the day, he went back into the ski school office and made arrangements for his sons' lessons for the next two weeks. When he tried to tell the director who he was requesting, the man knew exactly who he was asking for and smiled his approval. "Oh, yeah. Kristin, in that funny hat. She's definitely the best! Not only is she a great teacher, but the kids love her. She has a gift with the teenagers. I think you'll be very pleased."

Joe was pleased. His boys were everything to him, and he left the ski school office looking forward to the good time they would have skiing. For now though, he had to face the daunting task of getting moved into the house he had just purchased here. It hadn't been available to move into until late today, so they'd been spending the last couple days in the lodge of the resort. Hopefully, the movers and furniture delivery people would have everything unloaded and put into the correct rooms by the time they got there this afternoon, but they'd still have a ton of unpacking to do to get settled in. Then, he was going to let them take a couple of weeks off before they had to start back into school again.

He'd lived his entire life in the greater Phoenix area, but a few months ago he'd decided to make some drastic changes and had let the boys weigh in on where they'd like to relocate to. They had unanimously opted for someplace in the mountains. They weren't terribly picky about where, so Joe had done some research on where he thought would be a healthy, safe place to raise three teenaged boys and they'd ended up here in the mountains of southeastern Idaho, nearly on the border of Wyoming, in the little town of Driggs. They'd been here a few times on vacation and had loved it in both winter, and in the summer when they had ridden horses in the mountains here.

Joe hoped it would be a place where his boys could grow into adulthood with as few bumps in the road as possible. He didn't worry too much about seventeen year old Robby. He was so responsible and obedient that Joe hoped he was past the point of too much trouble, but fifteen year old Caleb was still testing the fences and fourteen year old Gabriel flat out worried him sometimes. He was the reason Joe had finally decided to take an extended break from work and pull up stakes. Gabriel had been suffering from depression for awhile before Joe recognized it, but even after recognizing it, he'd been completely blindsided when his youngest son had tried to kill himself with an overdose a couple of months ago. Needless to say, it had rocked Joe's whole world.

So Joe had hired a replacement administrator for the hospital he ran and was the major shareholder for in Phoenix, and had moved to Idaho. Or had almost moved. He had to finish moving this weekend.

****

Her own screams woke her up again. When she was awake enough to get control of herself, she lay there in the dark trying to blank her mind of the horrific images she'd been reliving, and tried to slow her heart rate. She untangled the sheets from around her sweaty legs and stretched to try to work the painful cramps from her muscles. Sitting up in bed, she pulled her knees up in front of her and hid her face and her tears. Even after three and a half years, the sadness that followed the horror was overwhelming.

Knowing it was hopeless to try to take her mind off the recurring nightmare and memories without getting up and doing something strenuous, she got out of bed, changed into her swim suit and went into the pool house attached to the back of her house and began to swim laps. She saw Murdock come by the glass wall between the pool house and the house to check on her. His presence helped her to focus and work toward some semblance of peace. She swam until her breath came in ragged gasps, but this time at least it wasn't from horrible nightmares and heartbreak.

When she was exhausted, she got out and dressed in warm gear, called to her black lab Teal, picked up her snowshoes and went out the back door. She crossed the yard on a well traveled trail and then let herself out the far gate. The moon on the snow made it light enough even without her light and she hiked up the trail that wound into the National Forest. It was 5:30 in the morning and bitterly cold, but she knew from three and a half years of experience now that sleep wouldn't return. The last years had made her nearly as comfortable in the dark as she was the day because she had spent the nights trying to escape from the images in her mind.

As she walked, she thought about her life. After all this time, the nightmares had only gotten marginally better. She'd tried everything from sleeping pills to hypnosis, to acupuncture to try to stop them. She'd done everything she knew of to remove herself from the time and place and memories as far as she could. She'd put away all the photos, sold the property and nursery, and moved as far from the flats of Kansas as possible. She'd even changed her last name back to her maiden name, hoping it would help to ease the pain.

After the explosion that had destroyed her life, it had taken more than six months just to recover from her physical injuries. She'd almost bled to death before help had arrived that day, and then she'd been through two surgeries and months and months of rehab to repair the damage done by the chunks of metal from the propane tanker that had hit her in the thigh.

On the day they'd buried her husband and her beautiful, sweet daughters in a combined grave, she'd been fighting for her life in the intensive care unit.

The propane company had given her a huge settlement to try to somehow make up for the loss of her family, but even though the money was something, she'd almost given up hope that she would ever get far enough over it to be able to actually sleep through a whole night. She'd finally decided that nothing could ever heal the scars on her mind, and had moved here into the mountains in a house almost completely away from people, and hired a retired policeman and his wife to come and live with her. They were the only ones in Idaho who knew anything about her past, and mostly they only knew enough to know that the nightly horrors were a regular occurrence and if not normal, at least they were to be expected.

She wasn't crazy. She knew that now, but it had taken her a long time to stop wondering. She was just hopelessly scarred emotionally. She had no doubt that the few people in the area who knew anything about her thought she had gone over the brink, but she was doing the best she knew how and had somehow managed to survive this long.

The days she could handle. Wide awake, and in the light of day, she had learned to control her thoughts enough to live a relatively normal life. In the summers, she took trail rides on horses up in the mountains for a local resort company and in the winter she taught skiing at nearby Grand Targhee Mountain Resort. Her day jobs were the only way she could survive the solitary life she was stuck in. She loved working with the teenagers, and as long as she steered clear of really little girls, she was okay. At least as okay as a woman who woke up every single night of her life having horrible nightmares could be.

Nothing helped the nights.

As the sky in the east began to lighten, she snowshoed back into her yard and wearily headed for a hot shower and breakfast.

****

Joe was up sitting in front of the fire, still surrounded with unpacked boxes and with their chocolate lab Hershey at his feet. He had just picked up his cup of hot cocoa when he happened to look out the window and glimpse what looked like a woman snowshoeing down a trail in the woods behind his house in the gray light of predawn. He did a double take, thinking he had to be seeing things. Who snowshoed in the dark, in the frigid wee hours of the morning? He was almost tempted to train the spotting scope they'd set up the day before to see if he was really seeing what he thought he was. He'd explained at length to his boys that it was only for spotting wildlife, and that looking at people was unethical, so he had to abide by his own rules, but he was tempted.

A couple of the locals had mentioned that his only neighbor was a little peculiar, but when he'd asked the real estate agent she'd laughed and brushed off any concern. He drank his cocoa, not really sure what to think, and relaxed in front of the flames for a quiet hour before he went to wake the boys for church. It was the first day in their new ward and he was hoping to make a good impression, both on the locals and on his sons.

The next morning when he dropped his boys off with the new ski instructor, he told the boys to have fun and behave themselves. As they skied off toward the lift, to the instructor he said, "Please don't let the youngest one out of your sight."

He free skied by himself that morning, keeping an eye out to see how the boys seemed to be doing with the new teacher. They were all good, solid intermediate skiers and he felt like they were having a good time when he talked to them at lunch. He must have been right, because when he picked them up that afternoon at four o'clock they were all ecstatic about what a great ski day they'd had. It was going to be really nice living here. If he ever got finished moving in, that is.

Jaclyn M. Hawkes

# Chapter 4

Kristin took charge of her new ski students with a positive attitude.  These three brothers seemed like well behaved, happy kids and even the father's last minute caution not to let the youngest one out of her sight, didn't dampen her spirits.  She recalled that she had guided these guys on a few horseback rides a year or two ago in the summer.  She truly enjoyed teenagers and felt like it was going to be a fun day.

They were only halfway up the first lift ride when she decided to just come right out and ask what she was up against.  It sometimes helped to be well informed.  The two other brothers were on the double chair in front of her and she was riding with Gabriel, the youngest brother and had already been small talking about where they were from when she casually asked him, "Why did your dad tell me not to let you out of my sight?"

She was more than a little taken aback, although she tried not to let it show, when he answered, "Because I tried to do something really stupid a couple of months ago.  I tried to kill myself."  His big brown eyes under a lock of dark, almost curly hair were frank and honest as he said it.

She looked back at him and said, "That would definitely make a father a little cautious.  Life is incredibly precious.  And all too fragile sometimes.  Would you pull something like that again?"

He gave her a shy, embarrassed smile.  "Heck no!  Are you kidding?  I've never been so sick!  It was awful!  Not to mention the fact that now he feels like I can never be alone again for the rest of my life. I'll be living that one down for like, forever."

With a grin she returned, "It's terrible to be so cared about. You poor soul." She elbowed him gently. "He seems like a wonderful father who cares deeply for you."

"Yeah." He looked down at his snowy skis. "You never have to wonder where he stands. We always know he loves us. That's for sure. He loves me, but he thinks I'm crazy, too."

In her head, she wondered why he would say something like that, but aloud she mused, "I don't really think there's too much crazy in this world. Mostly, I think there's just a lot of mixed up." Her voice held a sad note.

He thought about that for a minute, and finally said, "I think you're right. There mostly is a lot of mixed up."

"Did he tell you he thought you were crazy? Or do you just get that impression?"

"When he brought me home from the hospital afterward, he said that what I did was crazy."

She hesitated, trying to say the right thing, "Do you know what I'll bet? I'll bet he used the word crazy when what he really meant was that what you did was foolish. Sometimes even parents make mistakes."

After thinking for another few minutes, he replied, "Maybe you're right. It was foolish. I know that now. At the time, I thought it would make me stop being so sad. In a way it did. I take some medicine now that helps me feel better."

"What were you sad about?"

"Everything. Or nothing. I don't even know, really. It all started when I found out that my mother ran away and left us when I was two weeks old. I realized I must have been pretty much unlovable for her to do that. I mean little babies

20

are so cute. I must have been extra bad for her to walk away and never come back. After that, it just kept getting worse and worse. I know exactly what you mean by mixed up. I can tell you."

She faced him. "Gabriel, when a mother runs away and leaves a two week old baby behind, it's not that something is wrong or unlovable with the baby. It just means the mom is really sick and needs to get some help. There's nothing the slightest bit unlovable about you. You're adorable!"

She put her arm around him and squeezed. "You're mom was just sick, buddy. It's sad, but sometimes it happens to women after they have babies. It's called post-partum depression. Somehow, the mother's body gets all the chemicals in her brain all screwed up and she gets sad or does strange things like run away. It's just a matter of getting the chemicals back in balance. Apparently, your mom didn't get hers figured out. It's too bad. She really missed out. You and your brothers are great kids." She smiled her thanks to the lift guys and bopped Gabriel on the helmet as they got off the lift.

They skied hard and laughed and had a rowdy, happy run, but about half way up the lift again, Gabriel sobered and admitted to her, "I know who you are. You're the lady in the house next door. I saw you when you pulled in on Saturday through our spotting scope. Don't tell my dad, though. He told us about ten times that we weren't to use the scope to look at people. Just animals."

She was surprised. "Really? You're the ones who bought that house? That'll be great to have you guys as neighbors!" She smiled and whispered, "Don't worry. Your secret's safe with me." But she felt like she had to add, "But your dad is right. Looking at people through the scope is like being a Peeping Tom. You know, someone who looks in people's windows. Nice people don't do that."

"You sound exactly like my dad. Well, only his voice is lower." He gave her a guilty smile. "You're the horseback riding guide too, aren't you?" After another minute, he added in an almost questioning tone, "Some of the people around here said our neighbor is a crazy, old hermit lady."

She looked him in the eye and asked, "Do you think I'm crazy?" He shook his head.

"I don't think I'm crazy either, but sometimes I'm definitely mixed up." The smile didn't quite reach her eyes.

"Why do you live all alone up in that big house?"

She patted his knee. "I don't live alone. I actually have a friend and his wife who live with me and work for me. I live away from people mostly so I don't bother them." He looked steadily at her for a minute, but didn't ask her what she meant and she left it at that.

It was a great day of skiing and they had a ball. She tried to teach them and at the same time encourage them to have fun and they all spent the day laughing. Caleb was having a harder time of it than the other boys, but she honestly attributed that to the fact that he couldn't see where he was going very well through his long hair that kept hanging down in his face. Even with his helmet on, it would block his vision a good portion of the time and she made a mental note to bring him a barrette the next day.

At lunch time, she skied them back to the lodge and left them to eat with their dad. "Meet back here at one, ready to go! You'd better eat well; you're going to need your energy!" With that, she skied off to have a little time to herself.

She'd been serious, and she skied them hard enough that afternoon that she knew they'd sleep well that night. Just before the end of their class, she swooped down on the three of them and sprayed them with a thick coating of snow and then took off, shouting over her shoulder, "Ski fast! That's the rule!" By the time they reached the lift line, they were laughing almost uncontrollably. She teased them as she dropped them back off with their father. She'd been right. They were great kids.

****

Joe was pleased to see the boys so upbeat when he picked them up. Even Gabriel, who had become more mellow over the last few months, was laughing and joined in telling the funny stories of the day over dinner. Several times they mentioned that they wished Joe could ski with them so he could see how much fun she was.

He finally did perk up and think about visiting with her when they mentioned that she was the same young woman who had taken them on all the horseback rides a year and a half ago. Knowing it was the same Kristin was interesting. There had been something incredibly intriguing about her to him then, and he wondered if he would still feel the same if he was ever around her again. It was almost a little frightening that he might be. He wasn't sure if he even wanted to go there. For all these years he'd felt he should focus only on his sons, but she had been fascinating.

That night, late, when he'd gotten up to get a drink, he was surprised to see lights on in the little cabin on the hill behind his neighbor's house, and he could see a fire burning in the fireplace clear from here. He glanced at the bedside clock and realized it was after three-thirty. The lights had all been out when he'd gone to bed at a little after ten-thirty. What were they doing up over there at this hour? Maybe the locals had been right. Sometimes his neighbor did seem a little strange.

Through breakfast and on the short drive to the resort, the boys continued to pester him to come and meet with Kristin, their instructor, so this time as he dropped them off, he stayed for a few minutes to talk to her before they left to ski. They were right; she was the same woman who had been their incredibly intriguing horseback riding guide in this same area the summer before last. It was a little hard to recognize her in her helmet and goggles, but once she took them off there was no doubt. She was still as beautiful as she had been then, and he'd been right to worry that she would be as attractive to him now as she'd been before. She definitely was.

Walking away from her as they left to ski, he headed for home to work at settling into his new house again and wondered at the strange fact that in fourteen years there had only been one woman who had made him want to be with her. When they'd gotten back to Phoenix after the horseback riding, he had eventually talked himself into believing it had just been a strange mood or something that had made him think she was so fascinating. But it had only taken a few moments of talking to her again this morning to make him understand that whatever he had been so attracted to the time before, had been very real and was still there.

She was on his mind all day, a fact that made him want to cuss a time or two when he hit his thumb with the hammer he'd been pounding a nail with to hang a picture. He shook his thumb and felt like one of his own teenage boys that had met a pretty girl and gotten flustered. He was apparently still a red blooded human male who could feel ridiculously attracted to a beautiful younger woman.

That thought didn't stop him from driving back over to the resort early to pick up the boys and stopping into the ski school office to add his name to his boys' lesson roster. He was surprised when the ski school director himself told him that would be impossible, "I'm sorry, Mr. Faciano, Kristin only takes kids. No adults. Although we've tried a number of times to talk her into it. There are actually a lot of men who request her personally, but she always refuses and she's such a great instructor that I let her get away with it. I don't know why she's so adamant about it, but she is. She's our resident enigma. No one ever really knows what's going on with her, but she's the ultimate model employee."

"What do you mean, no one knows what's going on with her?"

The director looked a little embarrassed and then asked, "What's the typical ski instructor type? You know, young, about half wild, ski bums who lean a little heavily to the party animal side and footloose. About three fourths of my instructors are single, seasonal employees who go from here to another seasonal resort in the summer. Typically, most of their paychecks go toward high end ski gear and beer. Kristin is on the other end of the spectrum. This is her third season with us and I've never had to let her have a day off to recover from a hangover yet. And she usually works seven days a week. Never calls in sick."

He got up from his chair and walked to the window and pointed. "See that shiny, pearl colored Mercedes SUV out there? That's what she drives to work. Sometimes it's months before her checks get cashed. It makes the internal auditor crazy. I send them to some address out in Kansas. Who works seven days a week who doesn't need the money?"

He continued, "She wears a wedding ring, but in two and a half years, I've never gotten a whiff of a Mr. Moran. She loves the kids, but refuses to take an adult class. The men get rather frustrated with her almost studied lack of interest. She doesn't even store her skis here in her locker, but loads them onto her car every night to take them home. Personally, I think she does that so she doesn't have to deal with the guys who are hanging around waiting to talk to her."

He gave Joe a conspiratorial grin. "The guy who owns the lion's share of this resort hates that. Been after her right from the start and she hardly gives him the time of day. It's very entertaining, but don't tell him I said that!" He went back to his desk. "Anyway, long story, but I can't sign you up for her class. She'd just refuse, and she's earned enough clout here to be able to call her own shots. I just wish I had about twenty more like her. My job would run a heck of a lot smoother."

Joe headed out to pick up his sons, more intrigued than ever. And a little disappointed.

# Chapter 5

Kristin started her second day's lesson with the Faciano boys by having Caleb take off his helmet so she could pin his hair back out of his eyes with a flat, metal barrette and then looked at him and said, "Perfect!" She put his helmet back on his head. "I'll bet you take your skiing to a new level when you can actually see where you're going! You'll be amazed at the big, beautiful world out there you've been missing!"

She teased him as he buckled the helmet back up and Robby and Gabriel laughed heartily. When he was safely ready to go, she said, "Come on! Last one to the lift is a rotten egg!" She sped off, but made a point of letting Caleb beat her to the line."

They all laughed together when a half hour later Caleb exclaimed, "Hey, I really can ski better when I can see!"

They had a great day. She could help them work on their weak spots without them even knowing they were learning. After an hour or two, she stopped and picked up a football and took them to a less busy part of the resort and they played football all the way down the run. It gave them more confidence on their skis, but all they knew was that by lunch they were hungry and their sides ached from laughing.

****

Once again she dropped them off for lunch and went off by herself for a few minutes.  Joe watched her kick off her skis, wave toward one of the employees, and walk toward the back of the main lodge, wondering about her more than ever.  The boys were hungry and happy and he sat with them while they ate, listening to them tease each other and regale him with their tales of snow tackles which were not really supposed to be part of the game, and Caleb's cute little barrette.  Apparently the three of them had even tackled her and when he expressed concern, they all laughingly assured him that she hadn't minded a bit and, in fact, got them all back.

They unanimously thought he should sign up for a lesson with them, but he explained that he already would have except for Kristin's policy.  Gabriel got a wicked grin on his face and said, "So what if you don't sign yourself up?  What if you sign up our other brother Joey who's been stuck out of town for the last couple of days?"  They all laughed, but it was definitely an idea.

****

That afternoon on the way up the hill on the lift again, Gabriel got quiet when he had been chattering most of the day and Kristin wondered where his thoughts were.  She didn't have to wonder long when he asked her, "Yesterday, you said you lived away from people so you didn't bother them.  What did you mean?  What would bother people?"

She was hesitant for a moment, wondering how to answer that question and he rushed to backpeddle, "You don't have to tell me if you don't want to."

28

Putting her arm around him to give him a squeeze again she admitted, "Actually, I don't talk about this with most people, but you and I are kind of buddies. And since I have one of your secrets about the spotting scope, I'll share one of my rather personal secrets. I know I can trust you, right?" He nodded his assurance and she continued, "It's not all that exciting."

She tried to keep the deep sadness out of her voice. "Once I saw something that was really, really horrible and now I have nightmares sometimes. A lot. Enough that it's better that I be away from people a little bit so I don't disturb them when I have to get up at weird hours of the night." She patted the knee of his ski pants with her mitten. "Not that great of a secret is it?"

He looked up at her with that steady way he had for several seconds and then said, "You should get a blessing."

She had no idea what he meant and asked, "I beg your pardon? What do you mean?"

His big, brown eyes were earnest when he went on to explain, "You should get a blessing. That's what I do when I have things that bother me so much that I don't feel peaceful inside. It helps me a lot. I'll bet it would help your nightmares to go away."

"What do you mean a blessing?"

"You know. Like a priesthood blessing." She gave him a blank look that made him ask, "You're not a Mormon, are you?"

"No, I'm not. I'm not sure I even know what a Mormon is. What are we talking about here?"

"Mormon's are members of the Church of Jesus Christ of Latter Day Saints. A priesthood blessing is when someone who holds the priesthood power lays his hands on your head

29

and uses God's power to help. Like to heal the sick, or help you figure out your troubles or whatever. It's the same power Christ used when he was on the earth to heal people and perform miracles. It could help you with your nightmares." He was absolutely matter-of-fact and Kristin simply stared at him for a second.

Finally, she asked, "Do you really think so?" She could tell he honestly did believe one of these priesthood blessings could help her. She wasn't even sure what she thought about the whole Jesus issue, but the thought that there was a power somewhere that could help her find peace was a hope she wanted to grab onto and hold with a vengeance.

He didn't hesitate. "Yes, I really think so. In fact, I know so. Blessings have helped me a lot in the last while when I've been having a hard time. You know, with being sad and stuff. And wondering about my mom leaving and everything. Before I got my medicine, the blessings were the only thing that really did help. They help me a lot more than the medicine. You should get one. My dad can give one to you. He holds the priesthood. I'm sure he'd be glad to, he always helps anyone who needs it."

She smiled at his championing of his dad. "Your dad does seem like the kind of person who would help people. He's done a good job raising you guys. You're all great kids, so he must be a wonderful father."

"Well, sometimes he's a terrible cook. Thank goodness for Gram, but he is a good dad. He thinks he made some terrible mistake taking care of me that made me want to kill myself. That's why he hired someone to take over the hospital. He's a hospital administrator. And we moved here so he could be a better dad. I tried to tell him it wasn't his fault, but he didn't believe me. I love having him with us all the time and I'm glad we moved, but sometimes I feel a little guilty about it."

She leaned a shoulder against him. "Gabriel, your dad is a big boy. You shouldn't feel guilty about the decisions he makes. I'm sure he decides what is in the best interest of his family by thinking and weighing the options and making informed decisions. He doesn't seem like the kind of guy who just does things on a whim. You need to let him take the responsibility for his decisions and not let them make you feel guilty. When you grow up and have a family of your own, then you can feel responsible. For now, just do the best you can and worry about you. Your dad doesn't expect any more from you than the best you can do as a great what? Fifteen year old?"

"Fourteen."

"A great fourteen year old. Do your best and let the guilt go. Life is too precious to waste it worrying." She changed the subject a little. "Who's Gram? Does your grandmother live with you?"

"Yes and no." A huge smile lit his face. "She's not really our grandma. I mean she's not my dad's mother or anything. His mother lives in Arizona, but Gram is definitely our grandma. She came to work for my dad when I was just a newborn baby. He says she saved all of our lives and that we'd have never made it without her. Now she's so much a part of our family that we'd never let her go even if she wanted to. Which she doesn't, of course. She loves us too much. She helps us do everything, although dad is always telling us boys that now she's not working for us. We're supposed to be taking care of her now that she's getting older. She laughs at him, but she let's us try to take care of her, too."

"So your mom and dad got divorced when you were a baby, but you've always had Gram? It sounds to me like you didn't miss out too much on the mothering end. Gram sounds like a wonderful person."

"Gram is the most wonderful person! We'd be lost without her. In fact, she's the one who helped us join the church. Without her my dad probably wouldn't have done such a great job being a dad. He's told us a gazillion times that he doesn't know how he'd have made it without finding the gospel. But my mother and my dad aren't divorced. My whole life until just a few months ago, I thought she had died. I mean, no one ever told me that, but she wasn't there and he still wears his wedding ring and he never said bad things about her so I just assumed she'd died when I was born. But then one day I asked my dad who he was writing a check to and he told me my mother and . . ." He wound down. "It pretty much killed me because I thought she left because of me."

He looked up at her and she met his eyes and said, "Sometimes life is a little weird, isn't it?"

"Yeah." They rode the lift in silence for a few minutes until finally Gabriel said, "I don't talk to anyone about all of this either. Just like your nightmares. For some reason you just seem easier to talk to than other people."

"I know just what you mean. You're easier to talk to than anyone, too." She smiled at him and gave his shoulder a squeeze as they got off the lift. He really was easy to talk to. She called over her shoulder to them as she skied away from the unloading platform. "Follow me!"

# Chapter 6

At three-forty-six the next morning, Kristin was thinking a lot about Gabriel's offer of a blessing as she set up her easel in the little cabin studio. Living like this was crazy. Tonight her throat hurt because of her racing breath when she had taken longer to wake up. Teal flopped down between her and the roaring fire she'd built and looked up at her with sympathetic sad eyes as she laid her nose on her outstretched paws. Kristin began to paint, wiping occasionally at the tears that overflowed her tired eyes and slipped down her cheeks. Her daughters had been the light of her life once.

****

Joe held off the boys all the way through dinner and most of the way through breakfast. Gram laughed at him from across the table and then added her two cents worth that finally tipped the scales, "Go ahead and go with their scheming, Joey. There will be no harm done and it's about time you had yourself more fun. Especially if it involves a beautiful woman. You've worked yourself to death for years to take care of these boys. Go enjoy yourself. It's not like you'll be neglecting them. You'll be with them."

The boys jumped up from the table and gave each other high fives, knowing their father rarely went against Gram's counsel. Joe shook his head at them and laughed, wondering if this was wise and knowing he was going to do it anyway.

They each gave their opinion about what gear he needed to wear that day to disguise the fact that he was their father and not their brother, and he ended up with a helmet, tinted goggles and a neck gator that he pulled all the way up to his nose. It would probably never work, but the boys thought it was great fun anyway.

He went early and added another "son" to the lesson roster. He left the age slot blank and only felt a little bit guilty when he wrote intermediate down in the skill level space. He was an expert skier, but thought he could hide that fact for one day at least.

****

Kristin knew something was up even before she saw the trio of guilty grins from the boys. When she picked up the note from the bulletin board, stating that she had an added brother to her class, she had to wonder. None of them had mentioned another brother and she knew there hadn't been one with them when they rode horses with her.

This new brother was taller and bigger and had a deeper voice and smile lines around his eyes that gave him away immediately, even under all the concealing garb. Still, he acted just like a teenager in class, cutting up right along with the others, until she had to threaten to call their father if he didn't straighten up. The three boys howled with laughter and "Joey" looked penitent enough that Kristin laughed with them before skiing off with her customary, "Follow me!"

She glanced behind her and grinned. How in the world was she supposed to teach this new "brother" anything? He probably skied better than she did! What were these guys up to? Whatever it was, they all seemed to be enjoying themselves immensely and she tagged along with their fun mood, letting the hilarity of the moment try to cancel out the ache in her throat and her heart from last night.

She had to stop soon after they set out to work on Caleb's hair again. He'd forgotten his barrette and she had to dig in all the pockets of her ski suit to find another one. Then, in the middle of the run, she turned around and noticed that Caleb's helmet wasn't done up. On the next run he had it off completely and strapped to his back pack. It must have been a testing his dad thing because she hadn't had any trouble with him wearing it the first two days.

She stopped at the top of the lift and dug her little first aid kit out of her own pack and pulled out the tiny scissors. Approaching the four of them at the top of the run she said, "Caleb, either the helmet stays on, or the hair comes off. What'll it be?" She came up to him and raised the scissors.

Caleb laughed and hurried to replace the helmet and she said, "Oh, good! It would have been a real pain to have to cut that much hair with these itty bitty scissors. Okay, let's see if Joey here can keep up. Ski fast! That's the rule!"

For the first several runs, they rode a high speed quad lift and she let them all four ride together while she rode with others in the chair behind them, and then when she led them across the mountain to another two person lift they rotated who rode with her. At first she rode with Caleb and she picked his brain a little about Joey. Where he'd been the first two days, how old he was. On the next one, she rode with Robby and found that Joey had been a completely different place and was actually twenty-one instead of nineteen like Caleb thought, and when she next rode with Gabriel, he'd been someplace altogether different and was, in fact, twenty years old.

At least he'd split the difference. They all had the most mischievous smiles and she went along with it all like nothing was going on. It would be interesting to see how old Joey thought he was.

After she'd joked with Gabriel for a few minutes, his face sobered and he said, "I saw your lights on in the little cabin in the middle of the night. And your voice is funny. Are you getting a cold?"

She sighed. "No, I just needed to get up and do something in the night."

"Bad dreams again?" His voice was sympathetic.

"Bad dreams."

"How long has it been? Since you saw the really, really bad thing happen?"

It took her a minute to answer. "Uh, . Three and a half years."

He was surprised. "Wow. That's a long time to have nightmares."

She nodded her head sadly. "It was a *really*, really bad thing to see."

He patted her glove with his. "God was there, too, Kristin. He understands what you're going through. Someday it will get better."

She just looked at him, studying the steady brown eyes. This kid was amazing!

The next run, she ended up riding with Joey, and she was hard put to keep from teasing him when he told her he had been away at a fourth place and that he was twenty-two. She laughed and told him what the others had told her. "Look on the bright side! You're all terrible liars! That's a good thing isn't it? None of you must have much practice!"

He pulled his neck gator off with a guilty grin. "Does that mean I can take off all this hot gear? I feel like I'm suffocating."

He went to take his helmet off and she said, "Uh,uh,uh. I'd hate to have to get my little scissors out again. The helmet stays on or the hair comes off! Class policy."

Joe groaned. "Can I at least leave it unbuckled?"

"Is that what you want the three little brothers to learn?"

"All right, all right. Point taken. They didn't tell me you were such a mean teacher!"

She laughed. "I threatened 'em to keep it hush hush."

"Hmm. Threatening. Now that's a tact I haven't tried yet. Somehow, I don't think it would work for me. I think they'd laugh if I tried it."

She nodded at the three of them laughing as they got off the lift. "Knowing them, you're right. They'd laugh. They do a lot of that. It's very refreshing. After this morning, I'd be inclined to think they got it from you. Whose scheme was this anyway?"

"I believe it was Gabriel who masterminded this. I tried to just sign up as a dad, but the ski school guy said no dads, only brothers. So we had to bring in another brother. It was the principle of the thing. By the way, is there a concrete reason for the no dads thing?"

"Yes, there is, actually. Brothers are much easier to control on the lift, and threatening to cut their hair is typically much more effective. Especially if the dads are bald." She smiled at him as she skied off. "Follow me!"

They skied one right after another behind her until she pulled up on a ridge top. "Do we want to ski groomed, powder, or moguls?" She looked around at their faces.

Almost in unison, they opted for football, but she said, "Football after lunch. We have to get poor Joey here up to speed or he'll never be able to keep up with us with the ball, and then he'd feel bad." She grinned at the boys.

They ended up skiing intermediate mogul hills for the remainder of the morning and then broke for lunch and when they met back at the lift forty-five minutes later, she had the football tucked under her arm. Looking at the four of them, she wondered if this was wise. It might turn out to be teacher against pupils. She could handle the three boys okay, but Joe would tip the scales in their favor.

Just for a minute, she thought that might not be too bad. He was incredibly good looking with his crisp dark hair and innate self confidence, and she had come to respect him as a parent before she had hardly even met him this time because his sons were well behaved and happy. She caught herself thinking that and it shocked her. She didn't think about men. Ever. It had become as ingrained to her as blinking.

For years, she had put every ounce of her mental energy into either trying to forget her past, or teaching the young people she was with on a particular day. There hadn't been any left over to use to think about a man in the first place, and in the second place, the men who inevitably wanted her attention didn't hold the slightest interest for her. Almost it seemed that the less she acted interested, the more intrigued with her they became. It was an exercise in wasted effort that went on surprisingly often.

As they got off the lift, she stopped for a second to explain the rules and then they were off. Joe held himself a little aloof and for awhile she was able to hold her own. One time when all the boys fell into a snowy tangle together, she stopped just long enough to spray them with snow and then grab the ball and head back down the hill. She'd almost made it to the lift when she glanced back and saw Joe ready to overtake her, so she quickly ducked left onto a trail through the trees and only just made it to the lift line with the ball still intact.

Joe skied into line beside her laughing at her victory dance until the boys caught up with them and then accidentally knocked all five of them down in the lift line. It took a second to untangle poles and skis and they all roared with laughter again when they saw that they had bent Joe's ski pole almost into a ninety degree angle. He made a huge procession out of attempting to straighten it and then chivalrously helped her to her feet again and began to knock the snow out of her long braid and off her clothes.

It had been a long time since a man had helped her to her feet. Usually it was the other way around. Her helping her students. She looked up into his smiling brown eyes and decided that, surprisingly, she liked it. It had turned out to be a great day in spite of the Facianos' ploy to dupe her system. She enjoyed them immensely, the father included. She rode the lift with Joe again and this time when she asked where he'd been he told her honestly about trying to get moved into the new house and how transferring the balance of power at the hospital back in Phoenix wasn't going as smoothly as he'd hoped. It was actually really nice to have an adult conversation with him.

With her students, even though she found it easy and fun to be friendly with them, there was always the element of supervising them. She always had to be responsible. With Joe, she didn't have to worry about that, at least for the duration of the lift ride, and it was delightfully restful to just be with him without being in charge. When they unloaded at the top, she was almost a little let down.

Jaclyn M. Hawkes

They had another rousing game of football during which she found herself tackled a number of times. Usually it was Joe who picked her up and dusted her off, but one time it was he who plowed her over into a foot deep drift of powder. She looked up at him, startled and wondering if he had done it on purpose. It was definitely the most rough sack of the day and she could tell that he was worried he'd hurt her and hadn't meant to do it, as he gently bent beside her in the snow with his face full of concern.

"Kristin, are you okay? I'm so sorry. I didn't mean to totally plow you like that. I thought I was going to miss you as I went by. Are you all right?"

The boys skied up beside them and Robby said, "Dad! You wiped her out! It's not the NFL, you know. You're supposed to tackle her gently. Remember?"

It was actually Caleb who ended up hauling her up, with a gently prod at his dad, "You gotta look out for those macho types. You know. Some guys just have to prove they're tough. Just try to ignore them. They'll eventually grow out of it." Joe laughed and finished helping her up and then lobbed a snowball at Caleb.

"Smart aleck!"

Then it was a huge snowball fight. Kristin didn't get the impression that they were terribly focused on skiing, and Joe wasn't that serious about getting his money's worth out of the lesson. Mostly, they just spent the duration of the afternoon having fun, while she attempted to channel the laughter in an instructor-like direction. When she finally told them all goodbye back at the lodge, for some reason, it felt like a Friday night instead of Wednesday.

Picking up her skis, she nodded to one of the snowcat drivers coming on for the night shift to groom the runs and turned her steps toward the parking lot. It had been a fun day, but the worse her nightmares were at night, the more tired she got earlier in the evening, and last night had been a bad one. She debated about picking up dinner on the way home instead of facing her kitchen.

Just past the lodge, she met Howard Cummings, the man who owned most of the resort. She sighed to herself as she saw him coming. She was too tired to deal with him tonight, but she pasted on a smile and did her best to be amiable, while she deftly slipped past him without really even stopping to visit. He was a nice man. And he was good looking and wealthy. She didn't know why she was so dead set against letting him get to know her.

At first, she was still mourning the loss of her family and it had just seemed so awkward after having been widowed so abruptly and recently, but now it was just that she didn't want to be bothered with him or any other men. She continued on to her SUV, mentally grilling herself. Today on the hill, she had thoroughly enjoyed Joe Faciano. Was it just that he was still married so he didn't threaten her, or was it just him? And why was she not the slightest bit interested in Howard? As she loaded in and turned for home, she decided to work on being friendlier to Howard, if only for the sake of being professional to her boss.

****

After Kristin had said goodbye to them all, she turned and skied a little further and then kicked out of her skis and bent to pick them up. Hoisting them over her shoulder, she stood for just a moment and then it almost seemed like her shoulders drooped as she resolutely headed down toward the parking lot. Joe watched her and then skied over to the edge of the hill to see her leave. She walked down to the lot where she stopped for a second to talk to a man in expensive street clothes, then went on and loaded her skis onto the top of the pearl colored Mercedes SUV. It looked just like his neighbor's. He continued to watch her car until it turned south onto the highway. It had been a great day, and she was a beautiful and fun young woman.

Joe didn't notice his boys watching him. As he followed her to watch her leave, the three of them looked at each other. Later that night, there was a rather clandestine meeting of the minds in front of their video game system. They unanimously agreed that they were all going to be too sick in the morning to ski and that their dad was going to have to take their lesson without them. They even got Gram into it so it would go more smoothly in the morning.

****

When Kristin walked into the kitchen from the garage she was ridiculously grateful for the wonderful smell that permeated her house. Either Murdock or Elena had been cooking and the savory smell gave her just enough energy to eat a minimal dinner and fall into bed. She loved her job and the diversion it was from her emotional prison, but sometimes the lack of sleep left her wondering if she was coming or going. She'd read somewhere that sleep deprivation killed brain cells. If that was true, then her intelligence was doomed. Teal came and rested her head on the edge of the bed to look at her and she patted her gently as she drifted off.

She didn't scream this time. At least not that she was aware of. The silence was almost eerie as she came fully awake, sobbing quietly into her soaking pillow. She'd never had that happen before, and while the thought that something was finally changed brought a modicum of hope that someday she would be okay, the suffocating sadness was almost harder to deal with. She couldn't calm down and get a handle on her thoughts the way she wanted to, and her grief was as deep as it had been the first week after the explosion. She struggled to control her tears as she quietly dressed and went out the back door.

The full moon drifting in and out of the patches of windblown clouds left the winter landscape alternating between a blue gray glow that lit the mountains around her, and mysterious, fleeting patches of dark that slipped across the landscape at will. The moving shadows reflected her deep heartbreak and she quickly saddled her black gelding Jet and led him out of the stable to mount.

Even her animals had come to understand that she had to be about in the depth of the night sometimes. It was as if they could understand what she and the rest of the humane race couldn't quite grasp. She walked him in a tight circle for a few minutes to let him warm up and then left the yard for the forest trail at a lope, the heavy, long cape she wore over her other gear to stay warmer when she rode in winter blowing in the misty night wind.

As she rode up the ridge and topped out on the windblown trail, the moon played hide and seek with the shreds of clouds and when it finally escaped, the glow on the snow became almost ethereal. She looked around her at the frozen ranges in the low light and the glorious moon over it all and thought back to the conversation she had had that morning with Gabriel. Was there really a God out there? And was He truly aware of her and what she had been through? Her parents hadn't believed in God and although they hadn't taught her that He wasn't there, they just hadn't ever even brought up the subject of His existence at all. He'd been a non-subject and it had been the same with Ryan.

She had felt the most unusual feeling when Gabriel had spoken. If she was honest, she'd secretly hoped her whole life that there really was a God. The struggle to find a meaning to life seemed a little pointless if there wasn't one. But, if there was, why had He let her family be blown up? A God could stop something like that, couldn't He?

She wondered how anyone ever knew for sure whether there was a God or not. There had to be a way. Gabriel certainly sounded like he knew for sure. When she'd looked into his earnest brown eyes, she had seen no doubt there. None at all. How could a simple fourteen year old boy know something so surely, when she was so much older and didn't even know how to ask for answers?

As she sat her horse on the ridge, the thought came to her. That must be how you find out. You must have to ask. But who do you ask a question like is there really a God? Suddenly a strong gust blew a cloud over the moon and the sudden darkness and wind chill made her shiver. Just as suddenly, the cloud blew away again to reveal a moon so brilliant and so huge there in the heavens that she wondered if she'd been given a sign. Maybe it was as simple as asking God himself.

It was a thought that had never occurred to her, but at the moment it made perfect sense. Having no knowledge of Godlike qualities to draw on, it seemed to her that if there truly was a higher being, He would be kind and gentle and approachable, wouldn't He? And if for some reason He wasn't, would He pardon her lack of proper deity etiquette because of her naiveté?

Her horse began to paw and prance in the cold with impatience, and she wondered if she honestly had the guts to address a possible God. Her decision was finally made by the realization that if there was a God and she was twenty-nine years old and had never so much as acknowledged Him, she was in deep trouble. And if there wasn't, there would be no one to witness her query anyway.

With that thought in mind, she humbly bowed her head and quietly, but surely asked the question aloud, "God, are you really there, somewhere?" She looked up and into the heavens and wondered if she got an answer, what would it be? How did God talk to mortals? She was realizing tonight that there were a lot of rather important questions that she didn't know the answers to.

She continued to sit her horse looking up into the night sky. She didn't hear or even see anything different. The only thing she noticed at all was a warm, sweet peace that seemed to fill her heart. It was a feeling she hadn't felt in years, if she ever had, and it wiped away the heavy burden of her grief like a light wind blowing away suffocating smoke. She inhaled a deep cleansing breath. Even if she hadn't answered her question about the existence of a higher being, the peace in her heart was more precious than gold. With a deep and contented sigh, she turned her horse for home.

Jaclyn M. Hawkes

# Chapter 7

Joe turned over and punched his pillow into shape. It was so weird. He'd never in his life had trouble sleeping, but several times in the last week, he'd found himself lying here in bed as wide awake as if it was high noon. He hoped he would soon get over it. It frustrated him to no end. It was four-twenty in the morning for Pete's sake!

He was laying there trying to remember how people put themselves to sleep by counting sheep, when he heard what sounded distinctly like a running horse. Knowing he had to be imagining things, he got out of bed to look out the window into the woods beyond his back lawn and almost immediately saw a woman riding through the leafless trees on a dark horse in a long, flowing cape. He blinked his eyes, wondering if he was, in fact, still asleep, and dreaming he was having trouble sleeping. He pinched his arm. No he was wide awake.

He looked back into the trees and from time to time where the trail wound in and out, he saw her again. He wasn't imagining this; he just didn't comprehend what he was seeing. First she was snowshoeing before sunrise and this time she's riding a horse through the woods in the dead of night in a cape like some eighteenth century heroine. The rumors were right, this woman was a fruitcake!

He got up and went into the kitchen and was surprised to encounter Gabriel standing in front of the big picture window in the dark, gazing out into the mountains glowing under the full moon. "You couldn't sleep either?" He put a hand on his son's shoulder.

"I was sleeping okay. Her horse woke me up. She must be having a rough night again." He sounded almost concerned about the woman.

"What do you mean, she must be having a rough night again?"

Gabriel looked up at him in the dark. "The neighbor lady. Why else would she ride a horse off into the night unless she was upset about something? I wish there was a way to help her. Maybe you could give her a blessing sometime. I'm sure that would help."

Joe looked down at him like he'd lost his mind. "I don't know. Maybe she just likes to do stuff in the dark and cold. That's no reason to assume she's troubled by something. And I certainly can't go over there in the middle of the night and ask her if she'd care for a blessing. She'd think I'm as crazy as we think she is."

Gabriel gave him a look that almost qualified as a crusty and then walked back toward his bedroom. He stopped in the kitchen doorway and said, "There's not really a lot of crazy in this world, Dad. Just a lot of mixed up. She's *not* crazy."

After Gabriel had gone on to bed, Joe stood and thought about him. This move had been good for him. In just this short time, his confidence seemed to have soared and there was something else about him. Some sense of sureness. Joe didn't even know what to call it exactly, but for some reason he didn't wonder any more if Gabriel was going to be okay. He just knew that he was.

It was a wonderful change for the better. Gabriel had been pretty vehement tonight about the neighbor lady, and Joe couldn't decide if he had been offended that Joe had called her crazy because he just didn't like people to be referred to as crazy after what he had been through, or if somehow Gabriel knew something about their neighbor that he didn't. Maybe he'd better delve in the morning.

When morning came, he didn't remember to delve. He was too busy trying to get his sons to hurry so they wouldn't be late for their ski lesson. He called three times and finally he went back into the hallway to see what the hold up was, but none of them were in their rooms. He found them all three in the TV room, still in their pajamas, playing Xbox. When they saw him, they all three began to act sick as if on cue. He was just about to call them on it when Gram walked in and immediately proclaimed them far too ill to ski and took Joe's arm to pull him back into the kitchen.

"You'd better hurry, Joe. Your instructor is going to be waiting." She propelled him forward as she talked, "Now don't you be tempted to ski without your helmet just because the boys aren't along." He was going to protest because he hadn't even had time to think about skiing without the boys along, but the protest died in his throat. If he went without the boys, that's just what he would be likely to do. Gram was watching him and he was sure she could read his mind. She clicked her tongue in disgust and then told him to wear the white turtleneck instead of the blue one. "It shows off your dark coloring much better."

He went back into his room and changed turtlenecks, wondering what in the world was going on in his house that he wasn't privileged to know. Gram met him in the kitchen with a thermos cup of hot chocolate and a blueberry muffin.

When he opened his mouth to ask what was going on with the boys, she deftly stuck the muffin in, handed him his parka and pushed him out the door into the garage. He just stood there for a minute chewing, trying to decide if he should protest his lonely exile and remind them that he was the head of this house, or make the most of it and just enjoy the day with Kristin. He waffled for a full minute before he climbed into his Suburban and backed out of the garage.

When he met up with Kristin, he was afraid she would refuse to take him without the boys, so he pretended to wait for them for a minute and then suggested they take a run and meet up with them on the next one. This happened about three times, before he took out his phone and called them and when he got hold of them he asked into the phone, "Robby, where are you guys?" He could tell by the tone of his voice over the line that his oldest son truly believed his father had finally lost it when he replied.

"Right where I was the last time you saw me, Dad. Playing Xbox. We called in sick today, remember? You're on your own. Tell Kristin hello and that we're truly thrashed that we have to spend the day stuck here playing. Love you, Dad. Don't forget to wear your helmet. See ya."

Robby hung up without letting his dad finish the call and Joe had to laugh as he turned back to Kristin. "He says they all three called in sick, but to tell you that they're pretty thrashed about having to miss your class."

She looked at him steadily for a minute as if she was trying to decide if he was serious or not and then she cracked up. "Right. I can see them saying they called in sick, but you added that last part. I'll bet they're somewhere playing video games." She paused while they loaded on the lift, and then laughed again and turned to him. "So, just exactly what am I supposed to be teaching you today, since I'm relatively positive that you can ski better than I can?"

He looked a little sheepish. "Technique? Form? I don't know. I think I need to brush up on my moguls."

They skied black diamond mogul runs all morning and Joe had a wonderful time both skiing and talking to her on the lift, but it was a good thing they had to stop for lunch because his legs were beginning to feel like noodles. She didn't look like she was wearing down at all. He talked her into eating with him since the boys weren't there and they spent over an hour eating and relaxing before they went back out.

It was the first time he'd seen her without gloves. He noticed her wedding rings and he wasn't sure what to think about them. He wanted to ask her about her husband, but hesitated, rationalizing that he was only taking a ski class from her and her boss had told him the husband was missing in action to a certain extent anyway. There was something odd about it.

In all the time they'd skied together, she had never once mentioned a husband or family, and she wasn't shy. She had talked openly about some things, so the marked absence of personal life, either meant that she was keeping him on the merest professional level, or the husband really was absent. Joe didn't think she was acting like she was only talking to him because she was obligated as his instructor, so he was left to wonder. At any rate, technically he was still married so it was a moot point anyway.

After eating, they were back at it on the mogul hill and she'd been right. He was a better skier than her, but only just barely, but his stamina couldn't even begin to compare with hers. After a particularly grueling run, he reached up and took off his helmet and held it in his lap on the lift and then just set it back on his head as they got off. In all honesty, he didn't realize he had forgotten to buckle it up until it was too late.

He was in front of her on a positively gnarly, steep run when out of nowhere his left ski popped off. The tip of it flew up and sideways and hit him wickedly in the side of the forehead as the binding caught him on the point of his funny bone, instantly numbing his left arm.

It didn't knock him out, but it dropped him like a rock and blood showered the snow like a miniature red sprinkler. He was still laying there, a little stunned, as she rushed to him, shedding gloves and poles wherever they happened to land. Instantly, she dropped to the snow beside him and tried to stop the bleeding with one bare hand, while she tried to open her parka pocket with the other. She couldn't work the zipper with one hand and he reached over to help her with his right hand. Finally she pulled out a bandana.

"Fold it quick. About a four inch square." Blood was dripping through her fingers, staining the snow and he tried not to look as he struggled to fold the bandana with his numb left hand. He knew he was fine, but on the pristine white it appeared a mortal injury. After handing her the folded scarf, he winced when she put it to the cut and then pushed on it hard as she said, "Sorry, I'm trying to get the bleeding to stop and it's kind of a gusher."

That was an obvious understatement as the scarf soaked through almost immediately and the blood began to drip again. He dug in his own parka and handed her another folded handkerchief and she put pressure to the cut again. This time she was able to slow the flow and then asked him to unzip the pocket on her sleeve and get out her cell phone. He handed it into her bloody hand and she pushed the button preprogrammed for the ski patrol.

She was perfectly calm as she spoke into the phone, "Hey, Lars. It's Kristin. Can you get me a snow machine to the bottom of Slaughterhouse ASAP? I have a head cut that's ruining all of our pretty white snow. No, he's okay, but he's really bleeding. Get an ambulance there so we can run him in as soon as we're down. Cool. Thanks, I owe you one."

She closed the phone and Joe zipped it back in her pocket, blood and all as she turned away from him a little. "Joe, can you reach my backpack and pull out the first aid kit? There are some gauze pads. We're gonna need 'em." The blood continued to drip and even though he tried to hurry, it took him a little while to wrestle her pack free and unzip it while she still held onto his head. Finally, he pulled out the pads and handed them to her. She tried to drop the soaked handkerchief and replace it with the gauze pad almost simultaneously, but the blood still spurted out in the split second delay.

He groaned as she put her other hand behind his head so she could hold even more pressure on the cut and said, "You're gonna have a corker of a headache."

"I already do. And it's making my vision go all screwy. If I was a medical professional, I'd guess I just gave myself a concussion, but I'm only a hospital administrator, so that doesn't count."

They could hear the snow machine approaching and she tried to explain to him, "I hate to tell you this, Joe, but we have to get to the bottom of this hill. They can't bring that machine up this steep of a slope and it'll be twice as fast if we can walk down rather than have them hike up and then hike back down. But we're gonna have to do it without bumping this bandage if at all possible. Can you do it?"

He nodded wearily. "Absolutely." He tried to gather up their gear.

"Just leave it. Lars will see that it's brought down and stored in the first aid room. Let's just worry about getting you down." Slowly, in unison, they got to their feet and then she walked backwards in front of him as they tried to make their way around the huge moguls on the nearly vertical slope. She was so close to him that she kept tripping them as she tried to maintain the pressure on his head and several times they slipped and slid together as they made their way down. Finally, she just let him try to hold it himself while they hurried, but it didn't work because his left arm was still numb and she had to take over again.

The snow machine arrived at the bottom before they did and the two ski patrollers with it rushed up the last several yards to assist them the rest of the way down. They had to load three of them on one machine in order to have a driver and still have her hold the pressure. By the time they made it to the waiting ambulance, Joe's head was aching in earnest and they were both a bloody mess.

Inside the ambulance, the EMT looked at the bandage she was holding from a number of angles and then asked her if she was okay to just keep on holding it until they made it to the clinic. "It looks like you finally got it stopped. If we move it, it's just gonna start up again."

She gave Joe a tight smile. "I'm good to go, just hurry and get us to a doctor." They got Joe to sit upright on the gurney and she sat next to him almost in his lap as they headed out. Although it was only a fifteen minute drive, her arms were so tired it felt like ninety. When they finally made it to the clinic, the nurse asked her to let her look at it and got a little testy when Kristin kindly, but firmly refused until the doctor was standing there ready to stitch. When the doctor did come in, the nurse whined to him.

When he was standing there, ready to stitch it, Kristin finally released her hold and the nurse gasped right out loud as it began to gush blood again.

Even the doctor was a little flustered as he tried to hurriedly anesthetize it and then staunch the flow again. It took forty five minutes, twenty three stitches and two nurses to finally get his head stitched back together, confirm his diagnosis of a concussion and get his face cleaned up.

****

Kristin had called Elena while they worked on Joe and Elena was there to pick them up and get them safely home. It was only four-thirty in the afternoon, but they both felt like it had been ages since their peaceful lunch in the lodge. Kristin dropped Elena at the lodge to pick up her SUV and then she took Joe home to his house. He was so out of it that he didn't even notice she never asked him where he lived before she drove him home.

She pulled up in front of the house and left him sitting in the front seat while she knocked at the door. When the woman she assumed was Gram opened the door, her face blanched when she saw all the blood covering Kristin's uniform.

Hurriedly, Kristin asked, "Are you Gram?" She shook the sweet looking elderly woman's hand. "I'm sorry. Joe cut his head. It looks bad, although he's actually going to be fine. But he isn't feeling so great. Could I ask you to help me get him in and settled? Someplace where he won't need to do much for the rest of the evening, if possible."

Gram followed her to the car and immediately began to fuss when she saw the shape Joe was in. "Joseph Vincent Faciano, I swear I can't even let you out of my sight. What have you gone and done this time?" Her words were stern, but she handled him tenderly as they helped him to the house. The boys arrived and all three of them were speechless for a few seconds when they caught sight of him and all the blood.

Kristin hurried to assure them. "It's not as bad as it looks. I promise. Heads just bleed a lot. He's going to be fine. Don't worry."

Caleb came and put an arm around him to help him walk in. "I guess we can't ever let him go skiing without us, you guys. One day, and look at the shape he's in. Gee whiz, Dad, you could have at least gone through the end of the week before you crashed and burned."

Joe had enough starch left in him to tease back, "Hey, I get extra points for getting wounded this good without even crashing. My ski just popped off and wacked me in the head." To Gram he added, "Yes, I was wearing my helmet, and it was an honest mistake that I had forgotten to buckle it up." They got him into the great room and into a recliner and a huge chocolate lab came and put its head on his leg. With a sigh, he asked, "Could I have some aspirin?"

"No!" Kristin's exclamation stopped them all in their tracks. Joe looked at her. "No, I mean, take Tylenol or something. No aspirin. That only thins the blood and might make it bleed again."

"Oh, good." He sighed. "For a minute there, I thought you were going to make me tough it out."

She waited until he was settled and comfortable and then told Gram and the boys what the doctor had recommended for care. She went back in to Joe and gently took his hand. When he opened his eyes to look up at her she teased, "Maybe you should stay off the mogul hills until you can take the heat a little better."

Jaclyn M. Hawkes

# Chapter 8

That night the nightmares started in early and she was up at only one o'clock building a fire in her studio. Turning to pull her easel over, she jumped when she heard the door open. She spun to see Gabriel closing the door and asked, "Gabe, what are you doing up at this hour of the night? Is something wrong? Is your dad okay?"

He came in, looking all around as he did and took a seat on the loveseat beside her. "Dad's fine. He's dead asleep. I just came over to help you get through. You're not usually up this early. Are you okay?"

It was an earnest question and she turned to look at him. She knew it was obvious that she wasn't okay. Her eyes were red and puffy, her voice was strained, she was pale and her hair was a wreck, so she didn't try to sugar coat it, but she did say, "Gabriel, do you remember when I recommended that you let your dad worry about his decisions?" He nodded. "This is kind of one of those things, too. You need to not worry about me. I'm sorry I ever told you about my nightmares. I'm fine, and I don't want you to worry." She changed the subject. "How is your dad feeling, really?"

"Honestly, I don't think he feels that great. He went to bed right after you left and stayed there. We keep checking on him, but he just wants to rest. If he'd have felt up to it, I'd have brought him with me tonight. I really think a blessing would help you.

"You don't need to be sorry that you told me. I'm fine, really. I've been thinking about it and decided that trying to stay by yourself so you don't bother people is not what is best for you. People need other people. People help each other. My dad always says we're all in this together, and that we have to help each other out, just like Jesus would. Or the Good Samaritan. Jesus would come over and help you when you need it. That's why I came tonight. We gotta look out for each other. We're neighbors now, you know."

She smiled and reached for his hand. "I appreciate that so much, Gabriel. And you're welcome here always. But, I'm going to lay down a rule. You can't come over alone. If I was your parent, I wouldn't want you wandering around in the middle of the night visiting the neighbor lady who I didn't know very well. You have to bring someone with you. Deal?"

"Deal." He gave her a fist bump. "Are you ever going to tell me what you saw that was so bad?"

She turned back to look at him steadily for a long moment trying to decide what to do. Finally, with the most self control she could muster, she said, "I used to have a husband and daughters. They were killed in a propane tanker explosion. I was there when it happened. It almost killed me too."

He was watching her intently and at length he simply said, "I'm sorry that happened to you, Kristin." For awhile, the room was silent except for the crackle of the fire. Occasionally, she wiped at a tear that escaped, but he was right, having someone here did help ease the pain. She sat at her easel and began to paint him as he sat there in the leather loveseat with her dog at his feet, the firelight reflecting off of his dark curls. She had begun to concentrate on her art when he said, "I'll bet they were really beautiful little girls. Like you. Do you know that someday, when you get to heaven, you'll still be able to raise them?"

She looked up at him and her eyes narrowed, questioning. "How could you know something like that?"

"God talks to His prophets, Kristin. He always has and He always will. How else could we truly know what His plans are for us?" He got up from his chair and looked at her painting for several moments before going to the door. "I should go. Maybe when the dreams are really bad, you could think about when you get to see your little girls again and when you get to raise them. Maybe the good thoughts could overpower the bad. I hope you have a better night." He slipped out into the dark, not knowing how thought provoking his few comments would turn out to be.

She set her brushes aside and went to look out the window at the moon that was still almost full. She thought about both the things Gabriel had said and the feeling she had when he said them, then she looked back up, wishing she could talk to his God and pick His brain for a little while. She returned to painting, but from time to time, she got up to go stand at the window and think of all the things she would ask God if she ever had the chance.

Sometime toward three-thirty she sat in the loveseat and leaned her head back to look up at the ascending moon again. She'd turned out the lights and let the fire burn low so there was less glare on the windows and it felt peaceful sitting there. She almost wondered if she could fall back to sleep this time and then dismissed the thought as impossible, so she was stunned when she woke up there in the first light of day.

Wonder was the only word she knew to describe the fact that for the first time since the explosion, she had woken up not only without the nightmares, but in the morning. At a normal time of day, just like she used to before her life had been turned upside down. Not only was it heavenly to wake up refreshed and happy, but the hope it fostered was like oxygen. It breathed new life into her spirit.

She left the studio to rush into the kitchen looking for Murdock and Elena. When she told them, Elena cried for joy with her and Murdock gave her a big hug. These two dear friends who had been through so much with her, understood like no one else on the planet could, just what waking up like this meant to her. They'd been with her through thick and thin and the three of them rejoiced together.

She'd already told the resort that she wouldn't be in to work today, so she dressed and then she and Murdock went to pick up Joe's Suburban that was still at the resort. She drove it into his driveway and then knocked on the door to check on him, still bubbling over with hope. When Gabriel was the one to open it, she gave him a full out hug. "Gabriel Faciano, you are the best thing that has happened to me in years! Thank you!" She stood back and took his hands in hers. "Thank you. You've given me hope. Something that I haven't had the luxury of much lately. Thank you!" She ruffled his dark hair. "Now, how is your dad? I've come to check on him and tease him some more."

Gabriel rolled his eyes as he shut the door and said, "Good! Because I think Gram needs some help. He's not being very obedient. Come on in."

They rounded the corner of the hall, followed by the huge chocolate lab Gabriel called Hershey. She found Joe sitting in a recliner with a briefcase on his lap and a militant, elderly woman standing over him with her arms crossed over her chest. Kristin walked up, looking him over as she went. Even without considering the bandage, he looked terrible compared to how good he usually looked. He was pale and looked tired and the grimace between his brows attested to the headache. When he saw her, he broke into a weary smile. "Kristin, this is a surprise. I'm glad you're here. Help me. Gram is lecturing me to death."

Gram gave her a smile and then continued talking to Joe, "Yes, and I'm going to keep lecturing until you put that briefcase away and go back to bed! This is ridiculous!"

Joe looked to Kristin for help. As she came to his chair and put her hand on his shoulder, he said, "See what I mean? Help me out here, would you?"

Kristin searched his eyes before she answered. She knew he didn't feel well. Finally, she asked, "Tell me, is whatever you're working on here something that requires your best judgment?"

Joe inclined his head to consider this momentarily. "Yes, why?"

"Well, you are suffering from a brain concussion." She left it at that as she sat down in the chair Gabriel offered next to him.

With a sigh, Joe placed the paperwork back inside the case and handed it to Gram. "Women." He shook his head with a smile. "You two are in cahoots, aren't you? She probably asked you to say that before hand. You had it all planned." He leaned back in his chair and put up a hand to rub his right temple.

"Headache?" Kristin asked with empathy.

He grimaced. "The worst. If I turn my head too fast the whole world spins."

"I brought your car home. Robby gave me a key last night. And your things from the resort. They're all bloody, but they might survive. You probably will too, given time. Can the paperwork wait?"

"Yes, I was just hoping it would take my mind off of how awful I feel."

"Wouldn't a good book work just as well? Or a movie?"

"I tried a movie. It made me car sick." He gave a quiet laugh. "I'm afraid I don't have any terribly dynamic reading unpacked yet and none of the boys are in the mood for a game unless it requires a controller and screen."

She clicked her tongue. "Now you're whining. What kind of game are you in the mood for?"

"Don't you have to go in to work?"

"I took the day off. I tried to kill my student yesterday, and they figured it was for the best to let me have a day since my lesson was cancelled anyway." She smiled gently at him.

"Do you know how to play chess?"

She nodded. "Yes, I do. And if my opponent has a brain injury, I might even be able to hold my own. Are you up to it?"

He pulled himself to his feet. "I guess we'll see when we see how well I play." He led her to a small game table that held a beautiful chess set. "Do you want to be black or white?"

They talked quietly back and forth as they played. She wasn't really that great at chess, but he wasn't all that with it mentally, so the pace was leisurely and the conversation comfortable. After over an hour of relatively evenly matched play, he began to beat her handily and she lost just as Gram came in to ask if they wanted lunch. Kristin got up from her chair. "I should go, but thank you anyway."

When Joe began to stand up, she motioned him to stay sitting. "Don't get up. I'll see myself out. I hope you get feeling better. Thanks for the game. Honestly, that's the longest I've ever gone without losing. It was great for my self esteem!"

He laughed at her and asked, "Do you want me to have Robby run you home? He's a good driver."

She glanced over to where Robby looked up from where he was making a sandwich. "I'm sure he is, but no, I have a ride." She glanced at Gabriel and he gave her a conspiratorial grin. "Get some rest. Bye guys." She waved at the boys and stepped out the door.

****

When she was gone, Joe felt like the sunshine that streamed through the big windows toned down a notch or two. He enjoyed being with her and was disappointed that she was gone. For about the twentieth time that week, he wondered again about finally getting an official divorce. It had been forever since he wanted to be around a woman the way he did Kristin. He looked over at his boys and realized all three of them were quietly watching him. He wondered what would be best for them. When he looked at them they all went back to making their sandwiches and he wished he could see inside their heads.

He got a little bit of an inkling when Caleb brought him a sandwich and a soda. As he set it on the table in front of him, he said, "She's really pretty, Dad. And she's fun." He went back over to the others where they'd taken their sandwiches to the TV.

Jaclyn M. Hawkes

Gram weighed in, "That was nice of her to come and check on you and bring the Suburban home. She seems like a very sweet, young woman." Joe took a bite and leaned his head back. He wished he knew what was in the best interest of his sons. And he really wished he knew where Mr. Moran was.

Joe was up and watching the heavy snowfall at a little after two that next morning. His head still ached and sometimes it hurt to focus his eyes, so he wasn't sure he was really seeing the woman next door walk from the house to the little log cabin until he saw the first small flickers of flame as she started a fire in the fireplace. It didn't even seem unusual tonight, and he realized he believed Gabriel was right. There had to be a reason for all the middle of the night stuff. Something troubled this woman. He could never see her clearly. The only way he even knew she was female was that he could occasionally glimpse long hair, and she walked with an incredible grace. Maybe Gabriel was right. Maybe she wasn't crazy, just mixed up.

The next morning, Joe thought he was hearing things when he overheard Caleb ask Robby to take him to get a haircut. No way! Joe and Caleb had been discussing Caleb's too-long hair for months and Joe had finally given up to a certain extent, deciding that he wasn't going to lose a good son over bad hair. They'd hit a tentative truce where Joe didn't hassle him as long as he could see Caleb's eyes, and Caleb made a point of keeping it out of his eyes, at least around Joe.

Still wondering what was going on, Joe walked out of his bedroom and stood at the heavy wood railing overlooking the downstairs as Robby and Caleb went out the garage door.

Joe wandered down to the kitchen and asked Gabriel, "Where were Robby and Caleb headed?"

Around a bite of cold cereal, Gabriel said, "Caleb wanted a hair cut." He hadn't been hearing things. Gabriel laughed at his face.

Shaking his head in wonder, Joe pulled out a chair next to Gabriel and reached for the box of Cheerios. "What's up with Caleb that he *wants* a haircut?"

It took Gabriel a minute to finish his bite. "Kristin put barrettes in his hair so he could see where he was going. Caleb liked being able to see, but the barrettes made him feel like a sissy, so he decided to get it cut. You'd quit reacting to it anyway, so it wasn't all that much fun to him anymore."

That last stopped Joe chewing right in the middle of his bite, and Gabriel laughed again. Joe wondered if he'd ever have this fatherhood thing down. Sometimes he felt like he had less of a clue what he was doing now than when he'd first started.

When they got home forty-five minutes later Joe didn't know whether to comment on the short haircut or not. He settled for a, "You look nice, Caleb." over lunch and let it go at that. That afternoon, when the three of them folded the laundry on the couch in the TV room and put it away without being asked, he was even more perplexed. His head still hurt too much to worry about it, and he went to bed early, deciding to try to figure these guys out in the morning.

Sitting in church the next day, he was proud of his boys as they took part in their duties during the sacrament. It was only the second week in their new ward, but so far he'd felt wonderfully at home here with these people. Watching the married couples together was the only thing that bothered him a little. It had never bothered him back home in Arizona, and he wondered why he felt differently here. Maybe it was that there were only a couple of singles here in this ward and there had been more in Phoenix. He didn't know. He only knew that sometimes watching these happily married couples made him feel lonely.

The insomnia was still plaguing him and at two-fifty the next morning he found himself sitting in the hot tub on his back deck enjoying the feel of the snow falling on his head while the rest of him was luxuriously warm. Living here in the mountains was turning out to be nicer than they'd ever realized it would be. He closed his eyes and relaxed back into the steaming water, thinking about all the things he liked better here than he had in Phoenix.

As he thought about it, he realized just the act of counting his blessings made him more appreciative and happier. The fact that several of the things he thought about included a pretty ski instructor with brown skin and a thick blonde braid was a little disconcerting, but she truly was one of the best things about Idaho and he was grateful for her and the influence she had had on his family. He decided he had to get up the initiative to ask her about her husband soon. If she was married, he had to change his attitude in a hurry. He couldn't let himself think about a married woman the way he was beginning to think about her. He had the sudden awful thought that maybe her husband was in the military. It made him feel even more guilty.

The peaceful, silent snowfall was suddenly broken by a long, piercing woman's scream. It was drawn out and finally ended abruptly. It hadn't been loud. She must have been inside, but it made the hair on his neck stand on end and the snow was no longer peaceful, but made him shiver. He got up and rushed back into his room to change and then hurried across to the house next door and knocked on the side door nearest his house.

It was opened by a tall man in his fifties in a flannel robe. Joe felt a little foolish, but he never could have ignored that scream and faced himself in the morning. As Joe hesitated for just a moment wondering what to say, a woman about the same age as the man came into the room wrapping her robe around her as well. There was something about her that was vaguely familiar.

"I'm sorry to bother you at this hour, but I heard a scream. Is everything all right?" The older couple looked at each other and then glanced out the sliding glass door at the rear of the house. Joe could barely see the shape of the woman with the long hair that he had seen the other nights, walking through the falling snow toward the little cabin.

The older man sighed as he answered Joe, "Everything's all right. At least as right as we know how to make it. I'm sorry she disturbed you. I didn't realize you'd be able to hear her with all the windows closed."

"Actually, I'd been having trouble sleeping and had gotten in the hot tub on the deck. She didn't disturb me; I just had to make sure everything was all right. I'm Joe, by the way." He extended his hand. "Joe Faciano."

The older man took his hand. "And we're the Murdocks, Bill and Elena. It's good to meet you. I'm sorry it's under such circumstances." He glanced out the window again where there were now lights on in the log building. He hesitated and then said, "She has nightmares sometimes, and has to get up. Try not to let her bother you. There's nothing you can do. At least nothing we've found yet. She just has to get up and do something, to take her mind off things."

Joe's eyes narrowed as he tried to understand what they were telling him. She really was crazy then. As if Murdock could read his thoughts, the other man continued, "She's a wonderful, completely sane person. Please don't misunderstand. Once you meet her, if you ever do, you'll see that for yourself, but the nights are hard for her."

"Yes, well goodnight then. I'm sorry I intruded. It was nice to meet you." Joe turned and retraced his steps back home, stunned at what he had heard. A woman with recurring nightmares. But they thought she was completely sane. It was hard to compute, but the Murdocks seemed like dependable, stable people. What could make a person have nightmares that often?

Looking back, Joe knew he had noticed late night activity almost every night for the last two weeks, and it appeared she must have been up even on the couple of nights he'd been able to sleep through. Gabriel had been right. Their neighbor was indeed troubled. His heart went out to her, and rather than assume she was a loony, like he had last week, he felt incredibly sad for her. Thinking back on that scream, he wondered again what would cause something like this.

He met Gabriel in the kitchen on his way in and Gabriel asked, "Is she okay?"

Joe looked hard at Gabriel. How had he known she was troubled? "Yes and no. She's fine, but she's definitely not okay."

"Did you talk to her?"

Joe shook his head. "No, just the couple who apparently live there with her, why?"

"I just wondered." Gabriel turned to go and then turned back. "She's not crazy, Dad." He turned to the door again.

He sounded too sure of himself and Joe had to ask, "How do you know that, Gabe?"

Gabriel shrugged. "I just do."

Joe narrowed his eyes in concern. "Have you met her?"

"Yes."

"When?"

"I'd rather not say."

Surprised at Gabriel's borderline defiance, Joe asked, "Why?"

Meeting his eyes honestly, Gabriel replied evenly, "Because she trusts me."

At first Joe wanted to demand what was going on, but then he decided against it. Looking into Gabriel's face, he knew he could trust him, too. "Have you been over there?"

Gabriel hesitated for the slightest second, but then said, "Yes. Once. She told me I was welcome, but that I could never come alone again. Maybe you could come with me sometime and give her a blessing. It would help her."

Joe nodded. "I could do that sometime. Why did she say you couldn't come alone?"

"She said if I was her son, she wouldn't want me wandering around visiting a lady she didn't know very well." Joe thought about that. It was good reasoning. Whether she was nuts or not remained to be seen, but he was grateful for her sound judgment this time.

"She's right. I wouldn't want that either. What did you go over there for?"

Gabriel shrugged again. "It just seemed like it would be easier to not be alone when you have troubles. I was right. I helped her. She told me so."

"Now you're scaring me Gabe. You don't even know this woman. What if she's a child molester or something? It's not your place to worry about her. You're fourteen years old."

Gabriel came back in and gave his dad a hug. "You're right, Dad. In fact, she said the same thing. But I think we should try to do what Jesus would do. I won't go over there again without you, I promise." He hugged his dad again and turned back to his room, leaving Joe confused in his wake. How do you combat reasoning like that? Do what Jesus would do? And this woman had counseled his son, just the way he would have. He looked back up at the little cabin. What a strange neighbor.

Monday morning, Joe was still a little tired, and his headache wasn't completely gone, but he wanted to see Kristin enough that he intended to go skiing anyway. He was surprised that his boys said they didn't want to go again, and he would have insisted except that Robby and Caleb honestly had come down with a cold this time. Gram smiled serenely and encouraged him to go without them. She almost made him feel a little self-conscious when she mentioned that he looked very nice as he went out the door. He'd taken off the bandage and then put on a soft knit cap without feeling the least bit guilty for not wearing his helmet when his head was so sore.

Kristin met him with a smile, and only laughed when he said he was alone again, even though he'd still paid for all the lessons. She didn't even try to take him to any expert runs that day and took her helmet back into the ski school office before their first run after confiding in him that she hated to wear it too unless it was a cold day. There was almost a foot of fresh snow and they spent the morning making the first tracks on the back side of the resort where the powder was heaven. They took an early and long lunch and then spent an almost leisurely afternoon. On one of the lift rides, Kristin confided in him, "I feel guilty for getting paid for today. The snow is heavenly, and I haven't taught for one minute."

"You earned it after getting me off this mountain in one piece last week. You handled that very well, by the way. I'm glad the sight of blood doesn't bother you. It would have been awful to have been stuck with someone squeamish."

She leaned against him with her shoulder. "Thanks."

That night he mailed out the check to his wife with a letter asking for a formal divorce.

Jaclyn M. Hawkes

# Chapter 9

The door bell rang at eight o'clock Tuesday morning and Joe was pleasantly surprised to open it and find Kristin standing on his porch, wearing a bright blue ski suit that wasn't her usual resort ski school uniform. Motioning her inside, he said, "Kristin, come on in. What are you up to this morning?"

"I've come, hoping your boys are still deathly ill this morning so we can go heli-skiing instead of having mock ski lessons. It's been snowing all night and the powder is going to be awesome! Plus it'll be way cheaper for you than paying for four lessons and only using one."

"How's that," Joe inquired.

"The helicopter guys owe me one," she replied with a smile.

Caleb came in bleary eyed from his cold and gave her a one armed hug. "Hey, Kristin. I heard you say you hoped we were deathly ill this morning."

She laughed and ran a hand over his short hair. "I wouldn't have said it if I'd known you honestly were sick. Sorry! That's definitely going above and beyond the call of duty to get a cold, just to give your dad a break. You're such a server!"

Robby walked in on the tail end of that. "Am I a server, too? I'm way sicker than he is!" He came and gave her a fist bump. "Hey, Kristin. You look hot in that outfit."

She laughed and reached up to feel his forehead. "How much of a fever do you have, Robby?"

"Fevers don't make you blind. Do they, Dad? She looks great, doesn't she?"

Joe looked from one to the other of his boys and then back to Kristin. He'd started to answer when Gabriel and Gram appeared. Gabriel gave Kristin a huge hug. "I'm the only strong and robust son in this family right now, so I can hug you without giving you a bug. How are you?" He leaned back to look at her for a second, and Joe got the impression that it was a serious question, not just a figure of speech.

"Very well, thanks." Joe was amazed at how comfortable his sons were with this woman. They acted like they had known her forever.

Gram interrupted his train of thought. "You do look very nice, Kristin. All of you come in and eat. Breakfast is ready. You will join us, won't you?"

"Absolutely! Your kitchen smells heavenly!"

Gram herded them all in to the kitchen table and the boys pretended to fight over who got to help Kristin be seated. It ended with Robby and Caleb lying flat on the floor arm wresting while Joe actually pulled out her chair to seat her, and then seated Gram. When the two boys finally made it to the table, Joe asked Gabriel to ask a blessing on the food. He could tell Kristin wasn't familiar with the habit when she looked around and then bowed her head like the others.

Only the fact that Robby and Caleb truly didn't feel great kept that meal from becoming a hair out of control. Joe was almost a little worried Kristin would think his boys were heathens, the way they teased. At one point, when Caleb asked Gabriel to pass him a muffin, Joe put his foot down.

"Don't you dare throw that muffin at this table when we have company!" At this, Robby pointed out the window and when Joe glanced that way, Gabriel launched the muffin to Caleb and winked at Kristin. At least they all pitched in to help put it away afterward, although they appeared to be getting ready to arm wrestle again to see who had to load the dishwasher.

Once they had cleared out of the kitchen, Kristin turned back to Joe. "You never answered me about heli-skiing."

He gave her a grin. "I didn't have much of a chance between all the hugging and the discussion about what a hottie you were."

With a bland tone she asked, "Were they telling me I was a hottie? I thought they said my suit looked warm."

He laughed right out loud. "I'm sure you did. Heli-skiing would be great! Should I make us a lunch?"

"I've got lunch, my car and the helicopter waiting. And I brought you an avalanche beacon in case you don't have one."

"Are we skiing with a guide? Or do we have to figure out where the avalanche danger is by ourselves?"

"No guide, but I already checked with the avalanche guru. If we stay off of the steep, we should be okay."

They loaded into the pretty little Mercedes SUV and headed for the jump-off point with the helicopter. It was only the third time he'd heli-skied and he couldn't help the little pulse of excitement that hit him as they lifted off to the roar of the rotors.

Gliding down the huge expanse of unbroken snow, he thought to himself it was the perfect day to do this. The powder was thigh deep and although they could see other skiers on mountains across the broad valley, they had this whole mountainside to themselves. He wasn't sure how many feet of vertical drop they got with every run, but it was a lot. These Teton Mountains were some of the grandest on earth, and slicing through the pristine snow for miles at a shot was unbelievably exhilarating. To do it with Kristin made it even better.

She was incredible to watch. She'd lost the ponytail holder off of her braid on the last run and her golden hair hung loose down her back and glistened in the brilliant sun. She was a marvelous skier and he felt like he was twenty again, skiing beside her.

He got the guts up to broach the subject of her husband finally, as they waited for the helicopter at the bottom. "Would Mr. Moran be unhappy that you're here with me today?"

She hesitated for a minute before she looked at him. "I don't know." Her face clouded. "Probably."

Well, that was as clear as mud. He decided to press her. "Where is Mr. Moran exactly?"

They could hear the helicopter in the distance as she said, "He's away just now."

The chopper's noisy arrival precluded any further conversation at that point, but once they were loaded in, he turned to look into her eyes. She met his gaze and he couldn't imagine that she was the kind of person who would take marriage vows lightly. He was feeling pretty lost just about now. She could have answered him more directly, but she didn't and he was trying to figure out why. She was definitely not the kind of woman who played head games. Should he continue to ask, or let it go and back away from her?

When they reached the top, she headed down the hill before he had the chance to question her any further. They skied one more run before they stopped for a late lunch. Her unwillingness to tell him about her husband made him hesitant to ask any more questions, or even banter back and forth with small talk, so lunch was a bit strained and he was glad when they loaded back into the chopper for another trip up the hill.

He spent the next couple of runs trying to focus on the incredible skiing, and not the inevitable truth that he was enjoying a married woman's company far too much and that he needed to walk away. He knew it was the right thing to do, but he was still so disappointed. Ever since he had talked to the ski school director that day, he'd been hoping the elusive husband was really gone, but "away just now" was not gone. And he knew that fidelity in marriage was much too important to trifle with. Skiing at the resort in her class had been one thing, but today's trip was over the line if she really was married, which it appeared she was.

He was so engrossed in his thoughts about walking away from her, that at first the dull roar in his ears didn't register as anything more than the roar of the wind in the trees at the bottom of the run. It was several seconds before the fact that they were near the top of the run and above tree line kicked in. For a second he tried to focus to identify the sound and then he turned in panic to look back up the hill toward Kristin. He was horrified to realize that the huge cloud far above her on the hill wasn't a cloud at all, but an avalanche roaring down the hill directly toward them. He screamed a silent prayer in his mind for help.

At first, she wasn't aware the avalanche was behind her, but then he saw the moment of realization and they both began the ski race of their lives! He looked all around trying to decide which way to go to either try and out run it or get out of its path, but either course seemed impossible.

He breathed another prayer for guidance and protection. They were skiing in almost the middle of a wide relatively flat bowl that curved up steeply at both sides. There was no where to go to avoid it and outrunning it felt impossible. Even as he frantically searched, he was thinking that this isn't the place for an avalanche. They should have been perfectly safe where they were. It didn't make sense.

Far ahead of them was a large outcropping of rock that jutted up into the valley. It was their only hope that he could see, and while he didn't know if they could reach it in time, he thought about his sons and the woman behind him and knew he was going to get there or die trying. Literally. The first time he glanced back, he knew Kristin had the same goal in mind and they both skied harder and faster than he'd ever dreamed.

He could hear the terrifying roar bearing down on them like a living, breathing freight train of death and tried to quell the sickening fear that screamed in his head that it was already too late. The sound was deafening and he could feel the ice crystals from the flying snow becoming so thick it was almost hard to breath. The rocks were near, but not near enough! He tried to look back, but he couldn't see her at all in the flying snow. Had it already consumed her? With every ounce of determination he could summon, he focused on the rocks ahead and literally willed himself to make it past them.

At the last moment as he realized he was going to reach them, he turned his head to search for her again. He could see nothing but white. No! There! Not far above him he saw something. Unable to determine anything except that it looked different than the rest of the suffocating whiteness, he prayed again that she would make it as he swooped past the rocky bulkhead and ducked in behind it, frantically watching for her to make it as well.

For several seconds that felt like an eternity, he could do nothing except struggle for breath. He felt like he was drowning in the flying powder. The raging roar of the slide was deafening and it was impossible to see anything at all. He continued to pray, all the while trying to remember everything he could about what to do to find someone in an avalanche.

The roar began to subside ever so slowly, but there was still no visibility. He could finally breathe a little easier and tried to reach for the avalanche sensor with hands that didn't seem to be working. At last he could hear the beacon sounding and it was the sweetest sound he had ever heard. *Thank you! Thank you!* He prayed it over and over as he frantically kicked out of his skis, unstrapped the little plastic shovel from his back pack and struggled through the broken and convoluted snow toward the sound.

Sometimes it was hard to tell which direction and he prayed for more insight, knowing that Kristin was near, but buried somewhere in all this mountain of crushing, white death. He wasn't sure if it had been a few minutes or many when he finally felt like he had located her beacon but he could see nothing. He began to dig in the snow like a madman, frantically throwing it behind him. He prayed continually, willing his eyes to find the bright blue of her suit in the hole that was frustratingly nothing but white.

He was several feet down and the sickening feeling that was building in the pit of his stomach made him want to swear in despair. The beacon continued to sound stronger, but where was she? In desperation, he said, "Oh help me, Father! Help me save this woman! Which way do I dig?" Standing in the bottom of the deepening pit, he felt the urge to turn to his left and began to dig with a renewed passion.

There! He saw an unmistakable tinge of blue under the snow and focused on it like his life depended on it. Hers did!

He hit something hard and soon realized it was what was left of her ski. It was broken, but he could see a part of her boot still secured into her binding. Digging until his own lungs felt like they would burst, he continued the prayer that had become almost unintelligible. When he finally saw strands of her golden hair he tossed the shovel aside and tried to dig with just his gloves. He couldn't get any purchase on the uneven snow, so he ripped off the gloves and began to dig with both bare hands.

Finally, he unburied her face, but he couldn't discern whether she was breathing. Frantically he dug at her throat until he could fit a hand in near enough to feel for a pulse. The faint rhythm he felt made him want to shout for joy. Still unsure if she was breathing, he continued to dig her out as fast as his quickly numbing hands would dig.

At length, when he could no longer feel his fingers, he clumsily pulled his gloves back on and taking up the shovel again, dug around her as carefully as he could to get her released. She was so wadded and tangled in the snow and her ski gear that he feared for broken bones and worse, and when he finally got her body free only to realize that one leg was still stuck and was being twisted horribly by the weight of her body, it was almost more than he could do to support her weight while he freed her leg.

He had almost gotten her completely clear of the snow when he heard the helicopter approaching. For a second he was afraid it would start another slide, but all it did was hover for a second and dip it's rotor to signal him that they'd been seen. He waved a hand, and then carefully picked her up and pushed her out of the hole he'd dug to the relatively flat surface above and then scrambled out of the hole himself.

He still wasn't sure if she was breathing and his hands didn't have enough feeling to detect anything, so he leaned his face down until it was almost touching her lips. For an agonizing second he felt nothing. Another second, and then three. He was beginning to lose hope when finally he felt her breath on his cheek and then a moment later saw her chest rise. Instantly, he bowed his head and thanked God and then put his nearly numb hands on her tangled blonde head and quickly gave her a blessing.

With that done, the sick, tight knot of despair in his gut began to loosen and he knelt beside her in the snow to try and stretch her out and check her for obvious injuries. He'd had to worry more about speed and getting her out than about neck and spine injuries, but now that he knew she was breathing, and her heart was beating he hoped he hadn't hurt her any more. He removed the broken portion of her ski and loosened her boots. She'd lost a glove and at first he tried to warm her hands with his, but soon realized that was fruitless, as cold as his own hands were, and dug in his pack and broke out hand warmers. He stuck one inside her one glove and put two more on either side of her bare hand and then wrapped his own two around that.

His hands started to tingle miserably when the feeling came back and he wondered if the same thing was happening to her as she moaned in her sleep and tried to pull her hand free.  When she finally blinked her eyes and then opened them, he didn't think he'd ever seen such a beautiful sight in his life as their sky blue depths.  She closed them for a second again and whispered, "Ryan?  Enika?"  Joe thought she had slipped back into unconsciousness until he noticed the tears seeping out of her closed eyes.

"Kristin, are you okay?"  He asked it as gently as he could breathe the words, but the eyes that opened and looked up at him still held an immeasurable amount of heartbreak. He asked her again, "Are you okay?"

She wiped at the tears with her gloved hand and tried to sit up, but he pushed her back.  "Stay still.  Tell me if anything hurts.  Is anything broken?  How is your back?"

Slowly, without taking her eyes off of his, or removing her bare hand from his two, she stretched and moved and tried to see how badly she was injured.  Finally, she pulled her hand from his and struggled to sit up.  She turned away from him, wrapped her arms around her drawn up knees and buried her head and then unexpectedly, she cried like her heart was broken.  For some reason, Joe didn't think it had anything to do with the avalanche at all.

He couldn't help himself.  Whether she was married or not, he couldn't just sit there and watch her cry alone.  He moved over beside her and wrapped his arms around her and pulled her against his chest.  She turned her face into his neck and cried until he could feel the collar of his turtleneck become damp, while he gently rubbed her back.

He didn't know how long they would have sat there like that if the helicopter hadn't come back.  A long time probably.  It wasn't the same helicopter they'd been riding all day.  This time it was a rescue helicopter and it lowered an EMT as it hovered over them.  As soon as he was on the snowpack, they pulled the cable back in and sent down a toboggan. The EMT tuned to Joe and shouted to be heard, "How many people were skiing with you?"

He covered her ears and shouted back, "Just her and me. I don't think anyone else was caught in this. They were all on other mountains."

"Are you okay?"

Joe met Kristin's eyes, and then returned, "I'm fine. She was the one buried in it."

The EMT turned to Kristin who looked at him with huge, tired eyes as he asked, "Where are you hurt?"

She shook her head and said wearily, "I'm a little banged up, but I'm fine. Can we just go home?"

"Sure thing, just as soon as I check you out." After several minutes of examining her, he finally asked, "Can you move okay to get into the toboggan?"

She nodded without saying anything and let the EMT take her hand to help her up and over to the waiting sled. She sat down and then laid down in it and let him strap her in and they hauled her up. Next, they sent down a harness and the EMT helped Joe strap in and then handed him his pack and sent him up while the man gathered up Joe's skis and poles and then followed him up next. Once inside, the pilot took off immediately while Joe and the EMT knelt on the floor next to Kristin to help her unstrap. Once she was free, she just wanted to lay there and the crew insisted Joe buckle into a seat for the trip.

Jaclyn M. Hawkes

# Chapter 10

At the hospital in Jackson, where they landed, the EMTs let her sit up and then stand up and helped her out of the chopper and into a waiting wheelchair. They took them down into the hospital to the emergency department and insisted she change into a hospital gown and be examined, which she wasn't very happy about, but she agreed to anyway. She peeled off her ski suit and then stepped into the adjoining restroom to change. When she came out, Joe could tell she was cold and asked for some warm blankets and dry socks for her.

She was tired and almost lethargic and Joe worried that somehow he hadn't been fast enough rescuing her and that she had gone too long without enough oxygen. She still seemed sad and when she reached up and wiped away a tear, he went to stand beside her and took her hand. A nurse took her vitals and put an oximeter on her finger and then almost immediately strapped on an oxygen mask.

A doctor came and did a cursory examination and then sat down beside her with a clip board and began to ask her questions. Some of them were about how she was feeling now, and then he began to ask her about her medical history. When he asked her about any past surgeries she had had, Joe was floored when she said, "Three C-sections." The dates of them were seven and a half years ago, five and a half years ago and four years ago.

His head was spinning as he tried to digest this and the rest of the interview and exam went by in a haze. Three babies! Something didn't add up here. Where were her children? Even only having known her this long, he knew without question that she wasn't the kind of woman who could leave her children. Not even just for the day to go off to work, especially not if she didn't need the money and not seven days a week. So then, where were the babies? The strangely absent husband was one thing, but the babies brought a whole new level of not adding up, and he'd known the second she answered that doctor's question that he had to know what was going on.

He wasn't surprised when the attending physician admitted her for observation. She was obviously not a hundred percent, her oxygen level was low and she needed more care. On the way to her room, Joe called Gram and explained what had happened, and then when they got her settled in, he offered her his phone. "Is there anyone you want to call?"

Her half of the conversation was less than enlightening. "Hey, Elena. It's Kristin. How are things at home? Hey, I had a bit of an accident skiing this afternoon. Actually, I got caught in an avalanche, but I'm fine. I'm in the hospital here in Jackson. No, I'm fine. Really, they've just admitted me for observation and I'm sure I'll be home soon. No, Joe's here with me. No. I'm going to ask them to let me go home tonight." She turned to look at him. "No, I haven't. No. It'll be okay. Sure. I have no idea. A little while. I'll ask. No, I just didn't want you to worry. Room 221. Thanks, I'd appreciate that. Talk to you later. Bye."

He didn't say anything, just sat in a chair and watched her, wondering how long he could wait to start asking her some questions. He knew she didn't feel great, let alone all the stress and emotions of the afternoon, but he had to have some answers. Trying to find her in that mountain of snow had made him see some things more clearly, one of which was how much she mattered to him.

Getting up, she went to the window to look out with her back to him. The sun was starting to go down in the west and the late winter afternoon behind her looked cold and miserable. She turned and got back in the bed and pulled the blankets over her and up to her chin. Their eyes met and then she looked down. He knew she was cold even with the couple of blankets she had and he got up and went out to the nurses' station to get her some that had been heated. When he came back in with them, he brought them to her bed and pulled her sheets and blankets back and put the new warm ones on her and then pulled the other linens back up over the top.

With a soft sigh, she said, "Thanks. That feels wonderful."

"Now we're even for last week and my stitches." He smiled at her and pulled his chair up beside her bed and reached over and took her hand.

"Holding a bandage on your head isn't exactly equal to being dug out of an avalanche. You saved my life. Thank you."

He rubbed a thumb softly over the back of her hand. "Anytime." After a few more minutes, he asked her, "There isn't really a Mr. Moran is there?" She shook her head. "But there was. Where is he?"

He could feel her tense, and several moments later he wondered if she was even going to answer him. Slowly, her grip on his hand tightened. Finally, in a voice that sounded as fragile as glass, she said, "He died." He continued to quietly watch her, wishing he could somehow comfort her. He stood up, and pulled her over toward him to hug her.

Gently, he asked, "Where are the babies?" She didn't answer, but sadness radiated from her like a searing heat as tears began to fall again and he whispered, "I'm so sorry." He repeated it, "I'm so, so sorry."

She didn't have to tell him her children were dead, too. Somehow he had suspected something like that the moment she had mentioned C-sections. He knew it had to have been something drastic to keep her away from them, the way she loved kids. He thought about his boys and wondered how he would ever survive it if something were to happen to all three of them. Or even just one of them. How in the world had this sweet woman survived whatever had happened?

He stood beside her bed and held her as she cried as if her heart was breaking, and he was sure it was and had many times before. Finally, he moved the head of her bed more upright and sat right on her bed and pulled her against his chest again. When her tears dripped down into her oxygen tubing, he gently pulled it off and mopped it out, then helped her put it back on. He stroked her hair and rubbed her back and at length she fell asleep with her head on his chest. He lowered the lights and leaned his head back against the head of the bed, thinking about what had transpired on this day.

He remembered thinking this morning that just having her show up at his house to ask him to go skiing had been a big deal. Then the avalanche had seemed like a huge thing. But even nearly being killed in an avalanche paled in comparison to what he had learned here this afternoon. And it wasn't just finding out about Kristin's life that was all that earth shaking. Finding out just how deeply he felt about her was both intimidating and exhilarating as well. He was concerned about how his feelings for Kristin would affect his boys.

In retrospect, he had to admit that even knowing her a year and a half ago had been instrumental in why he chose to move here out of all the mountains in the west. He hadn't realized it at the time, but now he did. It was almost a little disconcerting how easy it had been to talk him into taking ski lessons and then coming without the boys. He'd never done things with women, or even showed any interest before. Thinking about it, he was surprised his boys hadn't teased him mercilessly over it. They must have sensed that she was somehow different to him as well.

Holding her, even when she was so sad and hurt, was incredibly sweet, and he wished there was a way to comfort her better. But how did you ever comfort wounds as deep as hers. He pondered that for several minutes while she breathed an occasional shuddering breath against his chest, and came to the conclusion that some things were far out of the realm of mere mortals. This was one that would have to be given over to God. No one else could soothe a wound that deep and lasting.

He wondered how much she understood about God. She'd looked a little lost at breakfast this morning as Gabriel prayed. He hoped she hadn't had to survive losing her whole family without the comfort of knowing her Father in Heaven, or even knowing that she would someday see her children and husband again.

There were a million questions he wanted to ask her, but he had to be content with just holding her and letting her find some temporary relief from her sadness in peaceful oblivion.

He'd been holding her for awhile, when the room door opened and in walked the man and woman he had met in the middle of the night just the night before at his neighbor's house. He looked up at them and smiled a greeting, expecting them to realize they had gotten the wrong room, but they didn't. Instead they advanced into the room to look at Kristin and then sit in the chairs against the wall. In the half light, he couldn't really see their expressions and he didn't want to speak for fear that he would disturb her, but he had no idea what they were doing here.

Finally, it hit him like a freight train. He looked down so fast at Kristin's head laying on his chest that she stirred in her sleep and he gathered her closer into his arms. Kristin was the strange neighbor? It couldn't be! But even as he thought that, he started to compute all the things that began to make sense. The graceful woman with the long hair. The pearl colored SUV. Not needing a ride home the other day. Even Gabriel being so adamant that she wasn't crazy! Somehow Gabriel had known she was the neighbor. How had he found out? He felt another heavy layer pile on top of the day.

He'd just wondered how she had survived the loss of her family, and now he knew that she hadn't. That was the reason for the nightmares. She had to get up and do something to take her mind off of whatever it was that had happened to her family. Everything began to fall into place, but it left him with an almost sick feeling.

Here he'd thought she was beautiful and dynamic, a happy and energetic ski instructor. And she was, but what had she been concealing from the rest of the world? The ski school director had been right. She was the ultimate enigma. He understood now why she hadn't wanted to tell him about her husband. Her lifestyle was hard to wrap his brain around, even when he cared this much.

Looking over at the older couple, he wondered where they came in. Finally, he quietly asked them, "Are you relatives?"

Mr. Murdock shook his head. "Not technically, but we've been with her for over three years now, and love her like she was our own. She hired us when she came here from Kansas. I'm a retired cop, and she wanted to feel secure when she was by herself and at night so much." There was a great deal of sadness in his voice. "What happened today?"

"A few runs after lunch, we ended up below an avalanche. We thought we were safe where we were, but it started way above in the steep crags. I made it to safety, and she almost did. I had to dig her out by finding her beacon."

"How long was she buried?"

Joe smoothed the hair back from her face. "I honestly don't know. In the middle of that it felt like days, but probably a few minutes. She was unconscious, but breathing on her own when I got her out. She took a horrendous beating. I'm sure she'll be stiff and sore for awhile."

"Have they said how long they want to keep her?"

"No. I think they're hoping her oxygen levels will stabilize." He nodded at the monitor. "She needs to be around ninety-six breathing on her own, but she's just barely staying at that level with the mask. I'm sure they won't let her go if her levels are low. I actually thought they would put her in one of those chambers."

"She's not going to be happy about being here if they try to keep her overnight."

"Honestly, she wasn't happy about any of this. I'm afraid she cried herself to sleep."

Mrs. Murdock made a sympathetic sound. "I wondered why she was asleep right now. She wouldn't typically sleep anywhere but home."

Joe leaned a cheek on her hair. "She's had a rough afternoon."

The Murdocks looked at each other, and then the wife stood up. "Hon, why don't we wait in the lounge down the hall?" She took his hand to pull him to his feet. "Call us when she wakes up, or if the doctors make any decisions, would you?" With that, they walked back out the door to leave Joe to his own thoughts.

His brain was completely tied in knots over all the things it was trying to process. It was more than a little overwhelming. Mostly, he was trying to figure out where to go from here. What was in store for her and him and all of them? It wasn't like they could all go back to just acting like they had before. From the jumble that was his thoughts, he tried to pull out some key ones.

What would she want? She was obviously a very private person, and the grief she felt was by no means faded. He knew she had enjoyed being with him, but was it enough to make her want to let him into her life on a personal level now that he knew more about her? And what about the dead husband? Could she ever let another man into her heart?

And is that what he wanted? Last night, when he'd written to his wife to request a divorce, he wasn't sure what he wanted other than the freedom to be able to date again if he chose to. He'd had no idea at the time that Kristin's husband was for sure gone, and he certainly had had no idea that she was the stranger in the night with some incredibly hefty baggage. Moreover, he had no idea how vitally important it would be to him that he save her life today. He thought back to those frantic moments and could feel his heart start to pound again. Of course, he would have fought with everything he had to save anyone's life in the same situation, but it had been more than that. Much more.

All of this should be troubling to him, and to a certain extent it was, but not the way he expected it to be. He was devastated for her, but all of it just made him want to take care of her. Could he be in love with a woman he had only known this long? No, he couldn't be, could he? If his boys had asked him that question he would have told them no way. That it was just infatuation, but it didn't feel like infatuation or even just physical attraction, though it was certainly a part of it. There was something about her that had drawn him from that very first day horseback riding.

And what about all the coincidences? How had he ended up in the house next door to her? How had he singled her out to teach his sons when he didn't even know who she was? Or even picking this resort. He wasn't one who believed in too many coincidences, so what was going on then? Was this the hand of God at work? And if it was, why a woman who didn't appear terribly religious? Was that what was going on? Were he and the boys supposed to help her find the gospel? Finally, he'd asked a question that made a kind of sense, but then he reminded himself that he wasn't even sure what her religious background was.

And what about the boys? All this time, he'd felt he needed to forego any personal relationships so he could focus just on being a father and a breadwinner. Now, with three sons who he realized had never been able to watch their parents have a happy and healthy marriage, he wondered if that had been in their best interest after all. There was no question that Kristin had been good for them. He'd never seen a more ready friendship between an adult and teenagers. Moreover, religion or no, she had counseled and gently guided them in good directions in every instance.

Around and around his thoughts went, never really coming to many solid conclusions. At length he settled on the simple fact that she felt incredibly good and right here in his arms and that if he didn't know anything else, he knew that he cared for her enough to stick with her through this and whatever else they had to deal with until he could figure out what he was supposed to be doing. With that, he leaned his head back once more and closed his own eyes.

****

# Chapter 11

Kristin was just awake enough to know that she was drifting in and out of dreams and reality. She was afraid enough of the nightmares that even in half sleep she was tense, but there was something else. There was something or someone else that was keeping the horrible memories just far enough out of reach that she was able to focus on the sweet feelings of peace she could sense. Her mind let her body relax again and bask in whatever this feeling was. She felt someone brush back her hair and heard a deep, gentle voice speak her name. Cuddling deeper into the warmth and safety, she went back to sleep.

Later, when her body wasn't so incredibly tired, she felt herself begin to wake again. This time it was easier to turn from the fear and pain and horror, and snuggle down into the arms that held her. It was his aftershave that finally prodded her brain awake. She opened her eyes without moving and became aware that she was still cradled against Joe's chest with his arms around her gently.

A sense of wonder filled her. She could almost remember that her psyche had struggled to drag her back into that terrifying place where she had to live through the explosion over and over, but somehow being here in Joe's arms had protected her. Her body was miserably stiff and sore, but her heart was incredibly grateful for this gentle transition to waking. She laid there on his chest for a few minutes, enjoying the peace and the safety she felt there. His strength felt good under her cheek.

Finally, she remembered he was married and forced her sleepy brain to kick in. She started to push away from him. "Joe, you're married. You shouldn't hug me." Her eyes were as tired as the rest of her body when she looked up into his face.

He gently pulled her back down. "I know, darn it! But not for long, and under the circumstances, I think it's okay. It's for medicinal purposes." She could hear the smile in his voice. She rested there again for just a minute more and then pushed away again.

"Married is married, Joe. But thank you. I wouldn't have been able to rest without you. What time is it?" She couldn't see her watch in the dim light.

The same deep, gentle voice that had helped protect her from the nightmares said, "Two o'clock in the morning. How are you feeling?"

"You're kidding. It's honestly two o'clock?" She hadn't woken up reliving the explosion. It was almost too much to fathom. Her voice held a note of awe. "It's two o'clock. I slept 'til two and woke up. Just woke up." She turned to look at him and realized that he didn't know how inconceivable that was.

She also realized that he'd been sitting there holding her since early evening. "Joe, you've been sitting here with me for hours. You're probably miserable by now. Why didn't you just push me off and relax, or go home?"

He smiled at her and reached up to brush away a strand of her long hair. "I am stiff, but I'm happy. I was hoping that if I held you, you could rest better."

She ran a hand through her messy hair. "You have no idea how well you helped me rest. You're a miracle. Thank you. I'm sorry I made you stiff." She slid to the edge of the bed and started to stand up and had to take it in almost slow motion. "Aahh. I definitely do not recommend being caught in an avalanche." She slipped off the oxygen mask and went into the restroom and came straight back out, shocked. "I've got a black eye!"

He chuckled. "I wondered if you knew you had that. It goes very well with the blue in the hospital gown." He laughed at her again.

"Oh, brother!" She turned around and headed back into the bathroom again, amazed that she was this comfortable with him. What had he meant, 'Not for long'? She looked like heck, and tried to run her hands through her hair but gave it up as useless with the colorful eye and went and climbed back into bed.

He stood up from the chair he'd switched to and began to help her put the oxygen back on and she asked, "Do I still need this?"

He nodded at the monitor and explained to her the same things he had told the Murdocks and then said, "The Murdocks were here. When the doctor came back in at eight and said he was keeping you, I talked them into going home. It wasn't easy, but I can be very persuasive when I choose to be."

She was surprised they had left her asleep around other people. "You must have been. What did you say to them?"

"That I would handle whatever I had to in the middle of the night." His eyes burned into hers in the low light.

She looked down at her hands on top of the blankets. "That might have been a lot more than you bargained for."

"I was bargaining for whatever it took, Kristin. It was far better than I expected."

The room was silent except for the machines for several seconds. "It was better than it's been in three and a half years. Amazingly better. I don't know what happened, but I'm grateful. Thank you."

He took her hand. "You're welcome. It was actually very much my pleasure."

She pulled her hand out of his. "You're married, Joe."

"Kristin, I haven't laid eyes on my wife since the day she walked out when Gabriel was ten days old."

"He told me something along those lines, but did you ever get divorced?"

He pushed a hand through his dark hair with a sigh. "No." He went back and sat in the chair again. "Until just lately, I thought I was doing the boys a favor by avoiding personal entanglements. Now I'm beginning to wonder. I finally wrote her and told her my attorney would be in touch."

Kristin had so many questions, but wasn't sure what she dared to ask, "I'm assuming she had post-partum depression. Did she ever get better?"

"I honestly don't know. I was so hurt and so struggling to survive with three baby boys and a new profession, that it was  before I even considered that she might be sick. It was Gram who helped me understand a little better.

"When Gabriel was about six months old, I hired Gram to nanny for me and she has truly changed my life and changed me. Before her, I was just ticked off at Nicole, but

Gram helped me come to understand that it may have been my fault she left in the first place. At first, I thought that was preposterous, but in looking back, I was a terrible husband. I was entirely focused on school and getting a good job. I thought I was doing it for her and the boys, but in retrospect, she had three sons, the oldest of which was three and an absentee husband. I don't blame her for what she did."

"Did she ever come back or try to see the boys?"

"No. Not even once."

"Didn't you ever try to find her and patch it up?"

He shook his head. "I'm embarrassed to admit that it took me more than nine months to try to find her. By then she'd become quite comfortable without any responsibilities and refused to even talk to me. I did at least start sending her money every month. I figured I owed her that at least. The saddest part of this whole story is that almost fourteen years after she left, Gabriel somehow decided her leaving was his fault because he was so unlovable. That's when he tried to kill himself. The other sad part is that when she left, it didn't take me very long to realize I had never honestly been in love with her in the first place. That made me feel guiltier than ever."

The silence stretched between them until finally she said, "At least the boys were spared the hurtful custody battles."

"Yeah. There's that."

She decided she owed him an explanation for what had happened to her own family after he had been so kind to her and her tears the night before and slowly admitted, "I had three little girls." She used every bit of self-control to try to get the words out matter-of-factly. "They were killed when a propane tanker exploded."

He stood back up beside her bed, but hesitated for several seconds to reach for her hand. "Was your husband there, too?"

She swallowed hard. "We were both there. The girls were coming across the lawn to meet me."

Finally, taking her hand and giving it a squeeze, he gently said, "You saw it all. That's why the nightmares."

She slowly said, "Yes. How did you find out I have nightmares?"

"For some reason, living in Idaho has given me insomnia. It wasn't until the Murdocks walked in here last night that I realized you were the neighbor lady who rode horses in the middle of the night. I knew you would never be away from your children willingly, and put two and two together."

She looked up at him. "It wasn't Gabriel?"

He rubbed the back of her fingers. "No. He would never betray a confidence."

"I didn't think he would." She dropped her eyes. "I'm sorry I disturb you in the night. I thought I had moved to where I wouldn't bother people, but then they came in and built your house."

He squeezed her hand. "Would you think I was crazy if I told you I think God had a hand in that house being built and us moving there?"

"Probably. You sound like Gabriel."

With a long look, he asked, "That's a good thing, isn't it?"

She nodded. "Yes. I think he truly is an angel. He's a marvelous person. All of your boys are, but Gabriel has such a way about him. He's wise far beyond his years and is wonderfully thought provoking to talk to."

His voice was quiet when he said, "I wish I had known it was you next door. I wouldn't have been quite so uptight about him being friends with the neighbor."

She met his eyes. "You still don't know me all that well. There are those who think I'm crazy, you know."

He shook his head and said, "There's not a lot of crazy in this world, Kristin. Just a lot of mixed up. Gabriel told me that. I suspect he heard it from a wise woman who is incredibly good at building teenage boys' self esteem. It was actually a very comforting thought. It's good to know I'm not the only one who's a lot mixed up sometimes."

"I used to wonder if I was crazy." She sounded wistful. "Do you know that Gabriel believes you think he's crazy? It was something you said to him when you took him home from the hospital."

"You're kidding."

With a sad smile she said, "No. I wish I was."

He sighed. "So he tells you, not me."

She squeezed his hand that held hers. "Maybe he was hoping I'd tell you so that you could reassure him."

"He cares a lot about you. Sometimes at night he thinks it would help if he came to be with you so you're not alone when you can't sleep."

She quietly replied, "He did come once. He was right. That was the only night I can remember that I was able to go back to sleep after a bad dream. It was just last week. He told me I would be able to raise my little girls when I die. I asked him why he thought that and he said God always talks to his prophets.

"The next night, on my horse, looking at the full moon, I tried to ask God if He was there."

Their eyes met. "And?"

She shrugged and looked down. "He didn't answer me."

He tugged at her hand to get her to look back up. "How did you feel?"

"You mean, was I disappointed? Of course."

"No. I mean how did you feel inside when you were listening, after you asked?"

She thought about that for a second. "I actually felt a warm, peaceful feeling that night. It was weird. It was like the worry blew away on the wind for that one night." She hesitated and then asked, "Do you believe in God?"

"Yes, very much so. And I believe He sometimes answers my prayers with a warm, sweet peace of mind." She looked over at him trying to see his eyes in the dark as he went on, "Gabe was right; you will be able to raise your daughters. I'll bet they were beautiful."

She leaned her head back against the pillows. "They were exquisite. There were times that just looking at them amazed me. It's at times like that, I wonder the most about whether there's a God. Perfect little human bodies couldn't just happen could they?" She looked directly at him again. "I mean, there has to be a Creator somewhere, doesn't there? How could that many things happen so perfectly to create a body?"

With a nod he answered, "You're right. It couldn't be happenstance. But, Kristin, when you ask God a question, He isn't going to answer you with a huge, deep voice out of the clouds. At least I don't think so. He's never answered me that way."

He paused and his voice softened even more. "In the Bible it tells about how God speaks to us. It says there was a great and strong wind that broke the mountains, but God wasn't in the wind, and there was an earthquake, but God wasn't in the earthquake, and then a fire, but God wasn't in the fire. But after the wind and the earthquake and the fire, a still small voice. God was the still small voice.

"When He answers me, it's either with that feeling of peace, or He sends someone to help. Another person who's in tune enough to feel a prompting. Today, when I was digging and couldn't find you, He answered with a thought that popped into my head to move to the left. He's not in the wind. It's a quiet answer."

Wistfully she said, "I wish I could be as sure of Him as you. I've always hoped that there's a God. I mean, wouldn't it be great if there really was a truly good guy who was in control? Another thing I always wish is that I could find out that there is a point to life. There should be a point."

He sat back down in the chair beside her, but didn't relinquish her hand. "You're stronger than I am. I would never have been able to survive what you have without His help. I can't even survive a regular day without Him. You should keep asking and listening. Maybe you could find the peace you need, or at least a little more of it."

She touched his long fingers that held hers. "Gabriel thinks that if you gave me something called a priesthood blessing that it would help the nightmares. I trust his judgment. Would you be offended if I asked you for one sometime?"

He shook his head. "No, of course not. I'd love to help you, but did he explain what the power is that does the blessing?"

"He said it was God's power that Jesus Christ used that had been given to you to use to help others."

He looked her in the eyes. "You believe in Jesus Christ, but not God?"

She looked away and then looked back. "I think I believe in them both, but I'm just not sure. Do you believe in Jesus?"

"Absolutely."

"I trust your judgment, too. Could I have one of these blessings?"

He squeezed her hand again. "Absolutely."

The feeling in the darkened room was hard to even comprehend when this strong, confident, and successful man humbly placed his hands on her head and blessed her. She'd never experienced anything like it before. Peace that was almost palpable filled the room. He finished and sat back down beside her again and picked up her hand. Neither one of them said a word. It was as if talking would ruin something incredibly fragile and they just sat there for the longest time enjoying the feeling and the friendship.

It was the nurse, finally coming in to check on her, that broke the quiet. After the nurse left, Kristin turned on her side and put her other hand under her cheek while they continued to talk.

When she woke up in the morning, incredibly sore, but dream free, it didn't even come as a surprise. She'd known last night that the power she had felt in the room was stronger than the scars on her mind. She smiled tiredly to herself at Joe trying to sleep in the obviously uncomfortable chair. He'd become a hero to her in just a little over two weeks. She tended to agree with him this morning. God Himself must have had something to do with Joe appearing in her life.

Within minutes of opening her eyes she could hear his boys arriving in the hallway outside her door. They came through the doorway like a small tornado carrying flowers and balloons and candy. Gram followed them in more sedately and the Murdocks brought up the rear, grinning at the teenagers' antics. The boys approached the bed and gave her a knuckle bump, one after the other, and then Gabriel bent to give her a gentle hug while Caleb began to hassle their barely awake father about her getting a black eye on his watch. The doctor arrived in the midst of them all and smiled at her when he saw she finally had her oxygen levels up where they should be.

"You're out of here then. Which is good, because I'm not sure this hospital could handle these three." He smiled at the boys, but then asked Kristin, "Do you want something for pain? Or are you okay with ibuprofen and Tylenol?"

She opted for just over the counter stuff and thanked him as he left.

It took Joe almost half an hour to round up her clothes for her, but then they were headed to the SUV within just a few minutes. The boys insisted she ride down in a wheelchair, whereupon Joe decreed that the boys were not going to be the ones to push. He helped her down and loaded her in almost tenderly.

Murdock volunteered to drive and Joe accepted gratefully. The ride seemed long, but though Kristin was bruised and sore physically, her spirit wanted to soar with the knowledge she had gained there in the darkened hospital room in the middle of the night. She knew now that there was hope of someday having if not a normal life, at least a more normal one.

She called her boss that morning to ask for some time off to recuperate. Riding out the avalanche and then being buried had left her feeling like she'd been hit by a truck. Usually, she had to have her ski students to fill her days, but she was relatively sure that now that Joe knew it was her next door, she would have some company to help her pass the time. For the first time in literally years, she dared to lay down for a nap when she got home.

Elena came to check on her and Kristin tried to explain the blessing and it's effect, but she knew she wasn't able to communicate what it had done for her when Elena still gave her a hesitant look about trying to sleep. Maybe someday she would understand. As Kristin lay there resting, her mind went back to the time spent with Joe the night before. Even though it had been the middle of the night, or maybe because it was the middle of the night, she knew she would always cherish that mellow and honest conversation.

Thinking of Joe, she finally admitted that, for the first time in years, she wanted to get to know a man. Spending time with him made her feel young and almost normal again. Even after finding out about her suffocating baggage, he had sent the Murdocks home and stayed with her. She wasn't sure what the feeling was that that gave her, but she knew it felt good. There was something about him that rejuvenated her tired spirit and gave her hope. Sweet, comforting hope.

# Chapter 12

Joe came home and asked Gabriel to come into his office and talk to him. Gabriel came in with a tentative face like he wondered if he was in trouble, but Joe just wrapped him in a hug. "I want you to know how proud I am of what you've done to help Kristin. For talking to her about the church and for not betraying her privacy. She thinks the world of you and I do, too. And I don't think you're the slightest bit crazy. You were mixed up for awhile, and we're all a little nuts around here, but I know you're not crazy at all. In fact, I wish I were a lot more like you. Thank you for watching out for her. I love you."

Gabriel gave him that mellow smile. "I love you too, Dad."

After talking to Gabriel, Joe went straight back to bed after threatening to throttle the boys if they woke him up for any petty arguments. He didn't remember feeling this tired in years. He knew it wasn't just that he'd had a relatively sleepless night. It was more the mental and emotional rodeo he'd been on for most of a day now. He laid down thinking back over everything from the time he'd opened his door to her the morning before. They'd come an amazingly long way in little more than twenty-four hours. Some of his discoveries about her had left him reeling, but he respected her more than ever and knew that whatever her background, he loved being with her.

He was hoping she was feeling that way too, late that afternoon when he wandered over to the house next door to see how she was. She answered the door herself and led him through a beautiful lodge style house to the kitchen. She'd taken a nap, too, and was up and cooking. Other than the black eye, she didn't look like she'd had a rough day and night. In fact, she looked better and happier than he'd ever seen her. "I don't know what you've done, but it looks good on you."

"What are you talking about? I'm sporting a black eye!"

"You're glowing."

"Thank you, kind sir, but that was your doing, not mine. Do you know that because of your miraculous blessing, I just lay down and slept? It felt wonderful!"

"That wasn't my doing. I was just the messenger. Did you not realize that?"

She stopped stirring whatever she was making to think. "I'm not sure what I realize. I just know I want to know more. I want to know and understand it all. I want to have the unhesitant knowledge you and Gabriel have. I feel like I've been suddenly given a new sense or something. It makes me . . . I don't even know what it makes me but hope feels good. Hope feels really good."

He sat at a stool at the bar. "I know how you feel. I was the same way when Gram helped me to learn about the gospel when she first came. It changed my life, I can tell you."

She smiled up at him. "Do you mean to tell me that you weren't always Mr. Good and Honorable?"

With a shrug he said, "Well, I wasn't too bad, but knowing some things I know now has helped me to figure out what's important in this world. It was like a paradigm shift or something. My whole perspective on life changed. It was a change for the better. I'm certainly happier."

She met his eyes. "Happiness looks good on you, too."

"Thanks."

It was surprisingly easy to fall into a much more neighborly routine. The two households had forged a friendship that was extraordinarily comfortable, considering the circumstances. Even Hershey and Teal were buddies. The Faciano household pretty much just adored Kristin, and Joe had somehow passed the test of character strength with the Murdocks when he had helped her through the night at the hospital without flinching. He felt really good about the direction their lives were heading. This move had been a good thing for his family.

He was still feeling that happy and positive three days later when he answered his door only to realize that the woman standing there on his front porch was the wife who had walked out on him and the boys more than fourteen years earlier. When he'd awakened that morning, he'd felt refreshed enough that he thought he could face whatever came his way. Looking at the beautiful, raven haired woman in front of him now, he had to wonder. He was so shocked he just looked at her.

"Hello, Joe."

Hearing her voice, he finally thought to look around and make sure none of the boys were near before hastily stepping out onto the porch and shutting the door behind him. "Nicole." He hesitated, not sure what to say. "I didn't expect you. What are you doing here?"

"I guess saying I was in the neighborhood isn't going to work just now, is it?" She nodded at the mountains all around them. "I got your note and wanted to come talk to you about it. Have you got a minute?"

He decided to be completely forthright with her. "I've got a minute, Nicole, but I don't want to talk to you here with the boys around. I don't want to mess with their heads right now. I'll talk, but late tonight or somewhere else. Not now."

"Okay, I'll respect that. I'll come back later tonight. What time?" Her voice was a little lower, but she didn't look fourteen years older.

"Late." He tried to think when the boys would be good and gone to bed. "Eleven."

"Eleven it is. Thanks for agreeing to talk with me. See you tonight." She turned and walked back to her rental car parked in the driveway, while he watched. What in the world had brought Nicole here to the wilds of Idaho? She was a city girl to the bone. She was still beautiful. He could see what had attracted him in the first place. He went back into the house as she drove off, wondering if he had a strong enough heart to withstand all the shocks he was receiving the last few of days. He shook his head. Nicole! After fourteen years!

He spent the entire evening trying to figure out in his head what she wanted, but was still without an answer that made any sense when he heard her quiet knock at eleven o'clock on the dot. When he opened the door to her again, he couldn't help but compare her dark good looks with Kristen's golden blonde beauty. They were poles apart in every way.

"Nicole, come on in." He led her through to the great room, where they would be less likely to disturb the boys. "Have a seat. Can I take your coat?"

She shook her perfectly styled head. "Thank you, no. I'm having trouble staying warm here. I'm used to the Arizona heat I'm afraid."

"Would you like something to drink?"

"A dry martini would be marvelous. Thank you."

"I'm afraid I have nothing alcoholic. I joined the LDS church years ago. I'm sure I have milk and probably apple juice and soda. Will any of those do?"

She waved a slender, manicured hand at him. "Never mind. I'm fine thanks." She sat gracefully on the couch and patted the seat beside her.

He sat on the chair across from her. "So what was it you wanted to talk to me about?"

She smiled up at him, blinking her dark eyes. "You never were one for beating around the bush, were you?"

"No. I wasn't. I'm still not."

She laughed and it brought back memories. "All right then. I don't want a divorce."

He looked at her almost warily. "Why not?"

She tipped her head to look at him. "I don't know for sure. I just know that when I got your note it floored me. I mean, I know we haven't been in contact at all, but I've always still been married. Somehow, it just feels wrong to me."

With one hand, he kneaded the back of his neck. "Nicole, you walked out more than fourteen years ago and have never so much as looked back. What in the world would make you want to stay married now?"

Shaking her head, she said, "You don't know I've never looked back. I've kept track of you all these years. Watched you and been proud of how successful you've become. And to a certain extent I've tried to follow the boys' lives. I know it was wrong to walk out when Caleb was born. I was a mess psychologically and I recognize that now, but I'd like to try and make amends. I don't want a divorce. I came to try to talk you into giving our marriage another good, honest shot."

Joe stood up shaking his head in disbelief and went to stand and look out the window with his back toward her. Without turning around, he said, "Gabriel."

"I beg your pardon?"

He turned back to her. "Gabriel. Gabriel is the youngest, not Caleb."

"Yes, of course. Did I say Caleb? I meant Gabriel. That's not the point."

"It's a pretty big point to me." He was almost snapping. "You don't even know your own children. Hardly remember their names. Are you remembering that another shot at our marriage would affect them, too?"

"Of course." She folded her dainty hands over one knee. "I'm prepared to do whatever I need to do to make it all up to them."

He laughed a humorless laugh. "How on earth could you ever make up fourteen motherless years to them? Who do you think you're kidding, Nicole? You still haven't even given me a reason for why you want to do this. Why is it?"

Without blinking an eye, she said, "You're not making this very easy for me. I'm still in love with you. That's why. Why else would I come here and ask you this?"

He turned on her. "Why are you in love with me now, but not before?"

She met his eyes. "I've always been in love with you. I just never thought you'd ask for a divorce."

He ran a hand through his hair. "I should have asked for one years ago, but I wasn't sure what was in the best interest of the boys."

She almost purred, "To have married parents is what's in their best interest, of course. So let's try to make our's work, shall we?" She stood up and started to walk toward him and he could see her intentions in her eyes.

He put out a hand. "No! Don't even think about it. We may be married, but we are *not* married, so just stay over there."

She laughed again and sat back down. "You almost act like you're afraid of me, Joe. I didn't think you were afraid of anything"

He shook his head. "I'm not afraid of you. But there is no way I'm going to give you the impression that you can show up after all this time and expect me to act all husbandly to you. I think you're nuts to even consider this."

Her purr was back. "Marriage is supposed to be important, Joe. I know we haven't been respectful of that for a long time, but it's not too late. At least agree to think about it. Would that be asking too much?"

Looking up he answered curtly, "Yes, I think that's asking too much. You have no right to ask anything of me."

She smiled smoothly and went on in the same sultry tone, "I don't believe that, Joe. I don't think you would have been sending me money all these years if you didn't think part of the blame lies with you."

This time he did snap, "Of course part of the blame lies with me. I'll admit that straight up, but I don't see how this could ever work. And I don't want to do something that would harm the boys just as an experiment. It wouldn't be fair to them."

Unruffled, she pressed, "Would you please just agree to think about it for a couple of days? Just think about it. That's all I ask. I know you, Joe. If you're anything, you're fair minded." She stood up and walked toward him and put one dainty, red tipped hand on his arm. "Please."

He glanced at her hand and back at her. "Okay. I'll think about it, but no guarantees."

She stood on tiptoe to give him a single kiss on the cheek. "Thanks, Joe. You won't regret this."

He heard the side door to the kitchen open and turned to see who was coming in. "Joe? Joe, are you still up?" He could hear Kristin's loud whisper. "Joe, I . . . " She came around the corner of the hall and stopped short. Her blue eyes were wide and she instantly began to apologize, "I'm so sorry to intrude. Please forgive me. I saw lights on and I just wanted to ask you a question."

Nicole's hand dropped from his sleeve as he said, "You're fine, Kristin. Come on in." He turned and looked back at Nicole. "Kristin, this is my wife, Nicole. Nicole, this is my neighbor, Kristin Moran." Both women stumbled over greetings and then Kristin turned back toward the kitchen.

"I'll just ask Gabe later. Sorry to bother you." She disappeared back around the corner and they heard the door quietly open and close.

Joe turned back to Nicole. "Give me a couple of days. And in the meantime, don't even think about contacting one of the boys. I'll call you. Where are you staying?" He reached into the roll top desk and took out pencil and paper.

"At the lodge at the resort. I brought my cousin with me. You remember my cousin, Larry? I'm in room 114."

Absently he said, "I don't remember a cousin Larry. What's your phone number?"

After writing it down, he walked back through the house to the front door, giving her no choice but to follow. He held the door for her and backed away deliberately when she leaned toward him. "Good bye, Nicole. It's was nice of you to stop by."

She went into a pretty pout. "My goodness, Joe. You're practically throwing me out! That's not very polite."

"We're through talking, Nicole. I need to go see what she wanted. It might have been important."

"I see." Her voice was cool.

He shook his head once. "I'm sure you don't, but it doesn't really matter, does it? It was good to see you again, Nicole. Goodbye." He shut the front door firmly and threw the dead bolt, hurried back through the house, grabbed a coat and made a bee line for the little cabin lit up in the back of Kristin's house. The path to it was deeply worn into the snow and it was wider than it seemed from his house.

He opened the door a crack and knocked gently. "Anybody home?"

She stood up from behind an easel near the fireplace. "Over here. Joe, I'm so sorry to interrupt you just now. I never dreamed. Please forgive me."

"You think *you* never dreamed! I was so shocked when she showed up today I could hardly speak."

She looked up at him. "Does she do that often? Just drop in?"

Raising his eyebrows, he shook his head. "I told you I haven't seen her even once since the day she left." He walked around to look at her painting. "May I?"

"Sure. What do you think?"

He looked at the painting and glanced back at her, surprised. "For the first time, I think you're strange." He nodded at the canvas. It was the exact image they had glimpsed of the avalanche as it bore down on them before overtaking them. "What? Is this some kind of catharsis?"

She laughed at him as he went around to sit down on the loveseat next to her dog, while she continued to paint. "It was terrifying, but wasn't it also awesome? I mean like truly awe inspiring awesome. It nearly killed me, but in a way it was fascinating. Painting it somehow makes it less powerful to me."

He shuddered. "I didn't think it was fascinating. I thought it was awful."

With her brush poised, she admitted, "It was. I'll probably just paint over this sometime, but I had to get this image down." She changed the subject. "What did she want?"

He sighed. "You won't believe it. At least, I didn't believe it. She got my note, asking for a divorce, and came to talk me into giving our marriage another shot." He shook his head and gave a short laugh that held no humor. "She didn't even remember Gabriel was the youngest."

She gave him a sad smile. "She's missed out. They're great boys. Do I dare ask what you told her?"

He rolled his eyes. "That she was out of her mind. She pestered me until I finally told her I'd think about it for a couple of days. I'm sure I won't change my mind, but it got her off my back."

Kristin painted for a few minutes in silence. "Joe, she may have a point. There must have been a reason you got married in the first place. Marriage vows are supposed to be honored, come what may."

He was a little taken aback. "Kristin, she hasn't spoken a word to me in fourteen years. Not one. It's not like she's interested in honoring anything. I honestly don't know why she even came here. What does she want?"

She paused in her brush stroke. "It sounds to me like what she wants is you. You are quite a catch." She glanced up at him.

Returning her look, he said, "It doesn't sound like you think so. You're trying to talk me into staying married."

She spun on her chair to look at him mildly. "I'm not trying to talk you into anything. I'm just saying that in the first place, you told her you'd think about it. And you're a man of your word. And in the second place, a vow is a promise, and you're a man of your word."

He pushed a hand through his hair. "Now you're making me feel guilty. I'm not the one who walked out. Remember?"

She went back to painting and changed the subject. "I've been reading the *Bible."* He turned to look at her. Where had that come from? "Murdock and Elena gave me one. She recommended I start reading in the New Testament, but I read the part in first Kings about God coming quietly after the wind first. It's really beautiful. Almost poetry." She paused. "Then I went to the New Testament. It's good reading. Jesus was a great proponent of forgiveness. Did you know that?"

He laughed. "That was low. But you're good. Still, how would any of this affect the boys? They're the reason I've never pursued this before. Lately, I've been wondering if that was the worst thing I could have done to them. To raise them to believe that a happy marriage wasn't necessarily necessary. What's in their best interest?"

Looking back at him, she said, "Don't look to me for answers to the tricky questions."

She painted some more and finally asked, "What does the prophet say about marriage?"

His eyes flew to look at her, but she didn't glance up from her work as he answered, "That it's ordained of God and definitely a part of His plan for us. Of course, God is against divorce, but this case is a little unusual, don't you think?"

"Yes, so I'll quit teasing you. Just make sure this is what you really and truly want, and that you honestly believe it's the right decision."

He stood up to come stand beside her as she painted. "You're a wise woman, did you know that?"

She cleaned her brush. "I've had my moments in the stupid decisions about marriage department."

"What do you mean?"

"I don't think I was truly in love with the person I married, either. It's not very fun to wake up and realize you've made that big of a mistake. That far reaching of a mistake. I didn't dislike him, and he was a nice guy, but it was a mistake." She glanced up at him. "But the girls weren't a mistake. They were the best thing that ever happened to me."

He looked around her studio. "Do you have pictures of them? I'd love to see them."

Her face clouded. "Only packed away back in Kansas. Over time, I've tried to remove anything from that time in my life, trying to stop the dreams. Even Moran was my maiden name."

"If it hasn't worked, maybe that's backwards. Maybe the best thing you could do would be to try to remember as many of the good times and good memories as you can. Maybe you could dilute the bad images with good ones."

She spun on her stool to look at him with wide eyes and he said, 'I'm sorry. Did I offend you?"

Slowly she shook her head. "No. Not at all. You are a wise man. Did you know that?"

"I've had my moments, too, but every once in awhile I come up with something worthwhile. Have you ever painted the girls?"

She was lost in thought for a few moments. "Never. I started painting when one of the psychologists I was working with encouraged me to paint the images I couldn't forget. It took me about thirty-one seconds to figure out that was for sure backwards, but I enjoyed the painting. It's helped me at night."

He dropped a hand to her shoulder. "Maybe you could paint the most outstanding, happy memories. Maybe that would help, too. It's good to give weight to the positives in life."

Absently she nodded. "I'll try it. Thank you."

He began to wander around the little cabin studio, picking up curios and then putting them back down. "What did you need tonight? When you came to my house?"

"I was actually wondering if there was any way I could get more information about what you keep calling the gospel. The *Bible* is good reading, but it's gonna take me awhile. And I have so many questions. I'm sure it's just that I don't understand, but in some places it's rather vague. Or even contradictory. Is there anywhere else to get information?"

He laughed. "Oh, Kristin. You have no idea. What if we just started at the beginning and met with the missionaries. I do believe they might be interested in meeting you."

Her eyes followed his wandering. "How soon could I meet them?"

Still looking around he said, "They'll be at church tomorrow.  Would you like to come with the boys and me?"

She turned on her chair to look at him again.  "Would you be uncomfortable being seen with the local crazy, hermit lady who still has a bit of a black eye?  I'll understand if you say yes."

With a laugh he shook his head.  "There are tons of nutty people at church.  You'll fit right in!  It starts at ten, so we'll leave about quarter to.  Is that okay?"

"Perfect.  What do I wear?"

He came back to her.  "You can wear whatever you want, but most of the women will be in dresses.  If you don't have a dress, wear dress pants."

"I have several dresses, actually."

Smiling at her, he said, "And I'll bet you look great in them."  He headed toward the door, and then turned back to her, and she looked up and met his eyes.  "Sleep well, huh?"

"I'm planning to, thank you.  Good night."

\*\*\*\*

# Chapter 13

It was a good theory, but it didn't exactly work out that way. She woke herself up at a little before three, and it seemed to take forever to stop her racing pulse. The shock and fear was replaced by the ever familiar grief the nightmare brought on, and she quickly got up and dressed. She strapped on her snowshoes, and headed out with Teal, trying to deal with the dreams for the first time in five days. While she was disappointed the dreams hadn't subsided altogether, she was still unbelievably grateful for those five days.

He knew she'd had a nightmare as soon as he saw her face the next morning when she came to his house. He said, "You look very nice." But then he put a hand under her chin and asked, "Rough night?"

She gave the briefest of nods. "Do I look okay, really?"

His answer was interrupted by a whistle from Caleb, followed by a cat call from Gabriel. "Apparently you're a hottie again." Joe answered dryly.

She looked at him in concern. "Is that good or bad? In church I mean?"

Gram put an arm around her shoulder. "You look perfect, dear. These boys are going to be proud as can be to show up with you." She turned back to the boys. "It's these young men I'm a little concerned about. Pull up your pants more, Caleb. Robby, your tie is showing at the back of your collar, son. There, that's better." She began to herd them all toward the Suburban, and noticed Gabriel was wearing white socks with his dark slacks and sent him back to swap them out. She winked at Kristin. "They're starting to be as handsome as their father, but still need a little polishing from time to time."

"But polish or no, they're very good looking." Gabriel looked embarrassed and Kristin gave him a knuckle bump again. All four of them did look incredibly handsome in their white shirts and ties and Joe looked like the successful businessman he was in his dark suit.

Church was a little puzzling to her from time to time, but all in all, it was pretty straight forward, be honest, work hard, and do the best you can kind of stuff that just made sense. She felt right at home with the kind of people she met. Joe had been right about a few of the people being nutty though. He nudged her when they were approached by a large, middle-aged woman in a moo-moo and running shoes and wearing a positively outrageous fuchsia flower plastered in her hair. She introduced herself as Lou Lou and welcomed Kristin into the fold with a suffocating hug. After she left, Joe whispered with a grin, "See, I told you you'd fit right in."

Kristin whispered back, "How did her parents know to name her that when she was only newborn?"

During the second meeting, Kristin went with Gram to meet with the women while Joe and the boys went somewhere else, but Kristin felt comfortable. She figured out right away that they took a practical, womanly approach to studying home and family. She looked around her. She'd been pleasantly surprised when she'd moved here to realize most of the women here in Idaho and Wyoming were down to earth types to whom the word feminist was like a swear word. These ladies were right along those same lines and spent the hour being taught and discussing how to parent better. Kristin was very impressed. The world could benefit from more moms like these.

Joe and the men came back in during the third part of church and Kristin wondered where all the children and youth were. The Sunday school lesson happened to be on the same part of the book of John that she had been reading and she was thrilled to know there was an official doctrinal meaning taken from the prophet himself on some of the more nebulous passages. She wasn't sure what to think about any of this religion stuff, but she had come to honestly trust Joe and the boys and even Gram, and was willing to ride on their faith until she understood everything a little better.

It was a good feeling to sit beside Joe and try to learn more about her Father in Heaven and his Son Jesus. She no longer wondered if they existed; she just needed to study about them now, and come to know them better. They were a precious gift to her from Gabriel and Joe.

After the meetings, Joe introduced her to the missionaries. They were two young men who seemed to be about Robby's age and were enthusiastic about teaching her. They set up an appointment to come to her home and made arrangements for Joe and the others to be there, too. Kristin was grateful to know Joe would be there. She respected his judgment and insight. She had a lot to think about on the drive home.

****

So did Joe. In fact, he was a little heartsick. He'd run into his new bishop on the way to the Elder's Quorum and on impulse asked him if he could speak to him. The bishop had ushered him right into his office and Joe had explained to him what was going on in his life. He'd told him candidly how he felt about Kristin and his concerns for the boys and what had transpired between him and Nicole in the last few days. He'd explained that he hadn't even considered getting back with Nicole until Kristin had mentioned that marriage vows were just that, vows.

He'd put it all out there on the table and then asked the man outright, "Bishop, what do you think I should do here?"

Bishop Harrington had been quiet for a long time, thinking. He'd steepled his hands in front of him on the desk and finally said, "Joe, I'll be honest with you. I don't know you well, although I've been very impressed with what I've seen of you so far. I've only just met Kristin, and I certainly don't know a thing about your wife other than what you've just told me. I'm hesitant to counsel you in a situation I'm this unfamiliar with except to say this. Marriage *is* ordained of God. It is sacred and should be honored if at all possible. That being said, it doesn't sound like your wife is very committed to you and the boys.

"Now, I know whatever you decide to do will have an effect on your sons, and so do you. You've done a wonderful job raising them in your situation, and I'm sure you'll continue to keep them in mind. I guess what I'm saying is, I'm not sure what to tell you to do other than to pray and listen and follow your inspiration. I'm sorry to chump out on you like that, but I also know that whatever you decide will be the right course of action for your family. You're a good man. Follow the Spirit and you'll know without question what decision is right." He'd stood up and reached across the desk to shake Joe's hand. "Good luck, Brother Faciano. I'll be praying for you."

Joe had said, "Thank you, Bishop. I think." He'd given the man a tentative smile. "Are you sure you couldn't just ponder this for a moment and tell me exactly what to do?"

Shaking his head, his bishop said, "Sorry, Joe. That's not the way it works, I'm afraid. You'll be fine. Keep in touch and let me know how this all turns out." He'd slapped Joe's shoulder as he went out the door.

Now, driving toward home, Joe's heart was heavy at the thought that he should possibly reconcile with his wife. He really didn't want to do that. But then, this wasn't just about what he wanted. He looked over at Kristin and then back to the road.

Kristin invited them all to her house for Sunday dinner and looked at him several times as if she wanted to ask him something. He knew he wasn't much company this afternoon, but he couldn't help it.

It was after eleven o'clock that night when he heard her come in his kitchen door again. She didn't call out this time, just came through to the great room as if she knew she would find him there, sitting staring into the fire. She sat down on the couch without saying anything and he said, "Hey, Kristin."

"Are you okay?"

He shook his head. "No."

Tentatively, she asked, "Was it something I did at church?"

He sighed. "No, you were great in church. I've just been thinking a lot about what you said about being a man of my word and marriage vows. I even talked to the bishop at church about it. He's the man over this particular congregation. I feel like I should agree to try to work it out with her and I pretty much hate the whole idea. How's that for a bad attitude?"

"That is a great bad attitude." She looked up at him. "Will that work? Agreeing to do it because you think you should, but not giving it your whole heart?"

Feeling frustrated, he asked, "Would it work if I did give it my whole heart? I guess that's the problem. I don't think for a minute it will work. And it's certainly not what I want."

Neither of them said anything for the longest time while the fire crackled quietly in the hearth. Finally, she asked, "How do you feel?"

He sighed again. "Tired."

Gently, she tried one more time. "No, I mean how do you feel after you ask, when you're listening?"

He leaned his head back. "That's a good question. I think I feel good about it from an answer to my question stand point and bad about it from a that's not the answer I wanted stand point."

With a soft voice she asked, "Isn't God supposed to be all knowing?" He looked over at her and smiled. "So then trust Him."

He busted up at that. "You're making me look bad with logic like that. And making feel guilty for questioning. Thanks a lot." He chuckled and shook his head. "I guess I don't need to ask how you did today."

"But it would be polite, and go a long way toward stopping me from wondering how I offended you."

He grinned. "So, Kristin, what did you like about church today?"

"Several things."

He turned to her. "Like?"

Intertwining her hands, she hooked them over her knees. "Logic. This is not what I thought organized religion would be like. I guess I expected a lot of ceremonial hoopla and robes and chanting and all. It wasn't like that at all. It was logical. It all made sense. If I was a Higher Being, I'd have it the same way. Have everyone try to work together to make things better. I liked that."

He leaned back to look at her. "What else did you like?"

Almost dreamily, she said, "The way it made me feel. I'm not sure how to explain it. Somehow, just being there made me feel better. Strange, isn't it?"

Softly, he returned, "I don't think it's strange at all. I'm thrilled for you that you've found something that to me is absolutely vital. I think it will make your life happier. I know it certainly made mine and the boys' happier."

Looking back up at him, she wondered, "Who knows? Maybe getting back with your wife will make you happier, too. At least go into it expecting the best. If you expect the worst, that's what you'll get."

Sounding dejected, he admitted, "I know you're right. It's just hard to put my heart into something this big, that my heart isn't in."

In the same down tone, she asked, "While we're on the subject, are you the only one who can give me a priesthood blessing?"

He looked at her, questioning. "No, why. Don't you want me to give them to you?"

With a sad smile she said, "I don't think your wife would appreciate that too much. And wives have to rank. Always. It's what helps keep them happy."

Nodding gloomily, he asked, "Do you need another one tonight?"

"I'd certainly appreciate one."

He hesitated. "Is it okay if I'm the one to do it, or do you want me to call someone else?"

She met his gaze. "If you don't mind, I'd prefer you."


The next morning was the boys' first day at their new high school. Joe let Robby drive them in the suburban, and then immediately after they left at seven o'clock he climbed into his Tahoe to go talk to Nicole. Might as well get this over with. The whole way there, he kept questioning his earlier feelings that this was what he was supposed to do. It didn't make much sense to him, but he was willing to trust God just like Kristin had talked about. He prayed in the parking lot of the lodge, asking for strength and wisdom and help in doing what was best for his family, and then walked on in. If he didn't have peace of mind about all of it, at least he had peace of heart that this was the right thing to do.

He found room 114 and was surprised to see it propped open with the morning's paper. Absently thinking that Nicole should be more concerned with security, he squared his shoulders and knocked. A decidedly male voice said, "It's open. Just leave it on the table, and take the tip."

Joe pushed open the door and walked in. His wife obviously hadn't been expecting him, because at the moment she was in bed with someone else. The look of horror at seeing him was almost a little comical under the circumstances. Joe found it singular that finding his wife in bed with another man could give him such a sense of relief. He chuckled and folded his arms across his chest. "Please tell me he's not really your cousin."

"Joe! What are you doing here?" She pulled the sheet up higher.

130

He gave a wry smile. "I came to tell you that in the interest of marital sanctity, I was willing to give you your second, good, honest shot. That was the word you used wasn't it? Honest?" He pulled his phone from his pocket and quickly snapped a couple of photos before they knew what he was doing. "Just in case you get any ideas about dragging your feet on signing the papers."

He turned toward the door. "You know, before this mean hearted, little scheme I was prepared to offer you a rather decent alimony."

Stepping out the door just as the room service waiter came, he said, "The tip is on the table." He whistled all the way down the hall.

Getting into his SUV, he wondered if it would be appropriate to invite Kristin out to breakfast to celebrate. He turned the key in the ignition and shook his head, chuckling again when he recalled their faces when they saw him. Why she had even shown up in the first place if she was involved with someone else? It had to have been a money thing. And why had he felt prompted to be willing to try again with her when it was all going to unravel this morning anyway. As he thought about it, he realized that it was much better this way. He would never have to wonder if he should have tried harder, or if he made the right choice. He prayed again before he backed out, giving thanks for being watched over so carefully.

Jaclyn M. Hawkes

# Chapter 14

Kristin looked up at Joe in surprise when Elena showed him into her kitchen. She was sitting at the kitchen counter thumbing through a recipe book and making a grocery list when he set a box down in front of her with a small flourish, and a big smile. Her look was almost wary when she asked, "What's gotten into you this morning? Eight hours ago you were positively glum. What happened?"

With a cheery grin, he said, "Oh, I just went to tell Nicole that our marriage was back on first thing this morning." Her eyes got wide and her face became even more wary.

"And that made you this happy?" He flipped open his phone and showed her one of the pictures he'd snapped. She put a hand to her mouth to try to stop the smile.

"They'd propped the door open so they wouldn't have to get out of bed to let room service in. When I knocked, they thought it was their breakfast and invited me in."

She really covered her mouth this time, but a giggle escaped. "They'd do that to a poor waiter? That's awful! I can't believe you find your wife in bed with another guy and it makes your whole day." She laughed again. "And you thought I was strange!" She reached for the box. "What is it?"

"I was actually going to come invite you for a celebratory breakfast, but I decided that was in poor taste, so I stopped at the bakery instead. Do you like Danish?"

"Of course I like Danish!  All four of my grandparents emigrated from Denmark.  No, wait.  I think one of them may have been Swedish.  Or Norwegian.  I can't remember.  Oh, Murdock is going to love these!"

The four of them sat and ate Danishes and visited over breakfast, and then the older couple left to go to the grocery store.  Joe turned to her to ask a more serious question, "The black eye is looking better.  You can hardly even see it.  How did you sleep?"

"All the way through the night.  No nightmares.  Thank you for asking, and thanks for your help."

He raised his hand.  "Just the messenger, remember?"

"Yes, I remember.  But you were willing and worthy to bring me the message and I appreciate it.  I want to show you something.  Have you got a minute?"

"Absolutely."

She almost took his hand and then pulled back.  "Come with me."  She went out the back door and across to the little cabin studio, and led him inside to the easel.  She'd started a painting of two little blonde girls and a blonde baby playing with some dolls.  There was a vase of wildflowers in the back ground.  The colors were bright and although the images were painterly and the details muted, it was obvious it was a happy, pleasant work.  "What do you think?"

Softly he said, "I think they're beautiful."

She reached out and gently touched the canvas with the tips of her fingers and wiped at a couple of tears that escaped her eyes with the other hand.  "You were right.  Remembering the happy times and painting them was a good idea.  I think it will really help.  Thank you."

He brushed away one more tear with his thumb.  "You're welcome."  She looked up and into his eyes for a good two full seconds and then turned away. There was something different now. It was as if, now that he knew for sure he would be getting divorced and she knew it, too, the feelings they had never been able to admit to had been loosed. The look that had passed between them almost scared him.

She led him out of the studio and back toward her home but instead of going inside with her, he left her at the door. "I'd better get home and get something done in my office. I'll see you later." She didn't say anything as their glance met again, and then he headed around the house and home, wondering all the way what he'd seen there in the sky blue depths of her eyes.

When he reached his house, he stood for a minute to look back at hers, thinking. He felt like he was just starting out somehow. It was silly to feel something like that at thirty-nine years old, but that's how he felt. He pulled off the ring he'd been wearing now for almost two decades and looked at it. He ought to feel regret, he supposed, but the time for that had long passed.

He tossed it in the air and caught it again. The next time he put one of these on, it was going to be there forever. He couldn't help the fact that there was an image of a pretty blonde ski instructor that went along with that thought. He took the ring upstairs and tossed it into the wooden box that sat on his dresser, and whistled as he walked into his home office. It was several minutes later that he realized he was whistling the tune to Here Comes the Bride.

He booted up his computer and began to go over the financials for this month that had been e-mailed him from his hospital in Phoenix. Paradise Valley Regional Medical Center was one of the largest hospitals in the greater Phoenix area and generated a huge profit, but there was something off with these figures. He'd only glanced at them so far before being called away, but something was wrong. He just hadn't figured out what it was yet.

He pushed everything else out of his head and spent the next several hours sifting through page after page of numbers and then picked up his phone and called his former secretary, Maxine, at home. She'd been his secretary for most of his professional life and had opted to retire when he'd left rather than start over with a new boss, and now Joe was grateful for that fact.

She answered on the third ring, and her cheerful hello was comfortably familiar. "Max, it's Joe. How are you liking retirement?"

"Joe! I've missed you! Honestly I'm bored to absolute tears and Norm is going to move soon if I don't find something to do with myself. How are the wilds of Idaho?"

"Idaho is heaven and I'm so glad you're bored because I have a project for you. Would you consider working for me again for a short time? You can even do most of it from home."

She teased him, "I don't know, Joe. You were a terrible slave driver. And miserable to work with. What have you got going in Idaho?"

"My project is back there in Arizona, actually. There are some weird numbers on this month's financials and I need to get to the bottom of it without ticking off any of the new management. Since you are the paragon of diplomacy and discretion, and even more importantly, since I know that I could trust you with my life, would you consider helping me? I need your expertise here."

Her voice was more serious when she asked, "Like what kind of weird are we talking here? Innocent mistake weird or embezzlement weird?"

"Well, if it's an innocent mistake, it's a rather large one, although I can't pinpoint any single transactions or even accounts that have drastic changes, but the numbers on the whole are off like a hundred and sixty or sixty five thousand dollars. And that's even accounting for the occasional normal ups and downs. It's that much worse than the worst months for the past two years."

"Oh my! Okay, I'm on board. Nobody's gonna take my well-run hospital and trash it the month after I retire. Norm didn't pay you to call me did he?"

Joe laughed. "No, but is he good for financial remuneration if I take you off his hands a little?"

"He might be, but I'm not going to ask him. Send me what you've got."

"Max, you're the best!"

"Don't you forget it!"


That night at dinner, he calmly announced that he was going to get an official divorce. The table was silent for a moment while the boys and Gram just looked at him and then at each other. After a few seconds Caleb asked why and Joe replied, "Because I finally found someone I'd like to spend time with, but Kristin won't even let me hold her hand because I'm married."

The boys looked at each other again and Gram said, "Good for her."

"Don't get your hopes up, Gram. She may not let me hold her hand even after I'm divorced, knowing Kristin." The boys all laughed and the discussion smoothly turned to his sons trying to tell him what he had to do to attract chicks. Later, dressing for bed, he decided the whole divorce thing had gone over remarkably smoothly. He'd wondered if it might be a big deal, but apparently not.

The boys telling him how to attract chicks turned out to be singularly apropos, because the very next day he noticed a marked jump in the number of cell phone calls and texts being directed toward his sons. It was almost a little concerning because only Robby was even old enough to date. When Joe walked past Robby's room door and noticed a funny light and realized he was texting someone in bed at ten twenty at night Joe decided he was going to nip this thing in the bud. The next night, he laid down some new, tighter ground rules about electronics.

He'd already had the don't send or receive questionable stuff rule. And the don't even think about glancing at that cell phone when I am speaking to you rule. Now he added the fact that it was impolite to do so after the hours of ten o'clock p.m. and before seven o'clock a.m. and decreed no cell phones or IPODs in bed or during homework. It helped, but he was still a little shocked when he picked up Robby's buzzing phone one afternoon and read a message from someone named Tasha that said, "Hey hottie lets hang after school tomorrow"

He handed the phone to Robby with a look, but all Robby said was, "Thanks, Dad. Can we?"

"Can we what?"

"Hang out after school tomorrow?"

"I thought there was a basketball game."

"Well, can we hang out until the game?"

"Who is we? And where are we hanging?"

"I don't know exactly. Some of the kids from school, and I'm not sure where yet."

Joe looked squarely at him. "Rob, did I ever let you just do something back in Arizona if I didn't know who you were going to be with and where you were going to be and what you were going to be doing?"

"Well, no but . . ."

"Would there be an intelligent reason to change that policy now that I know none of your new friends here?"

"Can we hang out here then?"

"Of course. But I want to okay the movies before hand if you're going to watch something."

"We'll probably just play video games, anyway."

"That's fine. Just leave me a list if there's anything in particular you want to eat."

"Thanks, Dad." Robby gave him a high five on the way out. Joe enjoyed the kids and he was always a little more comfortable when they were right here at his house and he knew what they were doing. It was perfect to have them come here until he could meet some of the local kids.

He was sitting in the hot tub again that night in the dark because he couldn't sleep when he saw lights come on in Kristin's house. Immediately, he wondered if she was okay, and he knew that she wasn't when a couple of minutes later he saw the light go out and heard a door shut. He went in and hurriedly threw on sweats and went over to her house, expecting her to go up to her studio or walking. He was headed up to the little cabin when he glimpsed her in the darkened pool house swimming laps. He was just about to knock when Murdock opened the door. "Come on in. She's in the pool. Through here."

Joe went in and sat in a lounge chair on the side. For a few minutes she didn't even know he was there and then she stood up and looked over at him. He knew she'd been crying, but couldn't tell if she still was or if it was just the pool water streaming down her face. She took a deep breath. "What are you doing?"

"Sitting here, wondering what I could do to help you. It's hard to know what to do when I'm this far away from you."

She wiped a hand across her face and her shoulders slumped. "I'm sorry. I don't know what to tell you to do. It's hard to know what helps. If you're going to sit there, you might as well go get your suit on."

"Actually, I was in the hot tub when I saw your lights. My suit is under my sweats."

"Then I didn't wake you up?"

He shook his head. "Nope. The insomnia is an Idaho thang. Since the day I got here, almost every night. It's been a good thing in a way though." He gave a mellow, almost sad smile. "I discovered a beautiful night fairy who lives next door."

The exaggerated twang in his voice brought a smile that almost reached her eyes. "Can you swim?"

He grinned. "Arizona all-state two years."

"Come on then." She turned and dove back into the water. He swam beside her for almost forty minutes before she started to slow down and swam to the edge. He swam over beside her, but still wasn't sure what to do. Finally, he turned and pulled her over against him and she laid her head on his chest. "Talk to me, Kristin. Tell me what happens to you. What is it that wakes you up?" She shook her head. "What?"

She wouldn't look up. "I can't do that."

Gently, he asked, "Why?"

She looked down and shook her head again. "I could never make it through it. And I could never admit to you what's in the dreams."

"Can you tell me what's going on after when you have to walk or ride or swim or whatever? What is it that helps?"

Raising her head, she asked, "Have you ever had something on your mind that the more you sit and think about it the worse it seems?" He nodded. "You have to get up and do something else so you don't just sit there and focus on it?"

"Yeah."

She dropped her eyes again. "It's like that. Times a lot. I have to work it off or walk or whatever."

"Work what off? Are you afraid or sad?"

She shook her head again and hesitated. "Afterwards it hurts."

"Afterwards?" She nodded.

"So what now? What are you going to do next? What helps you get back to sleep?"

With the patience of years, she replied, "I don't get back to sleep. I've only been able to the one night. When Gabriel came. I'll just go ride for awhile and then come back and paint."

"Can I ride behind you? Would that help?"

She looked up at him and shook her head. "You're married, Joe. You can't ride behind me."

He gave a sigh and brushed a hand through his wet hair. "Kristin, that's stupid and you know it. If it would help you, would it matter?"

"I don't know, Joe. I think it does."

She sounded tired and his voice softened. "Kristin, in this situation it's a piece of paper. It's not like I'm being unfaithful to someone. It's simply a matter of sometimes a human touch can combat bad feelings, and fear."

She thought about that for a moment and then said, "Just come back to the studio and talk to me for a few minutes and I'll be fine."

"Deal."

He let her go and she climbed out of the pool, picked up her towel and turned away from him to walk into the adjoining restroom, but not before he saw the massive scar that ran all the way up one thigh. Holy smokes! What had this girl had to go through? He got out and toweled off and climbed back into his sweats, wondering how many more things he would find out she'd had to endure because of that explosion. She came back out dressed and with her hair in a wet braid down her back, and he followed her to the little cabin without saying anything and helped her start a fire. When it was going, she went to sit at her easel, but he stopped her.

"Wait." He met her eyes when she looked up at him and he softly said, "I have an idea. Tell me what happened the night Gabriel came and talked to you. What were you doing?"

She shook her head and shrugged. "I was just getting ready to paint and he came in the door and sat right here beside me on the loveseat and Teal came and sat at his feet with her head almost on the toe of his boot. I remember because I painted him for awhile."

She went to a pile of canvases stacked on edge and rummage through them. She pulled one out and came and handed it to him on the couch. "Then he just talked to me for a few minutes. It wasn't even all that long. And then he went back home."

"What did you talk about?"

Her brow wrinkled as she worked to remember. "Why I have trouble sleeping. My little girls. That was the night he told me I'd be able to raise them later and about the prophet and how God tells his children about his plan."

"What was the last thing you talked about?"

"He recommended that when things were hardest I think about when I'll get to see my girls again, and be able to raise them. He thought maybe the good thoughts could overpower the bad."

He gently prodded her, "Okay, so what did you do after he left?

She slowly shook her head, thinking. "I can't remember. Sat here thinking, I think. I believe I went over to the window and looked out at the full moon, and then ended up there on the couch in front of the fire, just thinking. That's where I woke up the next morning."

He stood up to go stand in front of the fire with his back to her. "Kristin, what do you think it is that stops you from being able to go back to sleep?" He turned back around to her.

She dropped her eyes. "Whenever I lie down and try, my mind just keeps going over and over . . . bad things."

"What do you think was different that night?"

She sat on the loveseat and leaned her head back against the top of the cushions. "Somehow, that night Gabriel was able to make me think about other things. Peaceful things that relaxed me."

He came and sat next to her. "After he left, what were you thinking about as you looked at the full moon?"

She looked a little embarrassed. "I was thinking about God. I was still wondering if He was really there and all the

143

things I'd ask Him if I could.  If God is really there and is the creator of all things, there are a lot of things He knows that I don't.  I was thinking it would be great to be able to pick His brain sometime."  She ended and looked down at her hands in her lap.

"It'll be awesome won't it?"

She looked up at him in surprise.  "I thought most people don't look forward to the day they have to meet God."

"I always imagine meeting Him is going to be the sweetest, most precious thing to ever be able to do.  Imagine the spirit He must have about him."

She yawned and he reached out and turned out her work light as she said, "Like Gabriel.  And you.  You have a wonderful peace about you.  It makes people trust you."

He smiled.  "I'm not so sure about that, but I know Gram is that way for me.  Her sweet sense of hope and serenity preserved my sanity when I met her.  I had a three year old, a one year old and a six month old baby and had just started running an extended care center that was huge and hadn't been managed very well.  A dependable, sweet and kind nanny was like a breath of oxygen."

"How did you ever manage that long?  I had a husband and close in-laws and still thought those babies were going to wear me out sometimes."

"How close were yours together?"

"Enika was three and Amy was almost two when Anna was born.  But Enika thought she was twelve, so she was a great deal of help."

Chuckling, he said, "Robby thought he was helping, but sometimes I worried he was going to love Gabriel right to death.  And Caleb had this obsession with touching his eyes.  It's a miracle he wasn't blinded."

She smiled. "One time I caught Amy carrying Anna down the hall by her knees, so I know what you mean. But Anna loved them dearly."

"I'll bet they were fun. My boys were."

"Your boys still are. They're a riot. You may be in trouble when the girls around here discover them."

Joe groaned. "I think they already have. They are going to be hanging out at my house tomorrow before the high school basketball game."

She nudged him with her elbow. "You love having them around and you know it."

He raised a hand. "Guilty as charged. I think teenagers are highly underrated."

She yawned again. "I think they are, too. Teaching them has been my lifeline for ."

"Have you been back yet?"

"Mm tomorrow."

"Do you already have a class assigned?"

She opened one eye to look at him and smiled. "If you want to ski, Joe, just tell me and I'll get the day off."

"Cool. 'Cause I'm semi-retired, and the boys are back in school."

Both eyes were closed when she asked, "What does semi-retired mean?"

"It means managing a large hospital is too time consuming for a single father of three teenagers. I hired a new administrator and moved. Now, I'm just the chairman of the board."

"That's still a pretty big job isn't it?"

"It is. I've lost more than a hundred and sixty five thousand dollars somewhere in the first month of handing over the reins."

She opened both eyes to look at him. "Maybe you'd better unretire."

He grimaced. "I'm hoping to avoid that actually. I've decided being somewhat retired is just right. Not crazed, but not bored."

She leaned her head against his shoulder. "I'm kind of the opposite. Working everyday keeps my head on straight."

"I figured it had to be something like that. If the blessings and the neighbors can make a difference, will you still ski seven days a week?"

Even her voice was mellowing as she shook her head. "Can't work Sundays anymore. It's the Sabbath. Plus, I've discovered organized religion. It's very enjoyable."

He stood up and reached for the throw draped over the side of the couch. "Here, Kris. Lie down and I'll cover you up." She stretched out on the couch and he covered her with the throw and then went and put another log on the fire. When he came back, he sat on the floor and leaned his back against the front of the couch next to her. They sat there in companionable silence and watched the fire. It had actually burned almost down again before she finally fell asleep.

He sat there with her for a few more minutes, watching her sleep. She was an extraordinary woman. He hoped she wouldn't think he was forcing himself on her when he showed up like tonight, because it felt truly good to be able to help her find peace. He would have liked to lean down and kiss her goodnight. With a gentle touch to her hair and a whispered, "Goodnight", he closed the glass doors on the fireplace, let himself out and locked the door behind him. He had no trouble falling asleep this time, and he dreamed about happy little blonde girls.

# Chapter 15

The next morning, he found a hand painted thank you note with the two simple words written in a bold hand above her signature sitting on the seat of his SUV when he went to run errands. He touched the quaint winter scene and tucked it into the sun visor, and then ended up thinking all afternoon about how she had looked there in the firelight the night before.

She was still on his mind when the boys and a handful of teenagers showed up after school. At first, it was all boys and then a little import pulled in carrying four girls. Joe answered their knock and invited them in.

Three of them looked like relatively nice young women, but the fourth was markedly underdressed for the weather except for little leather boots that hit her mid calf. She had a belly button piercing in the middle of a span of about eight inches of skin between her shirt and denim mini skirt, and wore a strappy tank top with black bra straps hanging out of it. She had blonde hair that was heavily high lighted and sported a tiny pink braided tail that hung out from the length of it behind her six ear rings.

When Robby introduced them, Joe was a little dismayed to find out that this was the Tasha who had texted. He tried to be a welcoming host, but was hard put to hold his tongue when she kept draping herself around the guys grouped around the video games. At least Joe was pleased to note that his sons were honestly more interested in racing virtual cars.

About five o'clock, Kristin knocked on the kitchen door and came in. She had started to smile at Joe when Tasha walked by and she raised her eyebrows at him with a concerned look. She came over to Joe and whispered, "Is everything okay?"

He whispered back, "Obviously not, but I had decided to wait until I had the boys alone to talk to them about it."

"Do you dare wait?"

"I just didn't want to embarrass the boys the first day they had friends over."

"She's probably the one who's embarrassing the boys."

"Oh, I don't know. Watch Robby." He'd been watching Robby and noted the look on his face whenever she wandered by, flaunting everything. Robby didn't appear to be too embarrassed.

Tasha sacheted past Robby again and Kristin made a disgusted sound and went and talked quietly to Gabriel for a minute. He subsequently went into his room and came out with a button down shirt and gave it to Kristin who went back over to Tasha. Joe perked right up to see just what she was up to.

"Hi, I'm Kristin." She reached out and took Tasha's hand. "It's nice to meet you. Now, tell me your name?" She listened to Tasha tell her who she was. "And you go to school with these guys?"

"Yes, I'm a junior."

"Well sweetie, I couldn't help but notice that you were cold in that outfit." She held the shirt for the younger girl to slip on. "Gabriel has generously offered to let you borrow his shirt for awhile." Tasha looked around and then slipped into the shirt like she didn't know what else to do.

"Thanks. I guess I was cold." She smiled up at Gabriel. "I thought I'd be fine. I'm usually so *hot.*" She weighted the last word a little and put a fingertip on Gabriel's chest as she walked by.

Kristin came back to Joe. "I'm sorry; I don't know what's worse. All the skin or her coming onto a fourteen-year-old. I guess we were better off before."

Joe and Kristin stayed around and talked while they watched, and he was immensely relieved when the girls left to go get ready for the basketball game. When they were gone, he asked, "Kristin, do you and the Murdocks want to come with us to the game? Gram is going with, too."

"The Murdocks went out to dinner, but I'll go if you don't mind."

"Actually, I'd love the reinforcements. Plus, I might need you to dress more girls."

"What if it backfires again?"

He smiled. "We could spill something on her and she'd have to go home."

She widened her eyes. "How could we be sure she wouldn't just take off whatever had been spilled on?"

"You've got a point."

They went and cheered on the local team, even though they lost, and had a good time together. When they were on their way back into the house from the garage, he finally had a chance to ask her how her night had turned out. "Were you able to sleep until morning?"

"Yes, I slept so well I was almost late for work. Thank you for helping me. Were you tired all day because of me?"

He shook his head. "No, actually you've been wonderful therapy for my insomnia. Would you like another blessing?"

She smiled up at him. "Tonight, I'm using my faith and I think I'm going to do just fine, thanks. See you later. Thanks for taking me with. Good luck with your Tasha talk."

"Thanks, I might need it."

His talk with the boys that night actually went well. The three of them knew exactly where he was coming from and agreed to avoid being around her if she was going to behave like she had, although he could tell that Robby had liked her a little too much. Robby didn't seem too thrilled that Joe encouraged him to stay away from her.

They all went skiing Saturday and every one of them commented on the fact that they missed "their" instructor and Joe made a mental note to reserve her next week. It was late February and the weather was fabulous although it had turned the snow to corn. He wondered how long the resort stayed open here.

Sunday, they took Kristin to church with them again and this time the Murdocks came with them. Joe got the impression that they wanted to check out the church for Kristin's sake. He didn't care why they came. He was just glad they did, and he was grateful that they seemed to take such good care of her. That afternoon, the missionaries came to her house for the first appointment and the Murdocks sat in on that, too, as well as his boys and Gram. It turned out to be a great experience for all of them and they set another appointment for mid-week at Joe's.

Kristin came back over to his house again late that evening and they sat by his fire this time and he answered questions for her for more than half an hour. When she got up to leave, he walked her to the door and mentioned that he was going to be flying to Phoenix for a day or two to check into things back at the hospital. "Take my cell number and if you can't sleep, you can call me and I'll answer more questions."

She took the number but told him she was sure she'd be fine and he doubted she really would call if she was struggling.

He flew out as soon as the boys left for school and spent the day trouble shooting and investigating at the hospital, and then had dinner with his long time attorney. His specialty was business law, but he agreed to have an associate work up the paperwork for Joe's divorce as soon as possible.

He went back to his old house for the night and was ridiculously lonely. He'd kept the house for trips like this, and it was convenient, but he had grown happy quickly in Idaho and wished he could have taken care of all of his business in one day instead of two. He called the boys and Gram to see how things had gone that day and then sat around wondering if he dared call Kristin to see how she was. He finally talked himself out of it, not wanting to crowd her, and went to bed more down than tired.

The next day, he wished he could have finished his business sooner even more when one of the women from the human resources department, a Cindy something if he recalled, walked into his office all smiles. "I'd heard a rumor that you were divorced and just had to see it for myself, Joe! Look at you! No ring! Idaho must agree with you nicely. You look great!"

He groaned inwardly and hastily assured her that the rumor wasn't true yet, and that he was just getting the process started. He'd hoped to be able to see to things and get back home without any issues like this. He concluded his business as quickly as he could and headed home weary and excited to get there at the same time.

****

When Kristin had assured Joe she'd do just fine, she had truly believed that would be true, so it was even more dismaying than usual when her own long screams tore her from her sleep the night he was gone. She turned over and tried to catch her breath and force herself to calm down. Her heart was racing in her chest and the muscles in her neck and upper back were in spasms.

She sat up and pulled her knees up tight against her body, slowly rocking herself as the tears of grief flowed. The images in her mind brought the sadness back with a vengeance. She knew she had to get up or she'd be a basket case. She dressed and let herself out the back door and pulled snowshoes off the cabin wall as she went past.

Teal was at her heels as she walked across the squeaking snow into the woods behind her yard. At the top of the first little ridge she turned to look back. Having Joe around had been so comforting and helpful to her lately and tonight felt positively lonely. She looked at his house in the darkness, wondering where he was tonight. Still wiping at her tears, she thought about his patience the other night as he'd helped her get back to sleep. If she wasn't careful, she would come to care for him more than was wise.

If she could get a handle on the nights, that wouldn't be so bad. She'd thought she was coming around, but tonight had been as bad as ever. She knew she could never even consider involving others in her life if she had a marked negative impact on theirs. She couldn't do it, and she wouldn't. Not to people who had been as good to her as the Facianos.

Resuming her walk, she trekked high into the wooded hills, both trying to soothe her mind, and think of good things as Gabriel and Joe had urged her. She knew they were right and that it helped. She stopped to catch her breath and then turned and began to head back with Teal traveling quietly beside her. Home was only a quarter of a mile down the trail when a low growl startled her.

At first she thought it was an animal growling at them, but then she realized it was, in fact, Teal growling at something in a thick clump of mahogany growing beside the trail. The deep, menacing sound made the hair on the back of her neck stand on end and her heart began to accelerate again. She wasn't sure what was going on. They were above eight thousand feet in elevation, and the game animals had long since migrated to lower elevations, with the predators following in their wake. In the dead of winter like this, there was usually nothing hanging around in these hills other than a few birds and rabbits.

Moreover, she had seen Teal react to both a mountain lion and a bear before and she had acted a little scared, not threatening as she was now. Her behavior almost made Kristin think it was a person she was growling at and not an animal hidden there in the dark. She stepped off the trail and gave the thick clump a wide detour before stepping back onto the trail to hurry the rest of the way home. It would be light in less than an hour and she waved a hand at Murdock as she let herself into the little cabin to read for awhile. Her fear of a few minutes ago had superseded her sadness, but she didn't know which was worse.

That day, she had a private lesson with a little girl who had been spoiled beyond belief and the parents stayed nearby the whole day while Kristin tried to teach her to ski. They effectively squelched every attempt Kristin made to get the girl to quit pouting and try, and at day's end she felt like she had wasted her whole day. She clipped her skis into the rack on the top of her car with a sigh. She felt incredibly sorry for the girl, and wondered how in the world the parents could stand her that way. Kristin had only been with her today and the little girl had worn her patience to the core.

She was just about to get into the driver's seat when Howard Cummings appeared at her elbow and said, "Kristin, I'm so glad I caught you. I've been wanting to talk to you. Keith in the ski school told me you've finally agreed to take on an adult lesson occasionally. Now, I know I own this place, so to speak, but I'm still not much of a skier. Would you be willing to take me on as a project? I'd probably only be able to get away a couple of afternoons a week. Would that work out for you?"

"Certainly, Mr. Cummings, after all, you're the boss. You get to call the shots around here. Just let Keith know when, so he can arrange my schedule."

He reached and took her hand in both of his. "Please, call me Howard, Kristin. Certainly you've worked here long enough for that."

She carefully extricated her hand. "Okay, Howard. I'll look forward to your lessons. Have a good day now." With that she climbed into her car and backed out, hoping she had walked the narrow line between showing respect to the owner and not encouraging his romantic ambitions. As far as she knew, he still believed she was married, so she hoped he would behave accordingly during his lessons. She pep talked herself on the way home that, of course, everything would go fine.

Pulling into her garage, she sighed. It had been a long day. She hadn't gotten much sleep and her mind had dwelt on whatever had been on the trail out there this morning. The more she thought about it, the more she was sure it had been a person. It was a troubling idea and she tried to put it out of her mind. She went through the kitchen to her room to change and looked out the window toward the next house, wondering if Joe had gotten home from Arizona yet.

Thinking about him helped to ease the fatigue, and she went in and started dinner. On second thought, she called next door and asked Gram if it was too late to invite her and the boys over to eat dinner with them. She was glad she had made the invitation when the three of them came rumbling in, teasing each other, with Gram more sedately behind them. Hershey snuck in behind them and immediately went over and flopped down on the floor next to Teal. They seated Gram and Kristin, and Murdock made a point of helping seat Elena, something he had gotten out of the habit of doing. Kristin loved it when they fussed over her.

She'd made buckets of spaghetti and salad because she wasn't sure how much they would eat, and she was glad she had when they almost cleaned it all up. She wanted to ask when Joe would be home, but decided against it. He'd told her he would have a full day today in Phoenix and then had to fly into Jackson Hole, Wyoming. That was a forty-two mile drive over the pass, so she assumed it would be late when he got in, and she was tired enough that she knew she couldn't wait up. She went to bed early hoping there wasn't a repeat of last night.

****

When Joe finally did pull in that night at a little before midnight, he almost selfishly wished she had been unable to sleep so he could go over and see her. He'd missed her ridiculously over the two short days. He wondered what she would think if she knew how much he thought about her. She had to know he was interested in her, and although she had insisted he keep his hands to himself because legally he was still married, he knew she wasn't opposed to his friendship at all. He checked on the boys and Gram, prayed for all of them, Kristin included, and got into bed, glad to be home in Idaho.

After he got the boys off the next morning, he took a loaf of the banana nut bread Gram had made for breakfast that morning and went next door. When she opened the door, he knew she had been up a good portion of the night and chided himself for not realizing it and coming to be with her. He handed her the loaf of hot bread. "Bad night?"

She just smiled a weary smile and invited him in. "The bread smells wonderful. I was just about to have breakfast before I head off to work. Have you already eaten?"

"I ate with the boys, but I'll sit with you."

"How was Phoenix? Did you find your missing fortune?"

"I'm still working on that. How did you do here?" Her "fine" was less than enthusiastic, and he reached to lift her chin so he could see her eyes. "Both nights were bad?"

She shrugged and offered him a cup of hot chocolate. "I'm okay, Joe. You don't need to worry about me. I'll be fine."

"Can I give you a blessing tonight after the missionaries leave?'"

"I would love that. Thank you."

He got up to go. "Call me, or just come over. Have you already got a lesson for tomorrow?"

She grimaced. "I'm not sure, but I think so. You ruined my no adult policy and the resort owner found out about it. He asked if he could be my project for awhile."

"You don't look very happy about that. Is there something wrong with him?"

"No." She hesitated. "It's just that he'd like to be more than just my student, and I'm not really looking forward to dodging him for the rest of the season."

He put a hand on her shoulder. "Look on the bright side. You've only got another what? Three weeks?"

"Four. And then I have to find something to do with myself for a few weeks until my horse rides start up."

"You'll find something. Have a great day."

Several times that day while he was working in his home office, he caught himself day dreaming about her. At first he felt a little silly, and then decided to quit worrying about it and just savor it. He thoroughly enjoyed her. He called and found that she was indeed scheduled for Thursday, Friday and Saturday all three, and he knew his boys would be disappointed that they'd have to ski without her again this weekend. He asked to reserve her class for the next Tuesday and Saturday.

That night, when he went to give her a blessing, she mentioned it. "I saw you on my schedule and asked my boss to give me those days off. Can we just free ski instead?"

He hesitated. "You're not going to suggest we go heli-skiing are you?"

With a laugh, she said, "No! I think I'm through heli-skiing at least for this season. Plus, there's probably not going to be a ton of fresh powder. The snow is getting kind of grainy."

"Can we free ski all day without you hassling me about being married? 'Cause if not, I'm willing to pay for a lesson."

She cracked up as she sat on the loveseat in his office. "I won't hassle you if you don't try to hug me."

"And I won't try to hug you unless you're terribly unhappy and sitting in a hospital."

"Deal." She nodded and then laughed as she added. "My boss thinks I'm taking them off because I want to avoid you."

Chuckling as well, he gave her the blessing, and after they talked for a few minutes she headed out of his office. As she passed the boys, she invited them to bring their friends and come swim in her pool anytime, at which they jumped up and gave each other high fives. Kristin smiled at Joe as she left.

# Chapter 16

The boys took Kristin up on her offer of the pool for that very Friday. She'd been able to sleep perfectly both Wednesday and Thursday nights, which was a good thing because she had indeed been scheduled to teach Howard Cummings both days, and not just in the afternoons. Friday evening Joe came over before the kids all got there so she was there to see his face when Tasha arrived.

Tasha made a commotion as she stood beside the pool to take off her cover up and reveal the skimpiest bathing suit Kristin had honestly ever seen. Joe was horrified and quickly looked around to see where his boys were. They were all playing with a water ball in the pool already and didn't notice her for a minute. When they finally saw her, it got a little quiet for a minute and then one of the other guys from their ward started to hassle her.

"Oh, Tasha, quit making a scene and either get in the pool or cover back up. How come you wore your baby sister's suit anyway?" With that, he threw the soaking wet water ball at her, hitting her with a splat in the side of the head. She got disgusted with him and that led to a water fight that thoroughly trashed her hair and make up and she ended up only staying for a short time.

The other girls seemed like really nice girls and so both Joe and Kristin weren't sad to see Tasha go. As she went past them in the kitchen on the way out, she touched Joe on the chest with a finger just like she had Gabriel that first day, and gave him a smile. Kristin would have laughed at his expression if she hadn't been suddenly so angry.

She was mad and Joe was floored! He looked over at Kristin in utter disbelief. "What is up with that girl? She's unreal! That is the last time she is going to be around these boys on my watch!"

"Amen. I wanted to walk right over there and choke her." She finally cracked a smile. "Or at least hit her in the side of the head with the water ball, like Nate did."

Later that night when Joe got a minute to talk frankly with the boys about Tasha again, he was troubled to find out that she had been flirting outrageously with all three of his sons. He was even more troubled to notice that although Caleb and Gabriel were openly relieved to know they were to completely avoid Tasha and that she wasn't to be invited to their home again, Robby didn't seem very happy about their dad's decree at all.

Joe's prayers that night included a longer plea than usual to help him know what to do as a father to help his sons. As he dropped off to sleep, he wondered if the reason Kristin had wanted to choke Tasha was that she was just a little bit possessive. He hoped so.

He was back in the pool at two-twenty that morning after going to be with Kristin. He'd been sitting in the hot tub when he heard her scream again. It was long and drawn out and filled with a horror that was haunting. Even before Murdock let him in, he could hear her crying.

She swam for over an hour this time, although Joe got out and toweled off after only forty five minutes. When she finished swimming, she dressed in outdoor clothing and he figured they were headed into the woods until she changed her mind at the last minute and turned back around and went to the little cabin instead. Joe built her a fire and then went to sit beside her on the loveseat, still without a word. She sat there looking into the fire with tears streaming down her cheeks. Finally, she turned to him and asked him to go home.

He didn't answer her, but he didn't leave either, and she turned to him. "Go home, Joe. I don't want you to see me like this."

Unsure of what to do exactly, he finally just decided to follow his gut. Just when he'd decided he had to hug her again, she got up and turned and took his hands to pull him to his feet. He knew she was trying to throw him out, but instead of leaving, he let her pull him up and then pulled her to him in a hug. At first she tried to resist him, but then she clung to him and sobbed. After several minutes, he backed up and sat down and pulled her onto his lap. Wrapping both arms around her, he leaned his cheek on her hair and just held her and let her cry as long as she needed to.

He didn't realize she was asleep at first, because she was still breathing with little hiccupping sobs. He held her for a few minutes more and then gently got up and laid her down and covered her up. He didn't even take her snow boots off for fear he would reawaken her and she'd have to go through that depth of heartache again.

As he walked back to his house, he was a little sick at heart because he knew that tomorrow she wouldn't want to see him.

He was right.

She was gone before he had even gotten out of bed in the morning, and he sent the boys skiing without him. As he went through the day, he wracked his brain, trying to figure out how he could help her without making her feel self conscious or intruded upon. On a hunch, he called Murdock. When he answered the phone, Joe asked him right out if Kristin had said anything about him before she went to work. Murdock was hesitant at first, and then admitted that she had instructed him not to let Joe in anymore.

He'd been afraid of that. He didn't blame her. His heart went out to her again for what she was going through and had been going through for years now. Finally, he called a florist and ordered a vase of wildflowers. He tried to order the same vase and colors she had painted with her little girls. All the card said was, "I'm sorry I intruded. Please know you are welcome anytime, Joe" He wasn't sure if it would do any good, but he didn't know what else to do.

That night he knew she was awake, but he stayed away anyway, knowing she wouldn't want him there. He tried not to, but from time to time he went to the window and looked out into the dark, wondering if she was okay. He knew she wasn't, but he didn't want to make her even more miserable than she already was. He lay back down and tried to go to sleep.

It was impossible and he worried far into the night. Finally, he got down on his knees again and prayed for her. And for him. He prayed for inspiration about how to help her, and how to have some peace of mind when there was nothing he could do.

After pouring his heart out one more time, he got back into bed. He decided to go on faith here because, much as he'd like to help, for the time being at least, there was nothing he could do. On the other hand, he knew God knew what needed to be done and he trusted that as long as he did his best to be faithful, it would all turn out, somehow.

Sunday morning as he and his family got ready to go to church, he was surprised when, a few minutes before it was time to go, Kristin tentatively knocked on his door. When he opened it, their eyes met for a few seconds before he said, "Come on in. You look nice." She looked like heck and he knew it and she knew it, but he was going to make this as no big deal as possible.

She was hesitant. "Could I get a ride with you?"

"Absolutely. Come in, we're just about ready to go."

She came in and the boys all said hi. Gabriel came over and hugged her and pulled back to look at her for a second, but he didn't say anything. Gram came in and gave each boy an inspection and then approached Kristin. She took her hand in both of her aged ones and patted it. "Good morning, young lady. It's so good to have a breath of feminine air here. My, but you look nice this morning. And you have such a sweet spirit about you."

"Thank you, Gram. It's so kind of you to say that."

Caleb interrupted to ask Joe if he could drive. Joe smoothly denied him because it was snowing out and then helped Gram into her coat. She said, "Thank you, Joe. Caleb's driving has been known to turn my gray hair to white at times." They all headed into the garage and Robby held the front passenger door for Kristin. The drive over was uneventful in that the boys were up to their usual teasing and no one but Joe and Kristin seemed to notice the strain. On the way into the building, Joe held onto Gram's arm on the icy walk and he offered Kristin his other hand, but let go of her as soon as she was safely inside.

He struggled to focus on sacrament meeting. Not only was he very aware of her sitting there on the other side of Gram from him, but he was still wrestling with how he could find a way to still help her. He finally focused enough to listen to the talks on faith. About half way through the first talk, he was able to actually tune in and he became aware, just as he had late last night, that what he needed to do again was to trust in his Father in Heaven.

He knew in his heart that as long as he did his best to do what he honestly thought he was being prompted to do, that it would all work out the way it was supposed to. He was willing to do that, but he realized he was still frustrated in spite of saying he was willing to trust in God.

He did a little soul searching and found that the conflict was in the fact that what he really wanted was to be involved in her life. He let the talks fade as he searched his own head and heart to try to figure out just what he wanted out of this friendship with Kristin.

He knew this wasn't just a Good Samaritan thing, or even a missionary thing. When he got really honest with himself, he admitted that unless he discovered skeletons in her closet that were far graver than what he had already discovered, he could see himself growing old beside her. Her baggage, heavy duty as it was, didn't intimidate him. Her struggles actually made him respect her all the more and they somehow brought out an almost primal protective instinct in him. At this point, it would take a major character flaw to get him to want to seriously back away from her, and from what he'd seen so far, she was a rock.

After sacrament meeting, he was headed to the Elder's Quorum when Bishop Harrington intercepted him. He put a hand on his shoulder and asked, "How'd it go, Joe? I've been praying for you all week."

Joe thought about the scene in the lodge last Monday morning and gave him the first real smile he'd felt in a couple of days. He pulled the bishop aside and gave him the no frills version of finding his wife in bed with another man, and his deciding then and there that he was under no obligation to honor her farcical request to reconcile. He ended with, "And Bishop it feels right and good to say that I'm going to make being single official. I have no idea what's in store for me, but I feel good about moving on."

He saw the bishop glance up at Kristin headed into Relief Society with Gram and added, "Bishop, she's a wonderful lady, but she isn't entirely sure she wants me around. I'll respect that, but I still intend to be the best neighbor I can, and my family too. That being said, I think she could use some home teachers she could depend on when she needs help but doesn't necessarily want to encourage me. I know she's not a member yet, but I think she's headed that way, and I know there are times that having the priesthood available would be a good thing. Just send someone in who isn't likely to crowd her personally."

"I think you're right. I'll see about having some arranged for her. She ought to have visiting teachers too. In your opinion, is Gram an option?"

Joe nodded. "I think Gram would be perfect."

"Is she still taking the missionary lessons?"

"She is having them over again this afternoon as far as I know. It will be their third visit."

"How is it going?"

"Well. She's a wonderful person, and wants to know the truth."

"In light of what you just said about her being unsure what she wants from you, are you still sitting in on the missionary visits?"

"I honestly don't know the answer to that. I'll ask her in Sunday School and let you know."

"Would you rather I ask her?"

Joe thought about that for a second. "She would probably appreciate that. Would you mind? You can tell her I told you she was a little tentative where I'm concerned. She'll understand."

"I'll see if I can catch her before she leaves today. If not, I'll call her before the appointment. It would be good to make sure and have someone she trusts be there to support her."

"Thank you. And Bishop?" He turned back. "She does trust Gabriel without reservation. If I need to, I'll stay home and he can be there for her."

The bishop extended his hand. "You're a good man, Joe. I'm going to keep praying for you."

"Thanks. I need it, I'm afraid."

After church, before she went home, Joe caught her and asked her what she had decided about having him there for the missionary lessons. She looked up at him and then down. "What do you prefer, Joe? Do you want to come?"

He put a finger gently under her chin to get her to look at him. "I would like to be there to support you, Kristin, but if it's going to make you feel pressured, then I'd rather you have someone with you who won't make you uncomfortable."

She looked up at him steadily for a long moment, "If you don't come today, could Gabriel still come?"

"Of course."

She dropped her eyes. "Maybe he and Gram could come."

"Are either of the other boys welcome?"

Looking back up, she nodded. "Yes, they both are, why?"

He shrugged. "Maybe I'll just plead sick to save face, and let them all come so no one feels uncomfortable. Would that be all right?"

She hesitantly met his eyes. "Sure."

"Plan on them then. Have a good day, Kristin." He looked at her one more time and turned away so she could go home. He knew he'd done the right thing, and he tried not to let it sting, but it did. He honestly did feel like going home and taking a long nap. He was tired.

He slept all the way through the missionaries and even through dinner, got up, ate, and then went back to bed again for the night. By morning, he knew it wasn't just that he was discouraged. He woke up with a raging head cold, feeling guilty for not even waking up in the night to see if she was sleeping. He got the boys off, checked on Gram and went back to bed with a cold pill.

This time he slept until he heard them arrive from school and dragged himself out of bed. He listened to the stories about their day and ate loaded nachos with them before leaving them to their homework and heading back to bed. He didn't know they had invited Kristin to family home evening with them until he saw her walk in the back door carrying a plate of brownies. They had planned to have a lesson and go bowling. He made it through a short lesson on integrity, only sneezing about two dozen times, and then begged off again to go back to bed while the rest of them headed out to bowl.

He slept through them getting home, but not through Kristin having to get up and go to the studio. He watched her walk up the hill and turned and went back to bed. How was a decent human being supposed to sit back and watch someone who so needed help? He heard a door shut and got up to look out again and realized Gabriel had gone next door. He smiled and sighed and went back to bed. Gabriel could get her to let down her emotional guard and give her the help she needed.

After breakfast he asked Gabriel if she was okay and he answered, "No, but I knew you didn't feel much like going so I took care of her." Caleb heard them talking, and looked from one to the other with a confused look.

Finally, he asked, "Is something wrong with Kristin?"

Gabriel and Joe exchanged a look and then Gabriel answered him, "Sometimes, she has trouble sleeping and it's better if someone goes to be with her when she's up painting in her little cabin. Dad's been going sometimes, but last night he was sick, so I went."

Caleb looked at them and then said, "I'll go take care of her if she needs it sometime."

Gabriel looked at Joe and back to Caleb. "I'll bet she'd like that."

Joe hadn't talked to Kristin about skiing with her today, but she knew he was sick and he knew she didn't want to face him, so it had gone without saying that they wouldn't be skiing together anytime soon. He watched her drive away headed for work and then he headed for his office as well.

He phoned Max and dug right into the mess back at the hospital, doing his best to put Kristin into a neat little compartment in his head so he wasn't so discouraged about her. When he stayed busy it worked to a certain extent, so for the next several days he pushed himself. Gabriel had gotten up and gone to her on two nights when he'd seen lights over there, and on three other nights he'd seen her get up and ride away on her horse. It had been over a week since the night he had held her when she cried.

Gram finally asked him what was going on Saturday morning after the boys were gone skiing with Kristin without him. He knew he couldn't put her off, so he was honest about what had happened to Kristin and what had transpired between them. Gram shook her head with that wise way of hers and patted his hand. "She looks like the wrath of Moses, you look like someone ran over your puppy, and Gabriel is taking it all on his shoulders. What's to become of us? Maybe we'd better take a trip in to the temple in Idaho Falls."

Jaclyn M. Hawkes

# Chapter 17

Having experienced Joe's help and then trying to go without it couldn't have come at a worse time. Ever since the night Teal had growled at something in the bushes, Kristin had been struggling worse than ever. At first, she had been too nervous to even go out onto the trail, and then after chastising herself mentally for being timid, she had gone out again, but only on horseback.

The first night that had been okay, but then the next time out, her horse had shied violently at the exact same spot in the trail next to the mahoganies and nearly unseated her. She tried to pass it off as coincidence, which didn't truly work, but when it happened again the next time she was there, she turned around and circling wide around the spot went straight back home. The next afternoon, as soon as she got home from skiing with Joe's sons, she took Teal and went back up the trail in the light to investigate. She found just what she'd dreaded finding. There were footprints in the clump of shrubs. Large human footprints. Lots of them.

For just a second, she wondered if Joe had been out here because she had refused to let him come to help her, but she immediately discarded the idea, long before she remembered that he had been in Phoenix the first night someone had been here. She knew innately that Joe would never do something like this. She didn't even understand what the man in the bushes had been doing here. Why would someone come up this trail and hide in the cold on a dark winter's night? No one but her ever even came up here.

As soon as that thought registered, she had to acknowledge the fact that she had been trying to skirt mentally since that very first night she'd been frightened. Whoever was coming here was coming here to watch her, or worse. The fear that she knew was compounding the nightmares like a one-two punch, made the skin on the back of her neck prickle and her stomach tighten. She didn't need this.

Returning to her house, she went to find Murdock. As soon as he saw her face, he abruptly asked, "What's wrong?"

She tried to be calm about it all as she asked him, "Have you got a minute? There's something I'd like your opinion on. It's outside, you'd better slip your boots and coat on." When they approached the mahogany clump, she pointed to the trampled snow inside the small stand of thick bushes.

She had tried to recall the first time Teal had reacted here. "A week ago, last Monday, when I was snowshoeing, Teal raised a ruckus right here on the way home. I remember thinking it was odd, because she didn't act like it was an animal she was afraid of. She snarled like it was a person. Then three nights ago, Jet shied violently right here and it happened again last night. So I came out here today in the light and found this. What do you make of it?"

Murdock looked up and into her eyes. He looked around for a minute and then came back to her. She knew he was trying not to frighten her when he hesitated and finally she prompted him, "Somebody is watching me at nights, aren't they?"

"I'll have to check around here more, Kristin, but honestly at first glance that's what it looks like." He mused to himself, "I didn't think any of the Facianos would do something like this."

She shook her head. "It wasn't one of them. I'm sure of it. You're right, none of them would do this, but Joe was out of town the first time anyway. And Teal would never growl at one of them. She would wag them to death and dive into the bushes to be petted. She adores them."

"You're probably correct, but I'd better check it out anyway. Let's get you back and I'll come up and look around some more. The snow is hard to hide much in, and he has to get here from somewhere." They began to walk back home, and he was quiet for several minutes and then said, "Kris, I know this is going to be hard for you right now, when you and Joe are like you are, but I don't think you should be out here in the dark by yourself until we get to the bottom of this."

She sighed. "I know." He hesitated again, but she knew there was something else he wanted to say. "It's okay, Murdock. Go ahead and say it."

"I was just thinking that if this isn't one of the Facianos, then they need to be told."

"I know that, too." She sighed again. "Joe's gonna have a fit."

He looked over at her for a long moment. "Is it so bad to be cared for? There are people the world over who would give anything for someone as good as Joe to be concerned about them."

"Oh, Murdock. It's not that. It's wonderful to be cared for. And Joe is good. That's the problem. He's a good man, with a wonderful family. Why should he and his boys have to deal with a mess like me? I can't do that to them. And honestly, I like Joe far too much to even want him to know what a wreck my life is. And I'm afraid he cares for me, too. Involving him is a terrible thing to do to a man as fine as he is."

"Don't you think he has the right to make his own decisions about what he wants to be involved in? If you don't like him and don't want him around, that's one thing, but do you really think his being there is coincidence? He's been good for you, Kristin. I was beginning to think that eventually he could help you heal."

Her voice was sad when she answered, "Me, too."

When Murdock came back into the house an hour later, his face was grim. "It looks bad, Kristin. I think we should call the police. He's been here a number of times, and it's not just out in the woods. He's been watching you in the cabin and even here in the house sometimes."

She'd known that would be the case. Somehow she'd felt it. She'd even felt like someone was watching her while she was at work or at church last week. That had to be her imagination, but she had known the trail wouldn't be the only issue. Looking back, she was sure the fear she had been feeling was the reason the nightmares had strengthened this last week. How she wished she could ask Joe for another priesthood blessing.

Murdock called the police, and then went in search of Joe, and Kristin went into her room and shut the door. She knew Murdock would know what to do to help the police, and she wasn't sure she felt strong enough to face Joe right now. She knew how he was going to feel about all this. She curled up on her window seat, and looked out at the late winter afternoon. Was Murdock right? She trusted him implicitly with her safety. She knew he honestly loved her like a father. Was he right to insinuate that Joe had a right to decide if he wanted to be there for her or not? Or was it her duty to protect him and his family from the ravages of her life since the explosion?

She saw Murdock return with Joe and Hershey. Teal wandered out to meet them, greeting Hershey with enthusiasm. Joe glanced up at her window and she knew he saw her, but she didn't wave. The fatigue from her short nights, coupled with the fear, and even more so the discouragement and loneliness she had been feeling this last week, had stolen every bit of her spirit's energy. She lay down on top of the comforter on her bed, considering going to bed without bothering with dinner. She had almost drifted off, when there came a quiet knock on her door. When she said, "Come in.", Murdock poked his head around.

"Are you up to talking to Joe for a minute, or not?"

Dragging herself up, she ran a hand through her hair. "Not really, but I probably should."

"He's in the entry, waiting." He left her and headed toward the back of the house. She headed toward the front of it, wondering what she was going to say to Joe, and a little disgusted with herself that she was so calmed by the fact that he was here to see her.

She completely surprised herself by walking up to him and taking his hand to lead him into the living room and sitting beside him on the couch. When they were seated, she surprised them both by not letting go of it. He just sat quietly looking at her like he was trying to read her mind for several seconds. In time, he leaned back against the couch and tugged on her hand until she leaned over against him. For awhile neither of them spoke. At length he asked, "How have you been?"

She shrugged. "Okay. And you?"

"Kristin, you may not believe it, but I'm tough enough that you can be honest with me."

She thought about that for a minute. He was right. She believed this man was strong enough to handle honesty. Honesty just wasn't very fair to him. "I've had better weeks. How is your cold?"

"Cold's better. Spirit's a little tired." She leaned back to look up at him, knowing exactly what he meant.

"I'm sorry."

He looked right at her and asked, "That my spirit is tired? Or that you've shut me out?"

Leaning against him again, she answered, "Both."

"Does that mean I'm welcome back, or just that you're sorry I'm not welcome?"

She sighed. "I don't know what it means. If you've come to see if I have all the answers, you're going to be disappointed with me. You know it's not a welcome thing. It's a what's fair to Joe thing."

"Why doesn't Joe get to decide?"

She looked down and fidgeted. "That's exactly what Murdock asked me earlier."

Gently, he asked, "What did you tell Murdock?"

She answered without looking up. "That you were too good a man to have to deal with a mess like this."

He asked her outright. "So Joe doesn't have any say and you're good with that?" She looked up at him again. He rubbed the back of her hand with his thumb, and leaned his shoulder against her again. "It'll never work. Joe's too stubborn. But if it'll make you feel better, you're welcome to try."

Neither one of them said anything for several minutes. Then out of the blue she asked, "Why?"

"Why what?"

"Why do you even want to help me?"

He looked down at her with a sad smile. "If you think I have all the answers, you're going to be disappointed with me. I don't know why. I wish I could say it was because it's what I should do. It would be easier to understand, but it's not that it's what I should do. It's what I want to do. You're going to think I'm a nut, but clear back two summers ago, I felt like I needed to help you somehow. Then I didn't even know about your struggles, I just knew something was missing. You'd laugh, but it never really reached your eyes. Now I understand that."

She took a deep breath and let it out with a sigh. "So what is it you want from me?"

Shrugging, he said, "I don't know the answer to that either. What is it you want from me?"

She studied him and then looked away. "I haven't got a clue."

He gave her another smile that was a little bit sad. "We're quite a pair."

With a shake of her head, she said, "Not really. You seem to have everything handled and neatly wrapped up. I honestly wonder if I'll ever feel that way."

He chuckled. "Maybe you should have a long talk with Gram. Ask her what I was like the day she met me. It would be very enlightening. As far as that goes. I have a long way to go yet."

She didn't say anything. Didn't even smile, and he knew that this new issue of a stalker hadn't eased her burden. He squeezed her hand gently and got up. "Kristin, comparing troubles isn't going to help. I'm never going to talk you into anything. I'm not even going to try. Your life is yours. You can decide to let me in or not. I'm not going to pressure you.

"I'm just going to show you that I'm here when you need me, and I'll leave you alone when you want to shut me out. It's not okay, but it's all going to be someday. In time you'll come to see that."

He continued, "Tell me what I can do to help you today. Without pressuring you, is there anything I can do for you?"

She shook her head. "With this new development of someone watching me, I don't know what I need. All the things I've been doing to be able to get through now have this underlying element of fear added. I'm afraid now, as well as being the crazy, hermit lady."

She tried to smile at him. "Honestly, the dreams have cranked up with a vengeance." She didn't even dare voice the fact that they had been worse this week than ever.

"Should I find someone else to come and give you a blessing?" He was sad about that question, but sincere.

Looking up, she said, "No. But would you mind giving me another one now?"

His brown eyes looked into her blue ones. "You already know the answer to that, Kristin. Of course not. I will never mind that. By the way, the missionaries can give you blessings, too. Have they ever assigned you home teachers yet?"

"The bishop called and said something about that, but I'm not sure what that is."

He explained to her and mentioned that her home teachers would be able to give blessings, too. Then he laid his hands on her head and gave her a sweet blessing of strength and it held the added promise that everything would eventually be okay if she exercised her faith. When he was through, he squeezed her shoulder and walked out of the room without even saying good bye.

She knew he was trying not to pressure her too much, and she appreciated it. She knew she should stay away from him and get back into being the hermit that helped her to survive without disturbing people, but when he was gone she felt that deep feeling of tiredness again.

When the missionaries called to check on her and make sure they were on for the next day, she confirmed, but she knew somehow it would be without Joe again. It was necessary, but it killed her, too. She almost wished she had never met him. Then she wouldn't know just how much she was missing.

She rode to church with them again the next day, but even the boys had figured out there was something wrong between the two of them. They were still friendly and upbeat, but there was an undercurrent she regretted with all her heart. The bishop introduced her to two elderly gentlemen and their wives. They were the two men who were going to be her home teachers, and one of their wives was going to be her visiting teacher with Gram as her partner. Gram explained all this to her on their way to Relief Society.

When Joe came back in, he took the seat on the other side of Gram again, and Kristin sighed. She'd gotten just what she had insisted on, and it was the best thing, but she hated consciously deciding to push away the one person she wanted to be with more than anyone. On the way out of the church she had that feeling again that someone was watching her, and she looked around. She knew she was getting positively paranoid, but she walked closer to Joe anyway.

That afternoon she had the missionaries to her house again, and even though Joe not being there felt like a gaping hole, she knew that what they were teaching her was good and right and true. Before they left, they asked her to commit to baptism and she agreed without hesitation. Gabriel and the boys cheered and high fived and Gram wiped tears from her eyes. The two elders told her the stake baptism was two weeks away, and set another appointment to come back on Wednesday.

After everyone had left, she went into her room and looked out the window toward his house. She wished she could have asked him to be the one to baptize her, but she knew that was out of the question under the circumstances. It wasn't fair to shut him out and then use him. She'd been studying on her own, and she had come to cherish what she was learning. She wondered what the days and months and years after the explosion would have been like for her if she had known then what she knew now. Before the explosion would have been different, she knew that.

Her home life with her parents and brother could have been so much more than it was and there were so many things she wished she had been taught as a child. A knowledge of the gospel could have helped to prepare her for so many of the bumps in the road of life she hadn't been able to miss because she didn't know better. Her marriage could have been so much more important and fulfilling. She had lived a much different life than she had been taught because she had made better choices on her own, but she was incredibly grateful to find the gospel at last.

She would have loved to share it all with Joe. Now that she had made the decision to spare him and his family from dealing with her issues, she could be honest with herself and admit that it would have been heaven on earth to have been able to just enjoy him like the woman she had been before would have. To just live and love and see where it all ended up. It wasn't hard to imagine herself the queen of the Faciano kingdom.

For the ten thousandth time she wished she could have a normal life. This time it wasn't just so she didn't have to go through the horror and grief and loneliness. This time it was because she absolutely knew what she was missing out on.

Although she saw the boys almost every day, she didn't see Joe much. He had been good about making sure the boys didn't hold the fact that she had shut him and his help out of her life against her. They still visited and were friendly just like before, and, in fact, were sometimes even better than before about making sure to help her in any way they could. She had a nightmare on Tuesday and Gabriel ended up in her studio with her for awhile. She carefully pulled the drapes now wherever she was, and she tried to explain to him without scaring him that he shouldn't come and visit her, but he insisted it was what neighbors did.

The fear of being stalked was wearing on her and compounded by the fact that she wasn't able to get out and work off the intense emotion by walking or riding in the dark by herself. The pool became her only outlet and she had thick blinds installed to stifle any would be prowlers. She purchased a treadmill and universal gym and put them on the pool deck to augment her swims, and Murdock became much more intensely vigilant and set up a sophisticated security system and surveillance equipment all the way around her perimeter.

In ways, it made her feel more secure, and in ways it made the fear move right to the forefront. It was as if the fear sparked off the nightmares and she was hard put to find peace even when she did her best to exercise her faith. Before the missionaries left on Wednesday evening, she asked them for a blessing to help stave off the hellish nights, and found herself praying several times a day. Sometimes, she wished God was in the wind. A still small voice of peace was hard to hear through her fears.

More than a week later, on Thursday, after spending the third day that week fielding more and more overt passes from Howard Cummings, she drove home to find Joe waiting for her with Murdock. Joe had bought her a tiny black pistol that looked like something out of a James Bond movie, and a holster she could wear right over her winter gear to go with it. She met his eyes and wondered if he understood just what being stranded without the mountain trail was doing to her life.

At first, she was hesitant to even touch the little gun, but Murdock encouraged her and promised he would help her learn to handle it safely. And honestly, she loved the thought of having it with her, even if it was only in case she encountered a mountain lion. She didn't think she could ever really shoot someone, but she was surprised at how reassuring that little chunk of metal turned out to be. As Joe left her with Murdock, he told her that he would be out of town again for a couple of days. He encouraged her again to call him there, and reminded her the boys would do anything she needed while he was gone.

# Chapter 18

She hadn't called. He'd suspected she wouldn't, but it hadn't hurt to hope. It was almost midnight on Saturday night as he was returning home from his trip to Phoenix, and it hadn't been the conclusive success he had hoped it would be. He and Max were getting closer to tracking down the missing money, but they hadn't unraveled it all yet. He'd assumed that one person somewhere had pulled something, but it was beginning to look to them like a collaboration of some sort.

Not only had they not gotten to the bottom of things, but Cindy Kunz had dogged him for two whole days. He'd finally remembered her name with a little help from Max. He'd tried to evade her by just being busy, but had finally had to remind her in no uncertain terms that his divorce wasn't final and he was technically still married. She had irritated him to no end.

He actually had met with his attorney over lunch Friday and signed his portion of the legal documents that had to be filed. Nicole had been served with hers over a week ago and had surprisingly signed and returned them right away with no fuss. Now all that needed to be done was have them make their way through the system. That was the one thing that had worked out well this trip.

He'd done a lot of soul searching after giving Kristin the little gun on Thursday. He wasn't sure how she would take his gift, but the fact that she had accepted so easily troubled him. He knew she was having a bad time of it, probably even worse than she'd been having before they had moved in next door, from the looks of her. She had always had that bit of a shadow in her eyes that hinted of a past hurt, but lately she looked almost haggard in spite of being strikingly beautiful. Knowing someone had been stalking her must be compounding the scars on her mind and heart.

It had been three weeks since she had pulled away from him, and whatever she was doing to get through didn't appear to be working so well. He'd thought he could keep his distance and honor her wishes, but he wasn't sure he could continue to watch her struggle and not offer to help again. At any rate, he didn't feel in his heart that it was the right thing to do anyway.

He pulled into his garage and went into the house, and was grateful when he looked over at her place that everything seemed dark and quiet and peaceful. Checking on the boys and Gram, he made himself some hot chocolate and then went to stand next to the big picture window that looked out over the snowy mountains to drink it while he wound down from his drive. Idaho had grown on him quickly and the view out that window had him feeling like he was home. He drank his chocolate and then set it down to rotate his head and stretch his neck after the flight and trip from Jackson back over the pass. He put up a hand to rub the back of his neck, and then stood stock still, wondering what he had just seen.

There was something moving out there in the trees. It had just been a flicker of movement, but he knew he'd seen something. He pulled the spotting scope over to train it on the spot, even as he dialed Murdock's cell phone number. Murdock's voice was tired but absolutely alert when he picked up. Joe had found what he was looking for with the scope and explained to Murdock that he had just walked in and was watching someone sneaking through the trees toward Kristin's yard. They spoke briefly, and then hung up, and Joe went to get out his own hand gun while he called the police.

Thirty minutes later, they'd found where the guy had left his vehicle and walked in, but somehow he had slipped back into the trees and gotten away. They'd managed to let Kristin sleep through it all, but it was to no advantage because Joe was still standing in her kitchen whispering with Murdock when he heard her cry out.

His eyes met Murdock's, who shook his head in defeat and said, "I'm losing this battle, Joe. The stress and her not being able to get out are making the nights worse than they've ever been. She's afraid now, as well as being troubled. And on top of that, there's some guy at the resort who's giving her fits. He's the owner or something and is insisting she give him ski lessons everyday. He apparently thinks she's going to fall for him if he spends every single second with her and he's driving her nuts."

Joe looked at him, wondering why he was telling him this. He'd been toying with the idea of trying to push his way back into her life on the way home tonight, and after the last while looking for her stalker and now this, he knew he had to. He was just about to ask Murdock to let him in to see her, when Murdock said, "I know she said she didn't want you there, but it was only to protect you from the problems. You helped her so much, in such a short time. Would you be willing to try again? I think she needs you."

"What she doesn't understand, Murdock, is that I need her, too."

"Well, go on in, then. Maybe she'll be realistic enough to admit that she's in over her head."

She stayed in her room for several minutes and then went out into the pool house.

He went home and got into his suit, thinking it might go smoother if he just swam with her for awhile rather than trying to talk to her right off. It seemed to be working when she got out and toweled off after only swimming for thirty-five minutes. When she came out of the dressing room, she came over to him with almost an air of defeat. "Hi, Joe."

"Hi, Kristin." He looked back at her for a second and then asked, "Is it okay if I come with you for a little while tonight?"

The war of emotions going on in her head were clearly visible on her face for a time, and he wondered if she was going to shut him out again, but her desperation won out. "I should say no, but I'd really love your company. Do you think it would be safe to walk for a minute if you're with me?"

Joe doubted her stalker would be back that night again, and he knew she needed some freedom. "I think so. We'll tell Murdock we're going, and we should be fine." He didn't tell her that he would be carrying his own gun in his parka, and he was glad to see that she automatically slung her holster on over her coat on the way out.

It was mid March, and although it was still cold, it was much warmer out than it had been during the dead of winter at this time of night, and was actually nice out. They began to walk up the trail and he just let her lead the way in silence, with him behind her. At the top of the first ridge the trail widened onto what must have been a Forest Service road and they were able to walk side by side. He reached across and took her gloved hand in his. The worry that she would totally reject his overture heightened when she pulled her hand back, and then melted when she took her glove off and put it into her pocket and then took his hand again. He finally felt like he was making headway when he took his off, too, and they walked on up the road with her small hand warm is his.

Later, when the trail narrowed back down and she dropped her hand and moved ahead of him again, he felt ridiculously bereft about its loss. It was a simple thing, but holding her hand had been incredibly satisfying and had gone a long way toward mending their rift.

They'd been walking for over two hours and were almost back to her house when he decided to broach the subject of her letting him do more stuff with her. He had no idea how to go about it and finally settled for pulling her to a stop so she was looking at him, "Are you going to be mad at me if I tell you I really miss you?"

She pulled him into a walk again and said, "After the week I've had with Howard Cummings, I might."

"Is he the suit at the resort who always tried to stop you to talk? Or is he the resort owner you were telling me about?"

"Both. It's the same guy. And his notion that he's in love with me is suffocating me. I only have fourteen days left, and the last two years I've been sad that the season was ending, but this year it can't come fast enough."

"Tell your boss you've changed your mind about adult lessons again."

She sighed. "I've already tried that. This guy is the main owner of the resort, and basically overrode my boss."

Glancing down at her, he said, "You could always quit."

She shook her head. "But I want to come back next season. It's okay. I can handle anything for two weeks. How about you? Did you figure out the money mystery at the hospital?"

"No, actually. Whoever did it has hidden the paper trail well. We're inclined to think it's not just one person. There are too many departments that are suspect."

"Who is we?"

"My old secretary was willing to come out of retirement to help me get to the bottom of it. When I left, she decided to retire. I know without a doubt it's not her, so it made sense to have her help me. Max has been my right hand organizing wizard for most of my working life, and I just happened to ask on a day she was bored."

"Do you have any ideas about who did it?"

"We think we know; now we just have to be able to prove it."

They had reached her studio cabin and she turned toward him at the door. Apparently this was it, and she wasn't going to let him stay with her. "Thank you for coming over tonight. I'm sure you're tired, so I'll let you go home. Thank you for the walk, it was great to be able to get out again. Good night."

He wanted to ask her so many more things, but she had neatly sidestepped his admission that he missed her, and it was obvious that she was dismissing him now. "Good night, Kristin."

She rode to church with them again, and he tried to think of her as nothing more than the neighbor lady, but when she'd walked in this morning, even a little tired, she was exquisite. He made it a point to not sit next to her in the meetings, and when she and the missionaries were confirming their appointment that afternoon, he discreetly stayed away. One thing was good about him not being invited anymore to join in her conversion process; there couldn't have been any question that she was doing this for the right reasons.

When they were discussing her baptism that week, he was grateful it was a full stake baptism and he could show up without being invited. She wouldn't even have to know he was there. He could sit in the back and leave early. He was trying not to let this whole situation bother him, but he did miss her and honestly, being unwelcome in her conversion hurt like almost nothing ever had. Their friendship had come so easily at first. He'd even thought she was beginning to care for him. How had it ever come to this?

The boys had gotten used to him not doing things with Kristin so it was not a big deal that they all went to her house for the missionary lessons without him.

Monday night she came over for family home evening again, and this time the lesson was on service. He hadn't been sure she would be coming, but he'd hoped so. Maybe reiterating that helping each other was what the Savior expected of his saints would encourage her to let him back into her life more. He wasn't sure if it worked, but she let the boys walk her home at any rate.

Later that evening, Murdock called him. He told Joe that they were thinking of going to visit their daughter who was scheduled to have surgery in about ten days. He was wondering what Joe's schedule was going to be like at about that time. Joe didn't have set plans, but he assured Murdock he would do whatever he needed him to do to help her, so they could be free to go.

When he got off his phone, he went into his office and tried to put a schedule together that could coordinate the schedules of everyone involved. He wanted to help the Murdocks have the freedom they needed, while watching over Kristin. Then there was the fact that he needed to travel back to Phoenix again sometime and keep the boys supervised, and sometime soon Gram needed to go back in to have cataract surgery. As he worked to arrange it all, he came up with a plan.

Gram wanted to have her surgery back in Arizona because her grown children there wanted to be involved with caring for her when she went in. The boys had a two day break from school at the end of next week. He wondered if there would be any way he could talk Kristin into coming to Arizona with his family for a couple of days to keep her safe while the Murdocks were gone. That way he could schedule Gram's surgery and handle everything at the same time.

When he first broached the subject with her one afternoon after work, she wasn't open to the idea at all. The next day, after he saw her pull in, he went over and knocked on her kitchen door. She opened it and invited him in, but he could tell she was tired. He couldn't help being encouraged by the look he had seen in her eyes when she'd seen it was him. There was no mistaking the fact that she had been glad to see him, even as obviously tired as she was. It gave him enough faith to try to talk her into coming to his other house with them.

When she understood that he wanted her to come with him and the boys and Gram to stay right in his home with them for a few days she refused immediately. He understood her reasoning and at first coaxed her and then explained that if they did it this way, the Murdocks would be free to spend some time with their daughters.

She was adamant. "Joe, they can go for as long as they need to without worrying. I'll be fine here."

He used his best negotiating voice. "Kristin, you know they'll never agree to that. Elena will end up going without him. Look, Kris, I know you're hesitant to spend time away from you're own home the way nights go for you, but we'll do whatever we have to do to make you comfortable. Maybe you'd even really enjoy it. The weather is already warm there at this time of year, and you'll have a great excuse to get away from Howard."

She was shaking her head. "Joe, I couldn't do that to you, let alone to the boys. They would never think of me the same again. I can't control what I do when I'm asleep."

He took her hands and pulled her to look at him. "Kristin, we'll put you clear in Gram's apartment at the other end of the house from the boys while she's gone, and I'll leave the TV or radio on at night so the boys won't even know you're there. I have a pool, home gym, and a whole basketball court we can work out in if you need."

He started to wheedle. "At least think about it Kris, that way Murdock won't worry about you and neither will I, and I could really use the help with the boys that weekend. Please at least consider it." He left it at that, and went home, fully willing to keep picking at her to try to keep her safe while Murdock was away.

Several times that week, he called to ask her to consider coming and the Friday afternoon before her baptism, after an apparently tedious day with Howard, she finally agreed to let him schedule the trip. He felt like he'd won a major battle for some reason. It had been awful that week to have to stay at home when he knew she was up and struggling. Knowing he would be where he might be able to help her better was immensely satisfying.

The morning of her baptism, he woke up to contrasting emotions. He was so happy for her to be baptized, but the fact that he had to be so far removed from it all shredded his heart. He sent them all off in the Suburban early to meet the missionaries at the church, while he intended to come over later by himself. He would come in late so she didn't feel like he was pushing himself in without an invitation, and she wouldn't even need to know he was there. It was a pain in the heart, but at least he wouldn't have to miss it altogether.

He spent the drive over mentally pep talking himself to get over it. He hated when he let things get to him, but this was a tough one. She mattered enough to him that talking himself out of being hurt and discouraged was no small feat. Once there, he slipped into the back of the chapel and prayed quietly in his heart that this day would turn out to be the best for her.

# Chapter 19

It had been a horrible week. The nights had been bad, the days had been bad, and the times in between she had spent feeling so lonely that she felt sorry for herself, something she worked hard never to do. Gram had warned her a week or two ago that sometimes the days preceding big things like this held extra challenges but this week had all but been more than she could take. Every single night, she had wished she could call him and ask for help to get through, but she knew she couldn't do that to him.

When she came in from the studio Saturday morning, she knew she looked as hammered as she felt, but she couldn't fix it with mere cosmetics. It was a soul deep struggle that left her battered inside and out. She'd have been all right with Joe beside her, but that wasn't an option.

She put on her white dress and she and the Murdocks went across to ride to the church with the boys and Gram. When Joe didn't come out to leave with them, it wiped her out even further, even though she had been the one to insist he be shut out of her life except on the surface. None of the boys were cutting up this morning and she knew they felt the strain of having to do this without their dad alongside.

When she got to the church, she was helped by so many people to get dressed and be seated and decide who would do the baptizing and confirming and witnessing that it wasn't until she was finally sitting in her white suit next to the missionaries that she even had time to settle down and try to get a handle on the Spirit.

Just before they sat down, the one elder looked her in the eye and asked, "Are you sure Joe shouldn't be doing this?" She swallowed her tears and nodded. He'd asked her that four times already this week. She wanted Joe to baptize her more than anything, but she knew she had forfeited the right to even ask him at this point. And he hadn't come anyway. That was what had her tearing up, not the Spirit like everyone thought.

The meeting started and Kristin had to work to focus. The joy she felt because she was being baptized into Christ's church was having to vie with a deep discouragement that dogged her. The elder beside her turned to scan the room behind them for the umpteenth time, and then turned back to her to whisper, "Kristin, I feel strongly that Joe should be baptizing you today. Are you absolutely sure we can't ask him to?"

A tear slid from her eye as she whispered back, "He isn't here, so it isn't even an issue."

"He is here. He just came into the back. Can I go back and ask him if he would do this?"

She didn't know what to do. Finally she nodded her head yes. As he slipped from his seat beside her, she felt guilty for not being strong enough to protect Joe from the problems of her life, but grateful beyond belief that the elder had insisted. Now if only Joe would agree without being offended.

****

The meeting had started when one of the missionaries sitting with Kristin got up and came to the back of the chapel. He approached Joe and beckoned for him to follow him out into the foyer. Joe knew Kristin wasn't having second thoughts about going through with this, so he wondered what the problem was. Once outside the chapel doors, the elder stopped and turned to him, "Brother Faciano, Kristin wants to know if you would be the one to baptize and confirm her?"

Joe looked at him questioning. He'd thought she didn't even want him in the building. "Are you sure?"

The young elder nodded positively. "I've never been more sure."

"Of course I'll baptize her if that's what she wants."

"Then hurry and come get dressed. We only have a few minutes."

They rushed to get him clothing and changed and then they returned to the chapel to slip in as unobtrusively as they could. When he sat down beside her, she looked up at him and he was shocked at how bad she looked. There was both hope and trepidation in her tired eyes and he reached down and gave her hand a gentle squeeze and then felt her take a deep breath and let it out in a quiet sigh.

He tried to listen to what was being said, but it was hopeless. The talks were being directed to the eight year olds who surrounded them and were on too elementary of a level to overcome the thoughts tumbling through his head. He was trying to figure her out, and decided he had been right all along. It wasn't that she wanted him away from her, she was still just trying to protect him from the negatives she dealt with day in day out. If he hadn't known she thought she was doing it in his best interest, he would have been a little bit insulted in her lack of faith in him. She didn't understand how strong he was and how much she mattered.

He'd just have to show her. And this time, he wasn't going to let her deny him.

Even as tired as he knew she was, she positively glowed when she came up out of the water. He helped her up out of the font and into Gram's capable arms and then went to change his own clothes. He didn't know why she had changed her mind at the last minute, but he would always be grateful.

Two hours later, he had confirmed her and then had taken them all out to lunch with the missionaries, and now they were back home. He left the boys with Gram and went to waylay Kristin on the way back to her house. He hadn't figured out yet how he was going to convince her that he should give her a blessing and then hold her and help her sleep, but he knew it had to be done, so he prayed and then forged ahead.

She actually met him between houses headed back toward his. He hadn't even fully decided how to begin when she surprised him by saying, "Joe, I know I don't have the right to ask, but I need you. Is there any way I could steal you for even a little while this afternoon?"

He would have laughed if he hadn't been so concerned about her. He looked down at her earnest, sky blue eyes. "Tell me what you need."

"A blessing and maybe you could talk to me for a little while."

She led him to her studio cabin and he automatically pulled the blinds against the early March sunshine, knowing it would be easier for her to rest with less light. He started a fire in her fireplace and then settled her on the couch so he could give her a blessing.

It was different this time. It wasn't a gentle blessing of peace. It was almost a reprimand for not being willing to accept heaven-inspired help from those who loved her. He blessed her that she would be able to know what she should do to help herself and those around her and to remember there were times to give and to receive, and there was extra emphasis on the receive. He ended on a gentle note, saying she was precious in the sight of her Father in Heaven and that He wanted her to be happy, and would bless her to be, if she would allow His servants to help her.

When Joe was finished, he didn't even hesitate, but sat down beside her and pulled her over to lay her head on his lap. He turned her away from him and brushed her hair back and began to rub the knots out of her upper back and shoulders. Then he began to massage her head and temples, all the while getting her to talk to him about what was going on with her and how she had felt this morning. He asked her what she'd been thinking about the time when she would get to raise her daughters, and about some of the happiest times with them. It took him most of an hour, but he could finally feel her starting to truly relax against him. He turned her back over toward him and pulled her up into his arms and held her to him.

She started to resist him for the first time and said, "Joe, you're married."

She went to push him away and he stopped her. "No, I'm not, Kristin. Not any more. Now sit still. It's past the point of what we should do, or guilt or protecting me or any of those things. You have to have some help, Kris. You know it and I know it. So let me help you." He was talking to her like she was a little girl, but she had to let him in. Trying to go it alone was killing her.

She looked up at him for several long seconds and then he could tell she knew he was right and she cuddled into his arms as if she was a little girl and closed her eyes and sighed against his neck. He gently brushed the hair away from her face. "Go ahead and rest. I'll be here to help slay the dragons when they try to wake you up."

He'd known she would sleep for a long time as tired as she was, but he hadn't realized she'd still be asleep at midnight that night. He hadn't been home to check on his boys and Gram at all, but he knew he couldn't leave her when he'd given her his word that he'd help her rest without nightmares. The boys would be okay; he didn't question that. He just didn't want to leave them with the impression that it was okay to stay out until all hours with a woman. He would have to have a candid conversation about this later.

****

Slowly she came awake, and was at first a little disoriented. It took her a few minutes to realize where she was and that the aftershave and the strong arms around her weren't her imagination. She pushed her hair away and rolled back to look up at him in bewilderment. She blinked, wondering if this was a dream. How was she waking up like this, and in Joe's arms? Her eyes flew to her watch in the dim light. She couldn't see the hands, but it didn't feel like afternoon. The pale light was coming in the wrong set of windows. She sat up quickly, and looked at him in surprise, as he calmly said, "Good morning."

She groaned. "That's just what I was afraid of. Joe, you stayed here all night?" She put her hands to her cheeks.

He looked a little guilty. "I didn't realize when I promised you that I'd slay your waking up dragons that you would sleep quite that long. Do you feel any better?"

She stretched. "I feel wonderful as far as the sleep, but you need to go! How are we going to explain this to the boys?"

"I've been a little worried about that myself. But I had promised." He put a hand to her cheek. "You look better. Sorry, that wasn't very polite. But you do." He pushed her off his lap and stood up. "I need to go. I hate to rush out, but I'm hoping to get home before they wake up."

She stood up beside him. "I'm so sorry. I had no idea I would sleep like that." She took his hand. "Thank, you. You saved my life."

"I just hope I didn't ruin your reputation. I'll see you in awhile."

He did manage to make it home just in time to go about waking them all up for breakfast and church. He was tired, but when she came in dressed in her white dress and looking like a completely different woman than she had yesterday, he knew it had been worth it. Gabriel came up to her and gave her a hug and then studied her. Joe could almost see the weight come off his son's shoulders when he saw that she was so much better.

She looked over Gabriel's head at Joe with a deep look, and he hoped she understood that she had to let him take better care of her so Gabriel could go back to being a fourteen-year-old again. Gram came and handed him her coat for him to help her on with. She gave Joe the same look that Gabriel had just given Kristin.

Joe glanced at Kristin again. It was as if she could read his mind this morning, and he knew she was thinking that they had to figure out a way to help her without him being a bad example for his boys. Their eyes met for a long second, and then he took her hand and led her toward the garage.

He'd had a lot of time to think last night while he'd held her. Having her in his arms for hours and hours had been both hard for him and heavenly. He'd known from the start that he honestly liked her. She was so much fun and thoroughly entertaining when the skeletons were safely in the closet during the day. He had been inexplicably drawn to her before he'd even gotten to know her, and the more he got to know her, the more attracted he was.

Even with the soul deep scars she had, or maybe because of them, he had come to have an incredible respect for her and her character strength. Rather than make him turn away from her, it brought out an almost instinctive need to protect and help her. There was something about the combination of her strength and her helplessness that made him feel like a knight of old. He was strong enough to help her find peace and be strong herself. He'd learned she was selfless and serving, and she had been a wonderful influence on his sons.

She was so different from all the women he was usually around. From the time he'd been little more than a boy, he'd found that more often than not he had to discourage female attention. He wasn't sure why that was, but he'd become adept at tactfully avoiding attachments. Even married, and while he was pseudo-married, women had a tendency to offer a great deal more than just their business skills. It had been worst at the hospital, but it was relatively pervasive in his experience. Kristin had never been that way. She was exactly the opposite, in fact, and while it had been much more comfortable to know he could trust her, it was also intriguing.

Over the last few months, that intrigue and attraction had grown, and last night, holding her, he had realized he was more than attracted or even infatuated. He was in love with her and for the very first time in his life he understood what forever was all about. He could picture himself growing old with her, and seeing her come up out of the waters of baptism yesterday had been one of the greatest experiences of his life. This was a woman with the character strength and conviction to stand beside through this life and beyond. Last night had been wonderful as far as knowing he could bring her the peace she needed so desperately, but he'd had to ask himself some hard questions as well.

Several times as she slept, he knew she'd been dreaming, and fearing the nightmares, he had pulled her closer and gently spoken to her. He'd been able to actually see the emotional strife leave her body and mind at his touch and voice. That was great, except for the fact that she lived next door and he had three sons and was terminally human. In order to be there to slay her dragons, he needed to be there. Last night had been one thing, but it wasn't a permanent option and he knew it.

Not only could he not be that kind of an example for his sons, but she was far too tempting there in the firelight and the night. Her body had been heaven in his arms, but the physical attraction had been through the roof. Being the mere mortal that he was, he knew better than anyone else that he couldn't take that kind of temptation forever. He was almost embarrassed to admit that at almost forty, but playing with fire would be foolish and he knew it.

So there in the dark of her cabin in the middle of the night, he'd decided to marry her as soon as he could talk her into it, but that appeared at this point to be a rather large obstacle. He knew she wouldn't just say, "Sure," if he got down on his knees with a big diamond. Even if she loved him back, which he suspected but had no way of knowing for sure, she would still try to protect him from her troubles. He knew it without even having to ask.

Holding the door of the Suburban for her, he looked into her eyes wondering if her thoughts wound anywhere near the direction his did. She was intelligent. She had to have come to the same conclusion about his presence being able to slay the dragons of her nights. He paused for a moment watching her before going back around to get into the driver's seat.

Once they were on the highway headed into town, he reached across and took her hand again and glanced at her. Her eyes were big and he could tell she was unsure of him this morning. He could almost feel the boys in the back seats looking at each other, wondering what was going on. He turned the radio on softly to fill the silence, wondering a little what was going on himself. He wished he'd had time to talk to Kristin this morning before he had had to rush home.

He didn't hold her hand on the way into the chapel, but he put a hand on the small of her back as he helped her into the pew and then he sat next to her. He hadn't done that in weeks, not since she had shut him out that night. Even without holding her hand, it felt right to sit there beside her in church and be taught about Christ's gospel, and he almost regretted having to relinquish her to Relief Society.

He met her in the crowded hallway on the way to the Gospel Essentials class. "Can I come into your Sunday School class with you this time?" She still had the big eyes with him, and he knew she knew he'd made some decisions about her during their long night together. She nodded her assent and when she took his hand he felt sure that somehow it was all going to work out.

It was becoming easier everyday to read her moods and feelings, but holding her hand made it easy to feel her suddenly stiffen. He turned to her and realized she was looking all around at the others in the hallway with them. His eyes narrowed, questioning, but she just shook her head and kept walking. When they turned the corner and were alone, he stopped. "What's wrong? What's going on?"

"I don't know." She shook her head again. "I just felt like someone was watching me. That's so silly, I know. It happens at work sometimes too lately. I don't know why it would happen at church." He dropped her hand and went back and looked around the corner, but the hallway was mostly empty as everyone filed into class rooms.

Going back around the corner, he took her hand again and continued on to their own class. "Kristin, when you get feelings like that, you shouldn't ignore them or feel like they're silly. You need to follow your gut if you think something is wrong. If you get an impression, even in church, sadly, you need to act on it. Especially when you know you have a stalker. Sometimes, often, I believe, those impressions are the Spirit."

Stopping, she looked up at him. "I know. It's just that I hate feeling paranoid." She was hesitant to add, "The fear makes the nights worse. I've been trying to separate it all, but I've had to admit that things are much worse since finding out I'm being watched." She looked away.

"Did you think I didn't know that?" She looked at him in surprise. "Kristin, come on. When you care a lot about someone, you learn what they feel and think. And it's not exactly hard to tell that you're not doing well nights. When it's this bad, it's pretty obvious."

Still watching his eyes, she admitted, "Before you, I thought I could handle it all. Maybe not all that gracefully, but I thought I'd survive. Now sometimes I wonder. Not being able to get out is hard."

In an infinitely gentle voice, he said, "I know, honey. But we've found some things that help, haven't we? We'll figure it out. Just don't fight me when you know I'm right, okay?"

"What do you mean?"

He started to walk. "Can I wait until we have a few more minutes and a little more privacy to tell you what I mean?"

She looked up at his profile and asked, "Why do I get the impression that I need to worry about this?"

He squeezed her hand. "Probably because I know how stubborn you are, so I'm gearing up."

"I am not stubborn. Okay, maybe a little bit stubborn. But only when it really matters."

Matter-of-factly, he said, "Well, this really matters, so get ready." They'd reached their class, and he led her in and sat down, not glancing up at her questioning look. When she still kept turning to look at him even after the class had started, he whispered, "You're not paying attention here. Eternal families is an important concept."

She gave him one more piercing look before turning back to the teacher.

On the way home, he phoned the Murdocks and invited them to his house for Sunday dinner. When he hung up, he turned to her. "I'm sorry, I didn't even ask you. You will stay for dinner with us, won't you?"

"Yes, but are you doing this to postpone telling me what you meant?"

He thought about that for a minute, then said, "I don't think so. Maybe. I don't know."

His face made her laugh. "It was so good of you to be succinct."

As he looked in his rear view mirror he said, "You must befuddle me."

"Befuddle?" She burst into laughter. "I'm not sure I've ever befuddled anyone before."

He looked over at her and glanced her up and down. "Trust me on this one. You've befuddled a lot of people. A lot of men people."

"How would you know I've befuddled men?"

"I'm a men, Kristin. I know exactly what effect you have." She looked up at him a little surprised, but he met her gaze.

After dinner, the boys challenged her to a game of Monopoly, and Joe gratefully stretched out on the couch in the sun. He hadn't slept a lot the night before and he was bushed. When he woke up, the boys were playing Xbox across in the TV room and she was sitting beside him on the floor leaning back against the couch. Sleepily, he reached over and touched her hair. "Did you win?"

She looked up at him and smiled. "No, I'm afraid Caleb whipped us all soundly."

He turned over toward her with a yawn. "You let him win. You should have taken him to the cleaners so he'll learn to be wary of women."

"I don't think you have to worry about that one. He's gorgeous enough and savvy enough to already know to be wary of women. They all are."

He looked over at them. "Why are you letting them play Xbox on Sunday?"

"Don't look at me. I'm not letting them. I wondered though when Robby headed that way. He intimated it would be okay because you were so tired from staying out all night that you wouldn't mind."

Joe groaned, and turned back over onto his back. "He probably thinks I'm feeling guilty enough that I won't make them turn it off. I think he's right. I guess I'd better figure out what I'm going to tell them."

"Wouldn't the truth be best?"

He leaned back up to look at her. "Wouldn't that be betraying a confidence? Rob and Caleb don't know about your family and your nightmares."

"I'd rather they knew about my nightmares, than think that you and I spent the night together."

"We did spend the night together. And it worked."

A little flustered, she said, "You know what I mean."

With a piercing gaze he said, "Yes, and you know what I mean, too."

Her blue eyes met his brown ones. "Joe, don't tease. I'm not up to it right now."

He turned onto his stomach and looked right at her. "I'm not teasing, Kristin. And don't play innocent with me. You're the one who's been dealing with this for nearly four years now and it's worse than ever. You yourself told me

206

you've tried everything you could think of. Even Murdock knows you're losing the battle."

Hesitantly, she asked, "What exactly are you suggesting?"

He avoided the question with one of his own. "What do you think it is that's made you be able to sleep okay the two nights I've held you?"

Quietly she considered this for a few minutes. "It's the most amazing thing. Both times I've been in that half asleep, half awake mode where you dream. Do you know what I mean?" He nodded. "And both times I could almost feel myself being pulled into the nightmares, but with you there it's like I can turn away from them into you and they can't take over. Is that crazy?"

With his chin on one hand, he reached out with the other to brush a strand of her hair back from her cheek. "I was there, Kristin. I knew exactly what was going on. That's why I know you'd be much better with me there all the time."

Her eyes flew to his. He could see her confusion and backed off. "Now you know what I meant. Will you at least think about it?" He wasn't sure she was even able to answer him and urged, "This is where you say, 'Sure, Joe. I'll think about it. I promise'."

She looked away and whispered, "I'll think about it."

Jaclyn M. Hawkes

# Chapter 20

After she left, he had a family counsel of sorts and told the boys and Gram what had been going on with Kristin with both the nightmares and the stalker. He made it clear that he had been helping her and had made her a promise he didn't feel could be broken last night. "I have held her hand now, but I've never so much as even kissed her. So don't be thinking anything questionable about either her or me.

"And don't think it's okay to stay like that even if you are behaving. It's not. I never should have and wouldn't have except that when I promised her I didn't realize she would sleep that long." Robby looked skeptical, and Caleb teased Joe that it was about time he took care of kissing her.

Caleb joked, but you could see the concern for her in his eyes. Finally, he asked, "Is she going to be okay now?"

Joe wondered what to tell him. "It may take her awhile to figure out what she needs to do to find peace, Caleb. But eventually we'll get there."

"We'll?"

"We'll."

She was fine that night and the next two, but Murdock called Joe on Wednesday morning and told him that during the night there had been someone prowling around. He had set off the alarms twice, two hours apart and Murdock had video surveillance of him, but it was too fuzzy for Kristin to be able to tell who it was. Joe went over to talk to her, praying as he went that this wouldn't set off the nightmares again. When he walked into her house, she was just about ready to head out to work. She didn't look very happy about it. "Howard again?"

"Howard again." She grimaced and he laughed.

He'd wondered how it would be when he saw her again. He'd made her promise on Sunday that she would call him if she got up, and she hadn't called, but he still felt better seeing her for himself. He needed to know she wasn't avoiding him, and went up to her. "You only have one more day of work. Have you been thinking about it?"

Neither one of them had to figure out what he was talking about. "Of course. More than thinking. I've worried that you've lost your mind for two days now."

That made him laugh. "Have you been avoiding me?"

Meeting his gaze, she said, "No. I haven't. I promise. Actually, you won't believe this, but I've spent most of both days sleeping."

He gave her a high five, and then kept hold of her hand. "You look good. Sleep suits you." He decided to change the subject before she felt pressured. "When are your puppies due?"

She looked at him puzzled. "What?"

He nodded at her dog. "Her puppies. When are they due?"

She looked at Teal in alarm. "What? She's not going to have puppies."

Joe began to wonder if he'd just opened a can of worms. "You haven't had her bred?" She shook her head still staring at her dog. "Oh." The word just hung in the air, and he could see the wheels turning in her mind.

210

He knew he looked sheepish when she asked, "You don't know anyone around here who has an unneutered male dog do you?" Murdock and Elena came in just at that moment and laughed as Joe put both hands up and backed toward the door.

"Hey, don't look at me. Hershey never leaves the yard unless he's with me."

"Well, there are no other dogs around here for miles, that I know of."

"Well . . . then it must be Teal's fault." He smiled as he turned to wave. "Have a good day with Howard. See ya later." He shook his head as he walked across to his house. He'd just been trying to have an easy conversation. At least Hershey was a lab. Maybe it wouldn't be too bad. He shook his head again and then laughed. Kristin had looked horrified, but even their dogs knew they were supposed to be related.

She came to his house as soon as she got off work. When he opened the door at her knock, he wasn't sure if he should be worried or not. He'd told the boys and Gram what he suspected had happened.

With a grin, he said, "You don't look *too* mad." Robby and Gabriel laughed.

She smiled and sighed. "It's just such a relief to get away from Howard that I've decided not to murder both you and Hershey as planned."

"I guess that means I'm in Howard's debt?" He smiled his best smile at her.

Giving him the look, she said, "Don't push your luck, Joe." She let him take her hand and pull her inside. "I've come in search of information. How did you know Teal was expecting puppies?"

"Uh, because she looks like she's expecting puppies."

"I figured that. I'd just been wondering why she was putting on weight. Apparently you're more familiar with dogs in her condition than I am. Can you tell about how far along she is, by any chance?"

"Actually, the boys and I have raised labs a few times, and I would venture to guess she is due in about three weeks, give or take. I'm assuming these will be her first puppies."

She nodded absently. "Three weeks! Are you serious?"

She had this look that was half wonder, half concern and Joe asked, "Would it help to tell you Hershey has excellent bloodlines?"

"I don't know. I suppose. I'm just so surprised. I have no idea how to have puppies."

Caleb had just come in and said, "Which is a good thing, 'cause you're a human." They all cracked up and Joe was a little worried that she'd still want to kill him.

Caleb came and gave Kristin a fist bump. "Hey, Kristin." He went over to Robby and Gabriel and then ventured over his shoulder, "This is just God's way of trying to tell you that we're supposed to be related." Joe didn't know whether to laugh or be horrified. When he looked at Kristin he could tell she knew exactly what he was thinking.

She tried to hide a smile and turned back to the door. When Joe took her hand, she asked, "Is this a conspiracy?"

He hurried to assure her of his innocence. "No. I haven't said a word to them about us except to be very succinct that we weren't sleeping together."

"Well, somehow even Teal appears to be in on it."

He flashed her a huge smile. "Honestly, I'm stoked about it! Puppies are the happiest creatures on the planet."

"I guess I'm going to learn all about them. I'd better get home and get my bags and double check on the kid I've asked to take care of my horses. I'm glad you talked me into this. Murdock and Elena are way too happy about leaving me. I should have realized they needed more breaks a long time ago."

Squeezing her hand, he said, "I'm glad I talked you into it, too." He just left it at that, deciding she was right, he'd better not push his luck.

They took the Suburban over the pass to Jackson to catch their plane. Teal and Hershey rode in the back together after Joe had asked Kristin if that was okay. She'd looked at him like she didn't think he was very funny. The plan was to have dinner in the airport once they got through security, and Kristin gave him the look again when he asked her if she thought both dogs would be okay in one big kennel for the two hour and forty-five minute flight.

Joe sat next to Kristin and the flight seemed to take only about one fifth as long as it usually did. Still, he was tired when they finally got to his house in Phoenix at eleven-thirty that night. They'd dropped Gram off at her son's house so he could take her in to have her eye surgery the next morning, and then headed on to Joe's home without her. The boys and the dogs slept all the way from the airport, but Kristin never even tried to close her eyes, and Joe wondered if she was just interested in the city lights or if she was as nervous as she looked.

He tried to distract her. "Have you ever been to Phoenix before?"

She shook her head. "Never. I've never even been in Arizona before. I had no idea Phoenix was this big. This is huge!"

213

Changing lanes, he said, "It's actually several cities, there's just no break between them anymore. It definitely makes Idaho feel more like home, doesn't it?" He rubbed his thumb across the back of her hand, and then squeezed it. "Are you doing okay?"

She sounded worried. "I guess we'll see. You know how I said I was glad you talked me into this?"

"Yes, why?"

"I think I'm chickening out."

Gently, he reminded her, "It's a little late to tell me that, we're less than five minutes from my house. You're gonna be okay, Kris."

She looked over at him and tried to smile. "I hope you're right."

Giving her hand another squeeze, he said, "We're tough. We'll handle whatever we have to."

Glancing up at him, she admitted, "Sometimes I don't understand you, Joe."

"What's there to understand? I'm a simple guy. I just follow my heart sometimes. This is one of those times."

"That's what I don't understand. I'm way more trouble than I'm worth."

They stopped at a locked gate and he punched in a code and the gate opened. Continuing through the development, he pulled into his garage that held another car already, shut the door behind them, and turned in his seat to look at her. "I don't believe I've ever heard you say something that negative before."

"It's not negative." He looked at her. "Okay, it's negative, but it's true."

He got out and let the dogs out and came around to open her door. "I'm a smart guy, Kristin. Give me a little credit here. You could never be more trouble than you're worth. You're of infinite worth. Remember? So you've got tons of leeway still to cause trouble. Welcome to Arizona." He opened the back door of the rental car. "Come on guys. Come in the house and go to bed." He rousted them out, picked up her bag and then took her hand. "Come on inside."

He led her inside and down a short hall to the left. "This is Gram's little kingdom. Max came and changed all the linens and I hope you'll be fine here. Make yourself at home." He set the bags on the bed, and then turned and took her hands in his. "I mean it, Kristin. Do what ever you need to do. Come with me and I'll show you around a little. The pool is out here."

He opened a sliding glass door. "I've already made sure it's up to temperature, and this is a relatively secure neighborhood so don't worry about coming out here anytime. The exercise room is just around the corner right here. Lights are on the left."

Then he led her back into the main part of the house. "My room is the first one this side of the kitchen, and if you're having a hard time and don't wake me up, you'll be in the dog house. Speaking of dog houses. This is the dog kingdom." He indicated an alcove off the kitchen with a tile floor, and cabinets above it. It had food and water dishes and a large dog bed that currently held both dogs piled up on it.

"Chivalry isn't dead after all. Hershey is taking good care of his bride. That earns him some points, doesn't it?"

"Some. He's still in the dog house for awhile though."

Grinning, Joe said. "When those puppies get here, you'll be singing a different tune. When you see how adorable they are, I'm going to send you a bill for services rendered." He walked across the kitchen and opened a door beside the garage door. "Basketball court is through here. Do you play?"

They went inside and she looked all around. "Wow, this is awesome! I haven't played since high school gym class, and I was terrible then, so I guess that would be a no."

"That will change fast. I have ten bucks that says you'll be out here before breakfast with the boys. They live out here sometimes. This spring I'm going to build one in Idaho, too. They spend far too much time with something electronic there." He continued on through the house. "You can give yourself a grand tour tomorrow while I'm working, but the boys are these doors here." He pointed. "I'll leave the stereo on here in the TV room so you won't worry about bothering them. Will that work?"

"I'll be fine." She said the words, but she didn't look confident.

He came to stand in front of her. "Kristin, I'm in this for the long haul, dreams or no. We'll handle whatever we need to. Just promise me you won't shut me out here at my own house." She wouldn't look at him and he put a finger under her chin. "Kristin, don't you trust me by now?"

"Of course I trust you."

"Then don't do this to me. It kills me. Don't you know that?"

She looked up at him for a long time, and then said, "I won't shut you out, Joe. I promise."

"Good." He took her hand and led her back into the kitchen where the boys were all three sitting around the kitchen table eating cold cereal. "'Cause I'd be ticked if you did. She doesn't want to see me ticked, does she, you guys?"

They all started to answer with their mouths full and Joe immediately put up a hand. "No! No train wrecks. Tell her after you've finished your bites."

216

Kristin laughed at all four of them and it helped to ease the tension. "By the way, Kristin, would you like something to eat? You don't have to have cold cereal. Max stocked the place up for me. We could probably find something you'd like."

"No, I'm fine thanks, but I'll sit with you while you eat."

He began to dig through the cupboards. "I'll bet I can find something that will tempt you." He opened the freezer. "Ah hah! Pizza! No one can resist pizza. Am I tempting you now?"

"Yes." She laughed. "So stop. I'll never get to sleep if I eat at this time of night."

"So then, we'll go play basketball, or watch a movie until you're sleepy. Pepperoni or Canadian bacon?"

"Anything is good. Don't you have to go into work tomorrow?"

"I do. But rank has its privileges. I'm the boss. I can show up when I want."

****

He'd hoped and prayed she'd be okay here. It was finally a chance for him to be able to watch over her and he'd wanted so badly for her to trust him, but sometimes what you want isn't what you get.

He wasn't asleep. Thankfully, the insomnia had followed him back to Phoenix this time, and the second he heard her start to scream, he was up and headed into her room.

When he got there, she was sitting on the floor beside the bed with her knees drawn up and her head buried in her arms, crying silently. Pausing at the doorway to pray for guidance, he humbly asked for inspiration to know how to help her and then proceeded inside.

He dropped to the floor beside her and without saying anything, gently put a hand on her tangled hair, She didn't appear to even know he was there at first and then she turned and leaned her head on his shoulder without raising her face. He put his legs out in front of him, pulled her up onto his lap, and turned her toward him. All he knew to do was wrap his arms around her, pull her in close, and let her cry.

It was the only thing that came into his mind, and at first it didn't seem to be working. Her sadness was overwhelming her. Finally, she stopped sobbing and buried her face even tighter into his neck and clung to him like he was her life line. He kept praying as he held on, completely at the mercy of whatever inspiration he could get.

When she finally settled down, he began to rub her back and eventually asked, "Do you want to try to go back to sleep, or get up and do something?"

He felt her draw a deep breath and sigh it out before she pulled back from him enough to speak. "I'd love to go back to sleep, but I can't, so I guess I'll get up." She pushed her long hair out of the way, and leaned back to look up at him. "You can go back to bed now. I'll be fine. I'll just go work out for awhile."

"You promised, Kristin."

Holding up a hand, she said, "I'm not shutting you out, Joe. I just know how hard it is to go to work exhausted. But thank you for coming in."

She went to pull away, and he stopped her. "Don't give up without even trying. Talk to me and let's see if we can't get you back to sleep."

She leaned back into his chest with another long sigh. "I don't know what to talk about." When she sniffled, he handed her a tissue from the nightstand.

"Do you ever have dreams about the girls that are good dreams?"

"I think I do sometimes. They're harder to remember because they don't wake me up like the bad ones."

He leaned his face on her hair. "What do you dream about that's good?"

"I know I've dreamed about swinging them. They used to love that. Even Anna. I had this little airplane swing I could strap her right into and she would laugh so much the other girls would stop swinging just to watch her.

"And we loved to go and play in the water. My husband was a landscape architect and he'd built this stream that wound all through his gardens. They used to love it. It drove him a little crazy, but some days we used to spend all afternoon in the water in the summers. Then we'd wander through the flowers and pick huge bouquets on the way back in."

He chuckled. "I'll bet your husband loved that."

She shrugged in his arms. "Ryan was actually pretty laid back. Especially about the girls. Nothing made him too uptight. Sometimes I wished he did get a little more concerned about some things. Especially the girls. That was one of the problems I hadn't really thought through before I married him. I'd actually kind of torn into him that morning and never got a chance to tell him I was sorry. It took me awhile to forgive myself for that one."

"But you did forgive yourself?"

He felt her nod against his chest. "Eventually. At first I didn't understand there was a hereafter. I mean, no one in my family or close to me ever even considered such a thing. In retrospect, I know that's silly. The plan of salvation, the pre-existence, the spirit world. It all fits and makes sense.

"It's an incredible relief to know we aren't just done when we die, but it's hard to say good bye and not have huge regrets when you think they are just gone. I didn't think I'd ever get a chance to tell him I was sorry. It wasn't a big thing, but . . . It was just hard. Finding the gospel has been a tremendous blessing for me that way. I sometimes wonder if any of this would be happening if I had known then what I know now."

She leaned her head back against his shoulder. "If I could have had priesthood blessings right from the first, I can't help but think I wouldn't be here, or there in Idaho I mean, struggling to make it through night after night. The knowledge of the priesthood power and the hereafter both could have made it so much easier to deal with from the start. But yeah, I finally did forgive myself. I had to tell myself that I was honestly doing my best to be a good wife and mother. I still have regrets, but realistically I'm sure Ryan has moved on to much more vital considerations."

She was quiet for a time and then asked, "What do you suppose it's like to die and get to the other side and find that your most basic values and beliefs are completely off base. I wonder what it was like to face a Father in Heaven he never even acknowledged existed."

"I don't know. It's definitely not something I'd ever want to face, and yet, He's a loving Father. I would imagine that how that situation turned out depended on what Ryan's attitude was. I'd guess that if a person was hard-headed and belligerent that would be harder to face than if you were honestly sorry for making that huge of a misjudgment."

"I think you're right. And Ryan wasn't hard-headed; he just never drummed up much of a passion for anything other than his work."

"Maybe that would have changed in time, Kristin. I used to be that way about work when I was younger and didn't understand what was more important. In some ways, I'm totally in Nicole's debt because I never would have met Gram and found the church if she'd stayed."

She turned back into him and snuggled into his neck again. "I don't believe that, Joe. You're a good man, and you're trying to do what you truly believe is right. God would never have left you hanging. If it hadn't been Gram, he'd have sent someone else. Remember what you told me about God answering prayers by sending someone who was good enough to listen for promptings? He'd have found you one way or another."

He stroked her hair in the dark. "It's probably terrible to say, knowing my boys have been without a mother all these years, but right now I'm glad Nicole took off. I would never have been here with you if she hadn't."

With a sigh she said, "You probably would have been much better off without me causing you strife."

Softly he asked, "What's better off, Kris? I'm happier now than I've ever been. You're a huge part of that. How can you begrudge me that?"

"I don't begrudge you that. It's just that sometimes I wonder what you and I would have been like if we had met under different circumstances. Wouldn't it have been much nicer to have gotten to know the Kristin who was happy and up beat twenty-four hours a day instead of only half of it?"

"I don't know the answer to that, but shouldn't true friendship come with a whatever-it-takes clause? Doesn't everyone have moments like this at some time in their lives? How would we ever learn to be strong and have a decent character without facing the refiner's fire willingly?"

She yawned. "You have a point, but I still would have liked to have gotten to know you with less troubling baggage."

"Who's to say we would have even wanted to be together if we were different people than we are?" He laughed softly. "I would have just been another guy you were trying to avoid. And you would have been married and I would have been frustrated beyond belief about that."

She leaned back in his arms to look up at him. "You're being a little over the top, don't you think?"

"Nope."

They sat that way looking at each other until finally she whispered, "Joe, don't you dare kiss me when I'm this much of a mess."

He began to pull her closer. "I think you're beautiful, even when you're a mess." He pulled her tight into his arms and lowered his mouth to hers without looking away. Finally, he closed his eyes and kissed her the way he'd wanted to for weeks now.

It was worth the wait.

A minute or two later, when he reluctantly raised his head, he kept her hugged tight to him. He let his breath out with a sigh and stroked her silky hair. "Sorry, but I really, really needed to do that. I promise I'll do it again when you don't feel like a mess."

She hid her face in his neck. "It's okay." Hesitantly she added, "It certainly helped me forget all the bad stuff."

He gently pulled her face up to look at him. "That's not why I did it." He leaned down to do it again.

When he didn't find her in her room the next morning, he went looking and he'd been right, she was on the

222

basketball court before breakfast. He walked in in his business suit and stole the ball as Gabriel went past, then ducked around Robby, faked out Caleb and made a lay up. On his way back out, he took her hand and stole her, too. Back in the house, he backed her up against the wall. His eyes searched hers for a minute before he asked, "Were you able to get back to sleep?"

Hesitantly she looked down. "Yes. It took me a minute, but it was your fault, not because I was thinking about the girls."

He leaned down to kiss her and then said, "You did better than me then, because it took me a lot longer than a minute to quit thinking about you and get back to sleep." She looked up at him with wide eyes, and he laughed and leaned in again.

They were interrupted by whistles and cat calls as the boys filed into the kitchen from the court. Joe smiled at her and gave her one last kiss and then led her on into the kitchen. "Okay, all three of you, hit the showers. You smell like a locker room."

They all headed out, but not before Caleb quipped over his shoulder. "He just wants us out of the way so he can kiss Kristin!"

Joe smiled at her. "He may be right. What sounds good for breakfast?"

"I'm good with whatever you're having."

"I'm having wheat toast and instant breakfast that I'm going to eat in the car. I'm sorry to bail on you, but Max called and I need to hurry. So much for being the boss. These guys will eat most anything as long as there's a lot of it, so you may have to arm wrestle them for it." He began to pull bread and butter from the cupboards. "Is there a possibility you would meet me for lunch?"

She hesitated. "I don't know. You look great in your suit, but I didn't bring anything very professional to wear. I wouldn't want to embarrass you."

He laughed as he put the toast in. "You're funny sometimes. Do you know that? You could show up in your swimsuit and you'd look great! Actually, you'd look way better than great! Why don't you go ahead and wear your swimsuit." She gave him the smile he was after. "On second thought, then I'd have to beat back all the men in the whole hospital, so maybe that's not that good of an idea."

His teasing made her roll her eyes. "Joe."

"Oh, all right. Wear anything you want. You're gorgeous in it all. There's no need to look professional, you're a ski instructor and a wrangler."

Buttering his toast, she admitted, "Actually, I'm a physical therapist, but I gave it up."

He turned to look at her. "I could see you as a PT. You were probably great at it!"

She smiled. "Thanks. I was."

"Did you give it up to be a mom, or because of the accident?"

Her eyes clouded. "To be a mom, but then I couldn't face it after."

He squeezed her shoulder. "Well, you're a kicking ski instructor. I know I'm being selfish, but I'm glad you took it up. And I can't wait for the horse thing to start." He took his toast and shaker cup and stopped to kiss her one last, long kiss. "Call me."

****

He should have stayed home kissing Kristin. The morning had been insane. He and Max had been making some fairly decent headway when he'd come in before, but this morning, from the time he'd said hello to the receptionist in the administrative office he'd been inundated with people stopping by to visit. At first it had been surprising, but it didn't take long to become obnoxious. The ninth person in the door was his friend Paul Sharp, his second in command for years. "Hey, Paul. Come in and shut the door. What are you up to?"

"Same as you. Paperwork. How's it going?"

Max laughed before he could even start to grumble, "It'd be going fine except that half the hospital feels the need to stop in and see me today. What's going on?"

"Let me guess. It would be the female half of the hospital. Am I right?"

Joe grumbled under his breath as Max laughed again. "It's not very funny, Max. I have better things to do than sit here small talking with a bunch of divorcees. Why today?"

This time it was Paul who chuckled. "You can thank Lori Duncan. She put a blurb in the employee newsletter about you being newly divorced. It was the big news of the month around here."

"What! You've got to be kidding! Someone printed that in the employee newsletter? My own company did that to me? I have half a mind to fire Lori."

"You'll have to fire Joanne at the front desk, too. She's the one who's been telling everyone you're in town today, which actually surprises me that she wouldn't keep it a secret so she could keep you to herself." Joe was horrified and Max and Paul both laughed. Joe got up and went out the door to let the Joanne know that under no uncertain terms was he to be interrupted for the duration of the day. He came back in and breathed a rather dramatic sigh as he sat back down, at which Max and Paul laughed in unison again.

"It isn't really all that funny, Sharp. I'm tempted to take out my own ad about your present single status. See how much you get done."

"I'm actually good with that idea. My personal life is dismal right now. I don't know how you've done it all these years. I think it's lousy."

"It beats the heck out of inane small talk with mindless women. Enough about our personal lives. What have you got for me on those reports I asked for?"

"Hmmm. That's why I came by. You thought I just wanted to say hi because I'd found out you were divorced, didn't you?"

"Very funny. What did you find out?"

"Bradshaw won't release them to me."

"What?"

"You heard me. Your new hot shot administrator has power issues. He said he'd look into it himself."

Joe got up. "Did you ever get over your hesitation at becoming the chief administrator, Sharp? Because you're just about to become one." He strode from the room, and headed for the administrator's office.

# Chapter 21

Kristin came through the huge revolving glass doors and stood for a second, looking at the fountains in the lobby. It was a huge and beautiful facility, and she was almost a little intimidated as she walked in. Joe had said he owned enough of this hospital to call the shots. She looked all around, wondering what that meant.

She had known money wasn't an issue to him right from the first, and then last night when she found that he had an indoor basketball court in his second home, she had begun to think he was wealthier than she'd first thought. But, now, standing in the lobby of this imposing hospital, she began to have an inkling of just how truly wealthy this man was. No wonder he hadn't seemed that upset when he mentioned he'd lost a hundred and sixty-five-thousand dollars.

She headed up the elevator to the administrative offices, following the directions the boys had given her and wishing they had opted to come to lunch with her instead of dropping her off and going to eat with friends. Looking down at her casual outfit, she tried not to feel underdressed. She would have been much more at home in her lab coat, heading for one of the patient floors. She shook her head at herself. All of that had been left behind a long time ago, and now she was just Kristin. A fact that Joe was okay with, if his behavior last night and this morning was any indication.

Thinking back to that kiss last night made something in her heart skip a beat. How was she ever going to resist him if he did that again? She was falling in love with him and because of the way her life was, it scared the daylights out of her. Or had she already fallen? She knew that could have lasting consequences for both him and his sons. And for her. She'd never felt this deeply in all of her life, even though she had been married for years.

If it didn't feel so comfortable and so right, she'd have panicked and run away from him emotionally a long time ago. Sometimes, she still felt like she should. How could someone like him want to deal with someone like her? She knew far better than he did what she was up against.

Then she thought back to the bombshell he had dropped the other afternoon about him being there with her at nights all the time. He had to have been talking marriage, didn't he? He would never intimate they sleep together otherwise. So then why had he never mentioned the M word or feelings or anything like that?

She knew he liked her, sometimes she even wondered if he felt more than that, but she had no idea how much more. As a member of the church, he would never even think about a marriage of convenience, would he? She hoped with all her heart that she hadn't fallen this hard for someone who only wanted to be with her so he could help her. Being nothing but a mercy mission to him would kill her.

She got off on the top floor and approached the receptionist's desk. "Excuse me. Could you direct me to Joe Faciano's office please?"

A slightly overweight woman with fake nails and dark roots looked her up and down and then said with almost an air of satisfaction, "I'm sorry. Mr. Faciano gave me strict instructions not to let one more female near his office for the rest of the day. He's in some very important meetings. I'm sorry to disappoint you, honey." She cracked her gum and picked up a nail file, and then studiously ignored Kristin.

More than a little stunned, Kristin turned around and headed back toward the elevator. Joe had confirmed lunch less than two hours ago.

A man who had been standing just inside the office when she'd been there followed her and stopped her halfway down the hall. "Excuse me. Could I help you with something?" His frank admiration and enthusiasm for meeting her went a long way toward healing her ego after talking to the receptionist. 'I'm Paul Sharp, assistant administrator, at your service." He put out a hand.

She shook her head. "No, I don't think you can help me. I'm afraid there's been a small misunderstanding. I was under the impression I was supposed to meet Joe Faciano for lunch. I was apparently mistaken. I'm Kristin Moran, Joe's neighbor from Idaho. I came with this trip to help out with his sons."

"In that case, it's my professional duty to take you to lunch in his stead. He would be very disappointed if we were to somehow offend you while you're in town. Would you like to go downstairs to the cafeteria or could I talk you into coming across the street with me to a restaurant that's a little less busy?"

She was still a bit floored that Joe had cancelled lunch. "Either one is fine, but don't feel like you need to come to lunch with me. I'm perfectly okay to wait for the boys to come back."

He hadn't let go of her hand, and she put the other one onto his with her wedding bands very obviously in plain sight and tugged her hand out of his grip, as he said, "We both have to eat anyway, so it's my pleasure. Joe truly would rather someone take you, I'm sure of it. Have you been to Phoenix before?"

He was right, she did have to eat, and if he was the second in command here he must be well acquainted with Joe. She absently wondered what had come up to make Joe cancel lunch without even a phone call. As she accompanied Paul down the elevator and across the street, she hoped Joe hadn't lost another huge chunk of money.

\*\*\*\*

Joe glanced at his watch for the third time in twenty minutes and Max questioned, "What's up? Why do you keep checking your watch?"

"I was supposed to be having lunch with a friend, but she's late. Something must have come up. I've tried to call her, but her phone goes to voice mail. I hope nothing has happened." He looked out the window. She was usually fine during the day. What could be keeping her? Robby was supposed to be bringing her, so he doubted she'd gotten lost enroute. He tried Robby's phone, but it was off, too. Maybe he shouldn't have kissed her again this morning. But if he'd scared her off, wouldn't she have said something when he'd confirmed their lunch arrangements?

He worked through lunch becoming more concerned by the minute about why she would change plans. He was enjoying her so much. He really didn't want things to go south right now. Finally, at three o'clock he reached Robby's phone. "Robby, hey, where's Kristin?"

"I thought she was with you. Why? Have you lost her?"

"I've never found her. I thought you were going to bring her here for lunch. What happened?"

"Dad, I did bring her there for lunch. I dropped her in the circle drive at a quarter to twelve."

"Seriously? Huh. Okay, I'll start looking. If you hear from her, have her call me right away."

"Sorry, Dad. I didn't realize. I thought she was with you."

"It's okay, Rob. I'm sure she's fine. Behave yourself."

"Always. See ya."

As soon as he was off the phone, Max asked what was wrong. Still confused, Joe answered, "Rob says he dropped her off. But she never showed. Where would she have gone?" They both had the same idea at once. "You don't suppose Joanne wouldn't let her in, do you?"

Max stood up. "That's exactly what I suppose. Joanne would probably take great pleasure in keeping any other woman away from you. You try Kristin's cell phone again. I'll go talk to Joanne. If you go, you really will fire her. Tell me what this friend looks like."

Joe smiled. "Five nine, Scandinavian blonde hair down to her, uh, below her waist, skier's tan, drop dead gorgeous, beautiful smile, sky blue eyes and a figure like a personal trainer."

Max rolled her eyes dramatically. "Is there anything else you'd like to add? Maybe her measurements?" She laughed. "I've never seen you like this, Joe. You're practically gushing."

"It's actually very nice to feel this way. I'd marry her tomorrow if she'd let me. She won't. I'm still working on her."

"Having Joanne send her packing isn't going to help. What's her name?"

"Kristin. Kristin Moran. Thanks, Max."

When Max came back in, she said, "I wanted to fire her myself. Kristin was here. Joanne told her and I quote, 'Mr. Faciano gave me strict instructions not to let one more female near his office for the rest of the day.'"

Joe groaned. "Great. Just great."

"There's more. Joanne thinks Paul came and told her you wouldn't want her to have to eat alone, and he left with her."

"Paul? Paul wouldn't do that to me. Kristin wouldn't do that to me. What is going on around here, Max?"

"She might do that to you if she thought you blew off lunch and had her ordered away from your office."

"Thanks, Max. You're very comforting." He picked up the office phone and had the switch board operator page both of them.

Two hours later Kristin called his cell phone. When he answered, she said, "Hi, Joe. I'm so sorry. I didn't realize my phone was on silent. I've been wondering all this time why you never called, and then I just saw that you tried. Can females come near your office yet?"

He chuckled. "Where are you?"

"About halfway between your elevator and your security guard receptionist."

"I will personally escort you past security."

"Thanks. See you in a sec."

Max looked up as he hung up. "Is she mad?"

He shook his head with a soft smile. "No. She's Kristin. I can't wait for you to meet her. She's at Joanne's desk."

"Can I come out and watch Joanne's face when you bring her back?"

He got up and walked to the door. "That's not very nice, Max. What would Jesus say?"

Joe had been planning to give Joanne and her circle of friends something to talk about when he saw Kristin, but he almost forgot to when he saw her. She'd obviously been shopping, and was in an exquisite business suit and heels. She walked up to him all smiles and came into his arms without hesitating, and she was the one who kissed him this time. When she pulled back, she laughed up at him. He must have looked befuddled again as she said, "Hi, Joe. Sorry about the mix up. Did you ever get any lunch?" She didn't even glance at the big eyed receptionist.

He tried to hide a grin. "Actually, no. Could I make up for the misunderstanding by taking you somewhere nice for dinner?" He put his arm around her and led her back into his office.

Max stood up and offered her hand with a dry comment. "Well, you did describe her to a T. Hi, Kristin. I'm Maxine. I've been helping him try to find you this afternoon."

"It's nice to meet you. I'm Kristin Moran. I'm Joe's neighbor back in Idaho. I'm sorry I couldn't be found. I decided to go shopping while I was in exile." She smiled at Joe, and then laughed at his expression, and asked innocently, "Am I to assume you have had a few female visitors today?"

He actually blushed and rubbed the back of his neck with one hand. Max explained, "A well meaning PR person published the fact that he was recently divorced in the employee newsletter. It took him 'til about eleven to get the crowds under control." Kristin and Max laughed together like old friends.

"It's not all that funny, you two. I've done nothing to encourage any of them."

Max gave him a grin. "Joe, with looks like yours, you don't have to *do* anything but breathe."

"Now even you're giving me guff, Max? Come on, I gotta have somebody on my side today. Even Paul jumped ship." He turned to Kristin. "Did you really have lunch with Paul?"

She looked at him innocently. "Yes. He chivalrously offered to take me since you had thrown me over."

"I'm sure he did. How thoughtful of him. I may just fire him, too."

Max cut in. "Unless I'm getting my facts mixed up, you offered him the administrator position just this morning. That's a pretty short tenure."

"Yeah, well, that was before I knew he was so chivalrous." He rolled down the sleeves of his shirt and put his jacket on. "We're leaving, Max. How late are you staying?"

She was stacking papers. "Just long enough to lock up. I want to leave in time to see Joanne's face, when you leave with Kristin." She put up her hands. "I know, I know. That's not very nice. I've got to have my fun when I can now that I'm retired." She turned to Kristin. "It was nice to meet you. I'm so sorry about your lunch. Have a good night."

Joe took Kristin's bags in one hand and her hand in the other. "G'night, Max. Thanks for your help today."

In the elevator, he set her bags down and rounded on Kristin, putting both arms against the wall beside her head. "Was that kiss when you saw me just for the receptionist's benefit, or was it for me?"

She put her hands against his chest, and smiled up at him. "I'm not sure how I should answer that. Am I safe with you here in this elevator?"

234

"That depends entirely on what your definition of safe is." He leaned down to kiss her and the elevator opened. She laughed when she heard him cuss the elevator as he picked up the bags, and led her out past a few wide-eyed elevator patrons toward the fountains.

"Your hospital is marvelous. I had no idea what to picture, but I could never have imagined this." She looked all around. "I'm surprised you could walk away."

"This . . ." He looked all around, too. "Was too much to do and be a decent father. It was this or the boys. What kind of food do you like? Phoenix has it all. What'll it be?"

"Actually, I was thinking maybe we'd better go get the boys. With Gram gone, I think we should take them with us. In fact, maybe we should check on Gram on the way to dinner and see how her surgery went. Would you be offended?"

"Of course not, but the boys will be okay. They can take care of themselves long enough to take you to dinner."

"I don't doubt that, Joe, but it's just been you and the boys for a long time. I don't want them to get the impression that it's them or me."

They'd reached his car and he helped her in, then came around and got in as well. Setting her packages on the back seat, he turned to her. "You're definitely a wise woman. Thank you."

****

They still ended up alone at an elegant Italian restaurant. When they called the boys to invite them, the three of them asked if they could go to a movie with friends instead. Gram hadn't really felt up to visiting for long, so they left her the flowers they'd brought her and went to eat alone.

Once they were seated, Kristin was almost a little shy with him. She didn't want to figure out how long it had been since she had been on a date, but it had been a long time. Moreover, she was still a smidgen self-conscious about having kissed him so thoroughly in front of the receptionist. It was hard to remember he was the same Joe she'd come to know as her neighbor now that she'd seen his hospital. He must have known how she felt because he took off his jacket, rolled up his sleeves and then reached across to take her hand while they waited for their menus.

"So . . . How was your first day in Arizona?"

"It was interesting. And enlightening." She paused and smiled shyly at him. "I've seen a whole new Joe I wasn't aware of."

"The Joe who kisses you, or the hospital administrator Joe?"

"Both, I guess. I knew you were a hospital administrator, but I didn't realize on what scale." She hesitated. "And I have absolutely no idea what to do with this kissing Joe."

His eyes sought hers. "But you like him. At least you kiss him back."

"I think that's what scares me the most, actually." The waiter came with water goblets and menus.

When he left, Joe started right back where they left off. "You didn't seem scared this evening."

"Now I've had time to think about it, I probably owe you an apology. It's just that your receptionist made me so mad earlier."

He smiled. "You definitely do not owe me an apology. I loved it and it will hopefully save me from a lot more unwanted visits when I'm working."

Worry creased her brow. "Yes, but I'm still wearing my rings. Now they probably think you're having an affair with a married woman. I can't believe I did it. I'm usually a pretty private person."

He changed the subject. "You looked great when you showed up. Did you have fun shopping?"

"Yes, in fact. I don't usually like to shop, but I needed to. Downtown Phoenix has some great places. I'm still more at home out of the city, but the shopping in Driggs is a tad on the limited side."

"Tell me. How does a girl from Kansas become a downhill ski instructor in Driggs, Idaho?"

The waiter interrupted again to take their orders, and then she said, "My brother and I used to fly out to Whistler, British Columbia a couple of times a year. We loved it. Ryan, on the other hand, thought going to the mountains of your own free will was just slightly psychotic. After he was gone, I wanted to leave anything behind that could spark the memories, so I left Kansas. I found the most opposite place I could. Teaching skiing was just a way to preserve my sanity. I love the teenagers. They help me not be too lonely."

"Where is your brother now?"

She moved her water goblet in a circle. "In Kansas. He's a farmer clear over on the eastern side of the state. He tried to get me to come stay with his family, but I couldn't do that to them. His children already thought I was scary just from visiting me in the hospital."

"And your parents?"

She looked away for a second and then back at him. "My mother passed away last summer from lung cancer, and my dad is still living in the same town I grew up in. He's the local pharmacist, and stops after work to have a drink with the boys almost every night. He never understood why I would give up a perfectly good career to go home and have babies. He's kind of the male equivalent of a feminist. He thought I should put the girls in daycare and make a contribution to society. Needless to say, we didn't see eye to eye very well. What about your family?"

"My parents and two brothers live in Tempe. They moved out here from New Jersey when I was four. They're your classic Italian gangster types, only gone western. It's like a cross between Al Capone and John Wayne. They should make a movie of my parents. It would be hysterical."

She smiled at his description. "Do you do much with them?"

Shaking his head, he answered, "Not much. They think I'm nuts to have joined the church and left all the fun in life behind. I think they're nuts to live like they do. Sometimes I'm surprised they've survived it all. We have basically opposite lifestyles. Gram is far more of a mother to me now."

Quietly she said, "So, you've seen both sides, too. It makes me more grateful for the church than ever. When I really think about it, I wish there was a way to thank Gabriel for having the guts to talk to me on the lift like he did. I owe a lot to you, as well, but he's the one who helped me start to find the gospel. It's the greatest gift I've ever been given."

He reached and put a hand on hers and said earnestly, "You probably don't know what a gift you gave him, too, Kristin, because you didn't know him before, but you've helped him in a big way. He's the reason I finally made the break, left work and moved. He wasn't doing well when we first got to Idaho. As soon as he met you, he began to gain confidence, and a quiet self assurance that has helped him find the old Gabriel again. I still worry about him. I'm sure I'll always worry about all three of them, but I don't doubt anymore that he's going to be just fine. I don't know what you've said or done, but I'm incredibly grateful for how you've helped him to know he's okay."

She dropped her eyes and played with her water again. "Maybe it was that he could see how much he helped me. I had just about lost hope that I'd ever get any better."

Gently, he asked, "And now?"

She looked back up. "I don't think I'll ever be like I was before, but now at least I know I'll be able to make it through. You could never know how huge that is to me. Thank you. It's almost as big a gift as the gospel."

He squeezed her hand and played with it on the table, fingering her rings. "We know now how to keep the nightmares at bay, remember? Have you thought anymore about that?"

She tentatively met his brown eyes across the table, wishing she could just come right out and ask him exactly what he meant, but she didn't dare. "Yes, a lot, actually."

"What do you think about it?"

Shaking her head, she glanced at him. "I don't know."

"That doesn't tell me much."

"It's being honest. I think if you really knew me, you would never have said something like that to me in a weaker moment. I know me, and I'm not entirely sure I know what you want from me, but I know being too close to me would harm you and your sons. It couldn't not harm you."

He watched her across the table for a few seconds without saying anything, and then their food came. They began to eat quietly and he changed the subject and they talked small talk during the meal, then went home.

The boys were still going strong on the basketball court, but she was tired and she knew Joe was, too. Their interrupted night was coming back to haunt them in more ways than one. She told the boys good night and would have headed for Gram's room, but Joe stopped her. He started to say something and then thought better of it and walked her to her doorway in silence. At the threshold, he turned her around to face him and looked down at her for a long moment. Finally, he leaned down to give her the gentlest of kisses. "Good night, Kristin. Remember, you promised."

She pulled his head back down just for a second. "I remember."

In her room, with the door closed, she chastised herself. She shouldn't have done that. She shouldn't encourage him, but sometimes she felt completely weak about fighting her attraction. She had been honest about not harming his family; she just hated to admit that she should stay completely away from them for their sakes. She had come to love them all a great deal, and now that she knew what it was like to have their friendship in her life, she wasn't sure how she could go back to being alone.

She prayed and lay down. For the time being, she wasn't going to go there. She'd just try to be more careful not to fall for him any deeper. Walking away later was going to kill her.

Somehow, even in the middle of the nightmare, she knew she shouldn't scream. No sound came out of her mouth, but she jerked awake in the same horror and anguish she usually felt when she relived that awful summer day. She kicked off the covers, trying to catch her breath and change the stage in her mind, but couldn't stop the tears that streamed down her face. She tried to think of other things or just nothing to blank the awful images in her mind, but nothing helped.

When she couldn't get her heart rate to even slow, she got up and put on her swim suit and then put a pair of long lycra shorts and a t-shirt over it. In case one of the boys happened to see her going through, she didn't want them to see the scar. She stepped into a pair of running shoes without lacing them up so she could work out after her swim, and almost jerked a towel off the towel bar in her bath.

She didn't want to wake Joe up. She didn't think she could face him right now, but she'd promised. She stepped into the hall, trying to think past the scenes flashing over and over in her mind, to figure out what to do about him. She hesitated at his door and then decided she'd just swim hard for a few minutes to see if she could get a grip on herself before she woke him as promised.

Just as she was about to step through the patio doors, she heard a noise behind her and spun to see Caleb come out of the hall into the kitchen. When she saw him, she quickly wiped at her cheeks trying not to let him see how upset she was. He walked toward her. "Kristin, are you okay?"

She turned away and willing her voice to be steady, she said, "I'm fine, thanks. I'm just going to swim for awhile."

He glanced at the kitchen clock before he said, "You're a terrible liar. Can I do anything to help you?"

"Actually, yes. In the morning, will you vouch for me to your dad that I talked to you just now so I can get away with not waking him up?"

"Sure. Whatever."

"Thanks." She stepped out, shut the door behind her, and hurried to the pool.

At first, she hoped that just the fact that she was in a strange place would help to displace the images, but when they were worse than ever she swam hard to get her mind to focus on the physical struggle instead of the mental, praying as she worked. She'd been swimming for awhile when she realized Caleb was sitting in a patio chair beside the pool looking up at the stars. She stopped and stood up and took a moment to catch her breath. "Caleb, what are you doing still up?"

"Oh, just couldn't sleep. I thought I'd keep you company."

She felt a pang of guilt when she realized he felt like he needed to be out here with her. "You're a terrible liar. Go back to bed. I'll be fine."

"Actually, now I'm wide awake. You've been swimming for almost an hour. Switch gears and come play me a game of basketball."

"I'm awful at basketball. All that would happen is you'd run me up and down the court."

He grinned and then sobered. "It might help."

"You have a point. Go on in and I'll be right there." He left and she got out and toweled off and dressed and then laced up her shoes. They'd been playing for close to an hour, their shoes squeaking on the court, when she finally felt herself calming. Physically she was exhausted and she started to wear down.

At the end of another game, she put her hands on her knees and bent to try and breathe. Caleb went to the foul line and began to shoot baskets and asked, "Feeling better?"

"Better and tired. Thank you for playing. It really helped."

"You're welcome, but it's still not going to keep you out of hot water with Dad in the morning. If you told him you'd wake him, you'd better do it. It's five o'clock. He'll be up in an hour anyway."

"Actually, I can probably face him now. I just couldn't earlier. I hate it when he sees me like that. I hate it when anyone sees me like that."

He shot a few more baskets. "It's not like he's going to like you any less because of the nights. Maybe if you just got married the dreams would go away."

She swallowed hard, wondering what to say to him. "Caleb, it's not all that easy. Marriage is a big decision. It's a forever thing, so it has to be the most careful choice you ever make. Your dad just barely got his freedom. The last thing he'd want is to marry me right now."

"You don't know him like we do. I think he wants to marry you."

When Joe spoke from the side of the court they both jumped in surprise. "Dad would marry her in a minute, Caleb. Keep working on her. Maybe she'll listen to you. Remind her that I love her, will you?"

Joe went back into the kitchen and Caleb looked at Kristin with a big grin. "I'm 'sposed to remind you that he loves you." Kristin looked from Caleb to the kitchen door. She looked back at Caleb and he laughed at her. "It wouldn't be so bad." He made another shot. "He's a nice guy. And he's rich."

Kristin was completely . . . She didn't even know what she was. Befuddled? Maybe that was the word. No. Floored was more like it. She didn't realize she'd stood there stunned, until Caleb chuckled again. She looked at him and sighed and went back outside to get back in the pool and swim more feverish laps.

Remind? Remind! He'd told Caleb to remind her that he loved her when he'd never so much as even intimated it before. It almost made her mad. She swam several more laps and then stood up while she thought to herself. He always treated her like he cared for her. He treated her special, but then he always had. She dove back into the water and swam some more. How was she supposed to deal with something like this?

She hadn't made any more headway into either understanding Joe, or figuring out how she felt and what she was going to do about any of this, when she realized he was in the pool with her. He swam several laps with her while she worried about how to face him before he reached out and stopped her as she went to swim by. He pulled her to him and she looked up at him and tried to read his expression in the dark.

"Good morning." His gentle voice helped calm her nerves. He wrapped both arms around her and hugged her to him. "How long have you been up?"

She shook her head, "I don't know. . I was going to wake you, but Caleb was up."

"I gathered that. I still wish you'd have woken me. Did you scream? I didn't hear a thing until I heard you playing basketball." She shook her head again against his neck. "Are you okay?"

"Yeah. No. I don't know. I'm okay right now as far as the dreams; I'm just really mixed up as far as you."

He tipped her chin up with a gentle finger. "What are you mixed up about?" She shook her head and looked down again. "What? Are you mad at me?"

"No. Mixed up doesn't mean mad, Joe." She looked up at him. "Mixed up means mixed up. How am I supposed to know what to do here? How can Caleb *remind* me that you love me, when you've never said anything like that before? And how do I deal with that when I'm as much of an emotional mess as I am? I'm a little lost here, Joe."

He chuckled and hugged her even tighter. "I think you're beautiful even when you're a little lost."

She rolled her eyes. "Oh brother."

His voice was apologetic when he said, "I'm sorry I've never told you how I feel. I guess I thought you knew. How can you not know? Do you think I would try to talk you into marrying me if I wasn't in love with you?"

She watched him and then looked away into the dark. "I don't know what to think. I mean, you hinted at that, but when you did you'd never even kissed me, let alone told me you loved me. I almost wondered if I was a missionary project or something for you. How can you even hint at marrying me? You know what my nights are like. I couldn't do that to your family. Look at just this morning. I've had Caleb out of bed for hours. I'm ruining all of your lives."

He put a finger to her lips and then moved it and put his mouth there. She couldn't help it and kissed him back. Finally, he said, "Don't you think if Caleb had a problem with you that he'd be trying to talk you out of marrying me, instead of trying to talk you into it?"

She looked up at him with earnest eyes. "Joe, you and I both know Caleb doesn't understand what's at stake here. This is between you and me. We have to do what we think is best, no matter how we feel."

"Kristin, I'm not going to argue with you, but I'm not going to agree not to do something I think we should do either. Pray about it, and give it time, but don't waste time struggling through the nights if you don't have to. In the mean time, I'm just going to be patient and enjoy the journey." He kissed her again. "This is a great journey."

Jaclyn M. Hawkes

# Chapter 22

That morning's basketball game was the start of an epic effort by the boys to try talking her into marrying Joe. It started right off and by mid morning she knew she was in trouble. There were whispers and grins, and she wondered what was coming. She didn't have to wait long to find out.

Joe had gone to work early and the boys took her on a sightseeing trip around their old stomping grounds, and then took her to lunch at their favorite Mexican restaurant.

When they first got there, Robby excused himself to go to the restroom, but he must have taken a side trip to talk the Mariachis into serenading her into marrying Joe. All the way through their meal three musicians kept returning to their table with a guitar and violin and some maracas to try to influence her with their romantic music. They had changed the words to all of the songs to end each stanza with a phrase about marrying Joe. The guys thought it was a riot and she couldn't help but laugh at all six of them.

They offered to take her several more places, but she had gotten a taste of what she was in for and begged off and took them to visit Gram and then back home. It was Friday afternoon and she was bushed from her hours of exercise in the night, but she was afraid to try to nap. Finally, she called Joe, wondering how late he was going to be working. When she admitted what was going on, he encouraged her to try to sleep and promised her he'd come home within a couple of hours and help her wake up peacefully.

She thanked him and got off the phone, wishing she could go ahead and marry him. He was so good to her. She went back to bed, thinking of how nice it had been to kiss him that morning in the pool.

****

After Kristin called, Joe spent the rest of the afternoon having to actively concentrate on the job at hand. He wanted to finish tying up all the loose ends as soon as possible so he could spend the balance of the weekend with Kristin while he had her at his house. When they got home, he knew he would have to find excuses to visit her at her house and share her with the Murdocks.

He let himself think about how nice it had been to talk to her in the pool in the dark this morning. Okay, so the kissing was better than the conversation, but he wasn't picky. He smiled to himself when he remembered the look on her face when he'd spoken to her and Caleb in the basketball court. He didn't remember her ever being that caught off guard before.

The rush hour commute had traffic snarled for miles and he worried he wouldn't get home in time, but he did. He said hi to the boys and then went into her room to help her wake up. Before he even approached the bed, he stood back and looked at her. In her sleep, she seemed younger than her twenty-nine years. She was truly beautiful, inside and out and he said a quick prayer of gratitude for the inspiration that had sent him to her at the right time.

She lay curled up on her stomach, and he sat on her bed and began to scratch her back and talk to her in a gentle, quiet voice. It didn't take long to wake her and the look of wonder that filled her eyes when she woke up was the same one he'd seen before when she'd awakened peacefully. It tore at his heart that just waking up without anguish was so eventful for her. He needed to talk her into marrying him sooner rather than later.

She lay still for a minute and then stretched and sat up and hugged him with a smile. He loved it when she forgot to think, and just reacted to him without reservation. "Good morning again."

She was still sleepy when she said, "Hi, Joe. Thank you. I was way tired. How was work?"

"Fine. Long. I just wanted to come home and see you." Her blue eyes widened.

"Have you found the money you were looking for?"

He didn't answer her. Instead, he leaned down and gave her one long kiss, and then said, "Get out of bed and come out and I'll tell you all about it. If I found one of the boys sitting on a girl's bed kissing her, I'd trounce them both, so I need to go out and let you get up." He leaned into her and kissed her again. "Hurry."

On his way to the kitchen to see about dinner, the door bell rang and he detoured to answer it. He'd been expecting one of the boy's friends, so he was surprised when he opened it to reveal Paul Sharp standing on his porch. "Hey, Paul. Come on in. What are you up to tonight?" He let him in and began to walk back into the kitchen.

"Uh, I was in the neighborhood, and I thought I'd stop by." Joe began to wonder if something else unusual had turned up at the hospital.

He turned back to Paul. "Is there something wrong? What can I do for you?"

"No. Nothing's wrong. I just thought I'd drop by and see Kristin again before she goes back home. Is she around?"

Joe turned to stare at him. "Paul! What do you mean drop by and see Kristin? What do you want to see Kristin for?"

Paul shrugged. "Because she's the most intriguing woman I've met in years. Why? What's it to you if I come by and see your neighbor?"

"Paul!" Joe paused in shock. "Paul!" He looked at his good friend like he had lost his mind. He had! What was he thinking, coming here like this?

Paul laughed and said, "Look, Joe. If you're worried that you think I want to see a married woman, forget it. Even as pretty as she is I'm not that kind of guy. But I already know she can't still be married. No husband on earth would let a woman like that travel out of state with another guy no matter how innocent it looked. She's just wearing those rings to keep the slugs away."

Joe shook his head. "You're good. It took me a long time to figure out she wasn't still married. Did it ever occur to you that she might still be spoken for?"

Paul looked confused. "What do you mean?" Joe watched him begin to run through things in his mind.

Exasperated, Joe said, "She's sort of with me, Paul. Isn't that a little obvious?"

"What?" Paul looked honestly shocked. "I thought she said she was your neighbor and came with to keep an eye on the boys while Gram was indisposed. She said you weren't dating. I asked her."

Joe became even more disgusted. "Paul! I may have taken longer to figure her out than you, but I'm not an idiot. We are dating and I'm trying to talk her into marrying me! So, it matters a lot to me if you come by to see my neighbor!"

Paul looked honestly penitent. "Sorry, man. I had no idea. I thought it was weird that even a woman hater like you could resist her."

At this point Kristin walked in. "Hi, Paul. I didn't realize you were here."

Joe turned to her. "Did you really tell Paul we weren't dating?"

Completely unflustered, she said, "Yes. We weren't."

"Kristin!"

"Our first real date was last night, Joe. When I was with Paul, I wasn't even aware we would be going. Lighten up. It's not like Paul is going is going to ask me out. He's your administrator."

"Yeah, well he just dropped by to see you!" He turned to Paul. "What? Did you think she was my nanny or something?"

Looking embarrassed, Paul said, "Something along those lines. Yeah."

"Paul!" Joe was getting more disgusted. "Look at her! Nobody has a nanny that looks like that! Robby's seventeen, for Pete's sake!"

Paul started to edge toward the door. "You know, I'm just going to go ahead and go. I'll see myself out."

Joe nodded. "I think that's a good idea!" When Paul was gone, he turned to Kristin and grumped. "Was that really necessary?"

She laughed, but she sounded sincere when she said, "Joe, I'm sorry. He was your assistant administrator; I never dreamed he would hit on me."

"Why did you tell him we weren't dating?"

"Joe, he'd just seen me thrown out of your office because I was *another* female. And we weren't dating. For all

Jaclyn M. Hawkes

I knew, you had decided to send me away.  He just said he knew you wouldn't want me to eat alone.  I thought he was being respectful of your neighbor."

Joe let out a disgusted breath.  "Oh, he was respectful all right."

She came up to him and hugged him and looked into his eyes smiling.  He wasn't sure he was ready to smile back at her yet.  The whole idea of another guy with her ticked him off.  She just kept smiling at him and finally he asked, "What? What's so funny to you?"

"All of it.  This whole, loony mess was a scream.  Don't you think?"

He finally smiled.  "I don't think any of it was very funny.  Yesterday or today.  Can you imagine him simply walking into my own house to come and see you?  I'm still mad."

"Ah, Joe.  Life is too short to be mad over this.  Just laugh.  You were actually very entertaining!"

He finally lightened up and hugged her.  "Well, in case any more of my administrative staff asks, will you please tell them that, yes, we are dating?"

"Absolutely.  Can I be forgiven?"

He pulled back and looked at her skeptically. "Forgiven for what?  You haven't had lunch with anyone else I'd be opposed to, have you?"

She laughed.  "You have no idea.  You'll have to ask the boys about lunch today.  I meant be forgiven for being female."

"Now you're being a smart aleck.  I happen to thoroughly enjoy the fact that you're female.  I just don't want to share."

252

Laughing again, she said, "I did get that impression. You were going to tell me about your day today."

He pulled her back in close with a grin. "No, I was going to kiss you some more. I just thought I shouldn't do it on your bed. Then I was going to tell you about my day."

\*\*\*\*

They ate on the deck, and then lounged and watched the sun set and the boys and their friends playing in the pool when Kristin reminded him, "You never did tell me about your day."

"I was busy, and didn't want to be interrupted." He smiled over at her lazily and rubbed his thumb across her hand. "I found the missing money, though. I just hope we're able to get some of it back. The new, highly recommended administrator and an auditor with an addiction issue, tag-teamed to embezzle nearly two-hundred-thousand dollars. They thought if they took a little from every department no one would notice."

"I guess not, huh?"

"No. I think they thought no one would look over the books too closely now that I live in Idaho. Neither one of them knew me very well."

"What happens to someone who steals that kind of money?"

"They get arrested and if they're convicted they go to prison."

"Is the money already gone?"

"Some of it. Most of it was seized by the police, so now we just have to wait until it's all over to get what's left of it back."

"So, is Max retired again?"

"She is."

"Her husband will be glad to hear it, I imagine."

He smiled over at her. "I'm sure he will. Men need their women."

****

That night after he walked her to the door of her bedroom, when he asked, she gladly accepted a blessing and then slept soundly until she heard the boys playing basketball the next morning. He regretted not giving her one two nights before. He worked Saturday and then offered to take her to any of the places Phoenix had that Driggs didn't. They ended up at an upscale French restaurant and the ballet, where she looked like a Grecian goddess in a dress she had bought the first afternoon.

She was okay again that night and then Sunday they took her to their old ward to church. He almost felt like showing her off as they walked in, and he was grateful that she was beside him when a couple of single women came around. The boys made no bones about showing her off, and there could be little doubt to anyone near that the Facianos were smitten.

That afternoon they picked up Gram again and, taking the two dogs that had become more than fast friends, they boarded the plane to head back home to Idaho.

# Chapter 23

After landing in Jackson Hole, they started back over the pass and finally pulled into Joe's driveway at after nine p.m. The Murdocks wouldn't be home until early the next morning, so when Joe walked her home he checked her security system to make sure everything was working. It didn't take him more than a minute to ascertain that the system had been disturbed by an intruder several times over the course of the last few days. He was appalled and was standing looking at the computer terminal wondering how much to tell her and how to do the telling when she rushed back in to where he was with an ashen face.

Glancing back out the door, he immediately asked, "What? What is it?"

She didn't say anything, just took his hand and went back the way she'd come. He followed her into the house and into her bedroom. Her hand was literally trembling in his when she pointed to the dresser. A beautiful card and a long wilted rose sat on its surface, and he took a nearby pencil and carefully opened the card without touching it to read. "Kristin, I've missed you and can't wait until you return. Seeing you is the best part of my life."

Immediately he turned and gathered her tight into his arms and then quickly called the police with his cell phone. While they waited for them to arrive, he quizzed her about anything else that looked like it might have been disturbed or taken. When the police got there, he kept an arm around her as they questioned her and had her show them around her place.

As soon as they were through, he took her back over to his house and kept her in his office with him while he made arrangements for two off duty police officers to stand guard over both of their houses for the night until he could arrange for twenty-four hour security the next day. By the time everything was handled as well as it could be, it was after eleven and the boys and Gram were long in bed.

He sat with her in his T.V. room in front of the fire with the stereo on in the background. The haunted look from the morning of her baptism was back and he hated the thought of what this fear did to her nightmares.

There was no way he was going to let her go back to her house alone, and he didn't want her to be alone tonight in his house either. He brought an armload of blankets from the linen closet and then three or four pillows and piled them on the floor in front of the fireplace. It was like a sleepover he'd had with friends when he was a teenager. He knew it was probably not the most ideal situation, but under the circumstances, he felt it was appropriate.

He fixed her a bed on the couch, gave her a blessing, and tried to get her to lay down to rest while he sat on the floor at her feet, but her wide open eyes as she lay there belied rest. He ultimately took her and a huge, fluffy down comforter to a double rocker recliner and literally rocked her on his lap like a baby until he could start to feel her relax against him. When he finally thought she might be able to fall asleep, he reclined the chair and turned out all the lights but the one near the stairs and attempted to help her get some rest.

He had unconsciously switched out of boyfriend mode and into almost a security guard mode and his instinct to protect and comfort her was powerful. Tomorrow he was going on the offensive.

He woke up several times in the night and made sure she was covered and comfortable before going back to sleep beside her. Toward two o'clock, he knew she was starting to dream and he pulled her close and stayed awake to talk to her and hold her when he could tell she was fighting the drag of the nightmares. He managed to pull her through all the way to morning without the horrors, and though he was tired, he felt like he had won the war.

When the boys got up to get ready for school, all of them came in to check on her after knowing what had gone on with the stalker, and he put a finger to his lips to warn them not to wake her. They dressed and ate cold cereal and headed out without him moving from where he was holding her, and she was able to sleep in peace until almost nine. When she finally woke up, she was fine as far as the nightmares, but he could feel the underlying fear when she gave him a tremulous smile and thank you.

She and Gram cooked breakfast and he went with her across to check on her horses, and then brought her right back to his house.

When the Murdocks returned, Joe left her with Gram and went across to talk to them. He and Murdock went over everything that had happened and together they made a game plan and went back to Joe's to run it by Kristin. The fact that she was okay with whatever they decided almost troubled him. It wasn't like her to be that subordinate.

They decided to find a security team that wasn't local that could actually patrol the area and then set up a trap of some kind and get this thing over with. With the guy in jail, maybe Kristin could have some semblance of control. In the mean time, they would keep the off duty policemen around during the nights. Murdock assured Joe he would use some of his contacts to find someone they could trust and Joe went back to his house to be with Kristin.

She was between her winter and summer jobs, couldn't get out and about, was afraid and was totally at a loose end. After literally pacing his house like a caged tiger, she let him talk her into taking a day trip into Jackson Hole. Away from their houses, she appeared to loosen up a little and they spent a leisurely day browsing galleries and shopping. She appeared to be okay, but she hardly let go of his hand during the entire day. After a late lunch in a rustic log cabin restaurant, they went back to one of the galleries they had been in and bought a painting Joe liked and went back to Driggs to be with the boys after school. The boys' teasing helped, but he could tell she was still uptight.

She finally insisted he take her home and she swam for and then locked herself in her studio behind the blinds and spent the evening painting. When the boys were down in bed, he could still see lights, so he walked over and then called her to tell her it was him who was knocking.

She let him in with a tired smile. "Hey, Joe. What are you still doing up? I thought you would go down early after not getting much sleep last night because of me. Thank you, again."

He looked down into her eyes instead of answering her. After trying to search her soul, he bent and kissed her gently. "There's no way I could sleep over there when I'm wondering how you're doing."

"I'm fine. You can see that for yourself. I'm just going to paint for a little longer and then call it a night, so go home and go to bed."

He looked at her steadily again and asked, "What do I have to do, Kristin, to get you to trust me enough to be emotionally honest with me?"

She sighed and took his hand and led him back to the couch, dropping her paint brush on her easel on the way. When he sat down she sat down beside him, curled up against him and said, "I'm sorry. It's not that I'm trying to be less than emotionally honest. I'm still so mixed up about what to do concerning you. I would love to be honest, Joe. I'd love to just turn this all over to you and lean on you and let you be my knight in shining armor. But I can't. I can't do that to you, and I can't do that to the boys.

"So be patient with me, huh? Until I can figure out how to be your friend on a give and take equally basis, I'm just muddling through here. I know that sounds ridiculously incompetent, but I've never been so unsure of what to do in my life. I'm on this emotional roller coaster that's making me crazy. Trying to understand if I'm supposed to do what I think I should, or what I want is so frustrating. I'm trying to listen to what God's telling me and I can't hear it. I'm sorry."

He wrapped both arms around her and let her lean her head against his chest. "I don't understand what you're trying to say to me, Kristin. Start at the beginning. What is it you can't do to me and the boys?"

Still leaning against him, she answered, "I can't ask you to be involved in my life like you seem to want to be. It's too much to ask. I can't let you take on my troubles and continue to let my bad nights and fear ruin your nights and days."

He thought about that. She wasn't asking him to help her. He was offering, and he was already involved clear up to his heart. He wanted to point that out to her and remind her that that's what people who loved each other did, but he decided to just listen for the time being. "And what do you need to figure out about having a give and take relationship?"

She turned her head to look at him like he was being a little dense. "How not to just take and never give, Joe. What do you think I'm trying to say?"

He bent and nuzzled her neck for a second or two before he said, "I'm just making sure I understand." He went back to kissing her neck before his next question. "And what is it that you're unsure of?"

It took her a few minutes to formulate an answer, and even then she didn't make much sense. "I don't know what to do with you, er about you. About how I feel about you and what I should do about how I feel about you."

Trailing kisses up her neck, he finally made his way to her mouth and focused on it for several seconds. Eventually, he asked, "What is it that you want to do with me?" This time he bent to the other side of her neck and she didn't even try to answer him.

Finally, she pulled away from him and scooted a ways away on the couch and said in a voice that sounded distracted, "What did you ask? I can't concentrate with you doing that."

"Sorry, I'll stop." He took her hand and pulled her to lean on him again. "I asked what it is that you want to do with me. You said you've never been so unsure of what to do in your life. What is it that you want to do?"

She shook her head. "What I want isn't really the issue here. What should I do is a more responsible question."

Facing her, he said, "I disagree vehemently. Since what I think we're discussing, if I'm not mistaken, is what you're going to do about the fact that I love you and want to be with you for better or worse. I definitely don't want to be a should. I want to be a want. I want to be a need. A can't live without. So, could you stop already with the responsibleness and just be honest with me. What do you want?"

"Is responsibleness really a word?"

"I'm not entirely sure." He looked at her mouth again. "If it is, I'd rather you not use it to describe our feelings for each other. How about attractedness or intriguedness or fascinatedness or happyness. Hey! That one actually is a word. Or foreverness. That's a good one. Do you realize that in the hereafter there are no nightmares or stalkers?"

He finally got a real smile out of her and went on, "So, that means in the big picture you can quit with the guilt trip because I'll get to have you nightmareless much longer than unnightmareless. Now, hey, there's a word!" She laughed right out loud. "See, if I could be with you all the time, you'd laugh a lot more. And, I could kiss you as much as I want, and . . ."

She turned to look at him and asked, "And?"

He paused and thought about it and then said, "And, I think that's all I'm going to say about that. You never did tell me what you want."

She laughed softly. "I think you're so tired you're getting loopy. You probably wouldn't remember anything I said. I don't dare tell you what I want anyway, which is probably a good thing."

The look he gave her was absolutely serious, but he continued to joke, "Well, if you're not going to tell me, then you don't need to concentrate, so I can kiss you and not worry about mixing you up." He started to do just that.

Between kisses she admitted, "I think we kiss too much. Kissing mixes me up more than ever. You totally cloud my thinking."

"So then quit thinking." He brushed her bottom lip with his thumb, and then leaned his head back against the couch and said, "To be honest, I've been thinking a lot about you. But my thoughts work out better than yours. My thinking leaves me realizing that I never really understood how nice being in love would be. It's much more fun than I thought. If I had known it was this nice, I'd have made all kinds of deals with God to help me find you sooner." She looked up at him with wide, questioning eyes.

His words had been teasing, but he met her gaze directly. "Kristin, can I tell you something?"

She nodded and he continued, "I'm sure I don't truly even begin to understand what you've been through, but I have seen some of the aftermath, haven't I?" Again she nodded. "I've seen enough to get a little bit of an inkling of what your life can be like." He played with a long strand of gold hair and then looked squarely at her. "And I want to be with you anyway." He put a hand up to her cheek, and then gently kissed her one last time and got up. "I hate going home to sleep without you."

When she stood up to walk him to the door, he turned to her. "Is there any way you could call me if you wake up?"

She sighed. "Joe. What do I do with you? Sure, I'll call you. How about if you just pray for me and I'll sleep fine?"

"I always pray for you. How about if you just promise to call so I can go to sleep without worrying that I won't wake up if you need me."

She looked at him in concern. "Joe, is that why you get insomnia?"

"It wasn't at the start, but it is now." They stood looking at each other, neither one knowing what to say.

Finally, he quietly asked, "Do you understand that being there beside you at nights would solve a lot of things? For both of us?" He brushed her lip again. "Think about it. Pray about it."

He walked out, carefully locking the door behind him.

That night Kristin lay awake deep into the night, but not because she was afraid of either the nightmares or the stalker. She lay there trying to listen for an answer to her prayers about what to do with her feelings for Joe. Her intellect told her she needed to pick up and move away from him, away from everyone again so her dragons didn't touch any more lives than they had to, but the thought of leaving Joe was almost unbearable.

For years now, she had fought to have things in her life that would keep the nightmares and grief from completely overwhelming her. She finally had something, or someone, that she thought about far more than the nightmares, but she knew that to embrace that and enjoy it would only harm him and his sons. He was a dream come true that she had to walk away from for his good, and she hated even the thought of it. Not only did she hate the thought of walking away from him, but she honestly didn't know if she was strong enough to do it.

He was becoming everything to her. She'd never dreamed she could be this comfortable and this happy with a man. The more she knew him, the more she liked him. Even in her head she hesitated to use the word love, although when she got gut honest with herself she knew she loved him.

Moreover, it wasn't just a love or attraction thing, even though now that he had broken the kissing barrier, the physical attraction had taken on a life of its own. It was an all encompassing complexity of emotion that was based on a foundation of respect and friendship and trust. He was a good man. A great man. She wasn't sure she'd ever known a man she admired more. There certainly wasn't one she could think of.

Knowing that made this all the harder. How could she stay with him, but how in the world could she go? The mental roller coaster was insane! It was a wonder Joe hadn't dumped her flat, the way she waffled back and forth.

Surprisingly, she was okay that night. Waking up calmly in her own bed in the late March sunrise was an unexpected blessing. She'd assumed the heightened fear of the stalker would preclude peace in the wee hours, but she was glad she was wrong. She laid in her bed thinking as the room lightened from the rising of the sun. Even after praying and pondering, she still didn't know what she should do about Joe. Sometimes, she wished God *was* in the wind. It would be so much easier to figure things out.

Murdock looked at her with such focus when she came into the kitchen that she felt like he was inspecting her. He just kept watching her and she finally came right out and asked, "What? Is something wrong? Why are you looking at me like that?"

He was his steady, dependable self when he simply said, "I don't know. There's something different about you today. Arizona must agree with you. Even with this whole security mess, you look . . . I don't know what you look. Happy and something else. Happy and stubborn maybe."

That description cracked her up in spite of her seemingly unanswered prayers for direction. "You sound like my brother. Only he termed it a bit differently. I was pig headed with a sweet attitude."

He shrugged with a smile. "That works, too. You slept well, I see. Didn't expect it, honestly. Glad I was wrong. Did he give you another one of those blessings he gives you?"

"Not last night, but the night before. Last night he just teased me mercilessly until I relaxed."

"Must've worked." He sipped his coffee. "I've never seen anything like those blessings. I would never a believed something like that would work if I hadn't seen it myself."

She hugged him as she went by. "I know exactly what you mean. I had never experienced anything like it and that first night in the hospital it was the most amazing thing. The power in that room was indescribable, Murdock. I would never have dreamed there was an unseen power like that. I'm so grateful I can't even tell you, but I'm sure you of all people know that without me saying a word."

"I do. I'm grateful, too. I'm happy for you, Kristin. He's a good man."

She took a glass of milk and toast to the table. "He is. Far too good a man, with way too nice of a family to be involved with a woman like me. I know it; I just don't have a clue what to do about it."

He leaned back against the sink and folded his arms across his chest. "What's wrong with a woman like you, Kris?"

A long sigh prefaced her answer. "You and I both know exactly what I'm saying, Murdock. Would becoming more involved with him be fair to either him or his boys?"

"So you have dreams. He knows that now and loves you anyway. They're getting better all the time. Look at you this morning, even with the added worries."

Her stubbornness showed on her face. "They're not better enough, Murdock. You know it and I know it. He's been up with me three nights out of six and the other ones he doesn't sleep for worrying about whether I'm going to dream. One of those three nights I had Caleb awake, too. What Joe calls insomnia is actually worry about me."

Gently, he said, "He worries because he cares."

"I know that. He cares too much for his own happiness." Her brow furrowed sadly. "I'm thinking about moving away from here because I care about him, too. It's what I should do."

Murdock was shocked. "You finally find someone who can help you get better and you're thinking about getting away from him? I thought you were really beginning to like him!"

She was able to answer him honestly, "I love him dearly. That's why I want to shield him from all of this."

Murdock shook his head. "I've never thought you were crazy, Kristin. But trying to take the right to make his own decisions away from a man as capable as Joe Faciano is sheer lunacy. What right do you have to choose what's best for him? He's not a kid, Kris."

"Trust me, Murdock. I'm one hundred percent aware that he is not a kid. If he was, I wouldn't worry as much."

"If you know he's all grown up, why would you try to take away his right to make his own decisions?"

She just looked at him sadly. "Doing something I know would harm him just to benefit me wouldn't be honorable. I care too much for him to do that, even if I could."

"So what are you going to do then?"

"I have no idea. For all my self-sacrificing talk, I'm not sure I can honestly make myself walk away from him. He's the best thing that's ever happened to me. How's that for selfish?"

"There's a difference between being selfish and using good judgment. Have you prayed about any of this? God knows better than you and me and Joe, all three."

She nodded. "I have prayed. I'm just not very good yet at understanding what I'm being told. That's what I get for spending most of my life ignoring God, I guess."

He drained his coffee cup, rinsed it, and put it in the sink. "Well, Kris, I love you like you were my own daughter, but I think you need to do some more praying. If you walk away from Joe Faciano, you'll regret it for the rest of your life." He put a hand on her shoulder and squeezed it on his way out.

She was restless, especially after talking with Murdock. She didn't know what to do about Joe and she didn't want to face him for some reason this morning. Knowing he was going to show up sooner or later, she asked Murdock if he thought she would be safe if she took a horseback ride somewhere far away from home. At first he was hesitant and then said to go ahead, but just to make sure no one was following her. "Let me know exactly where you are and keep in touch with me with your phone." With that, she made a fast decision, changed and loaded up a horse and Teal and left before she had to face Joe.

Pulling out of her drive, she mentally began to go over where she could safely ride at this time of year. She needed to be someplace she could be sure no one was following her, either in a vehicle, or on foot, so wide open spaces would be best. At this time of year in this country, there was still snow up high and in the lower country a lot of places were still water logged and muddy. She decided to go out on the flats west of the river bluff and at the crossroads headed that way, feeling a little guilty for not touching base with Joe at all that morning.

# Chapter 24

Even as tired as Joe was from his relatively sleepless night the night before, he still laid awake late after he prayed, thinking about Kristin. He knew her well enough now to recognize the inner turmoil she was feeling about their friendship aside from the other troubles she had. He knew without having to ask that she felt like she should protect him and the boys from the ravages of her life. Part of him wanted to just bully her into letting him take the burdens of her nightmares on so he could help her find some peace, but some other part of his brain knew if he pressured her right now, he'd lose her forever.

He resolved to back off and let her have all the space she needed so he didn't spook her into pulling away and shutting him out again. He had to trust that she would continue to pray and ask what she should do, until she was sure what God had in mind for her. He knew what God wanted, and he knew Kristin would eventually figure it out. He just had to hang in there until she did.

When he finally made it out of bed just in time to see her pulling out with a horse trailer hooked onto her SUV, he had to remind himself to be patient. He could understand her wanting to try to protect them all from her troubles, but it still made him want to swear. When she still hadn't come home at five o'clock that evening, he felt like swearing even more. It was a good thing he had three young men looking up to him to keep him from reacting the way he felt. He'd have probably cussed up a storm.

The boys were hopefully going to be his secret weapon through all this. When they got home from school, he listened to them joking and talking as they sat around the kitchen table, eating the brownies Gram had made for them. He didn't think they knew he could hear them through his open office door. In the time it took them to down half a pan, and most of a gallon of milk, they had made a game plan of how to start wooing Kristin into marrying him. It was rather involved and included multiple bouquets of flowers, as well as notes, gifts, candy, and at one point they considered jewelry.

He made a mental note to squelch that one in the bud. When someone finally gave Kristin jewelry, it was going to be him in the form of a set of rings to replace the ones she still wore.

Occasionally, he wondered why she did still wear them, but he had seen enough of the way men reacted to her to assume it was for the same reason he had worn his long after the sentimental feelings were gone. It didn't always work. There were plenty of people out there who had no qualms about flirting with someone who was married, but it certainly cut back on the sheer volume.

There was a little voice in the back of his head that nagged at him that maybe she wore the rings, and continued to hesitate about their relationship because she was still in love with her dead husband. He invariably tried to quiet that voice whenever it raised its obnoxious little head. She'd told him once she hadn't ever been truly in love with her husband, and Joe had to cling to that hope because he knew he could never have overcome a serious devotion to someone who wasn't even around to compete with.

She pulled in just as it was starting to get dark and he watched her unload an obviously weary white horse that had mud eight inches up its legs. Both Teal and Kristin limped on the way into the house and it was all he could do not to go straight over to see if she was okay. The boys must have had a sixth sense, because they took her a plate of brownies a few minutes later.

Joe was up several times in the night to look over and see if there were any lights on at her place, but she appeared to be having a good night, which was a double good thing. He didn't feel like he could have gone to her if he'd needed to. He lay back down for the fourth time, frustrated beyond belief.

He got up and helped the boys get ready and off to school and then watched her load up and leave again, this time with the black horse and no dog. Murdock was out and about with her before she left, so Joe knew he was up on where she would be going, and after she was gone, Joe went to talk to him. The handshake and steady look he gave Joe when he came up was incredibly reassuring. Joe had no doubts Murdock was on his team and knew Joe was in this for the duration.

They talked about the security people Murdock had been arranging. He had been able to find some men out of Washington state who worked as a team in situations like this and came with the highest recommendation. Two of them were retired Navy seals and the third was one of their brothers who had worked with them for a couple of years. Murdock was pleased that they were trained professionals who wouldn't hesitate to act if they felt inclined. They were supposed to be arriving within two days with their own large trailer that was their living quarters that they would park in the pasture on the other side of her house. He ended his description with, "They're expensive, but they've never failed to find their man."

Joe waved off the expense. "I'm picking up the tab on this, Murdock, so don't even consider the cost. She has to be able to feel safe in her own home."

Murdock sighed. "You know she's going to kick up a fuss about you paying."

"Please encourage her not to. Tell her I insisted. Tell her it's for my place as well. Tell her whatever you need to, Murdock, but at least let me do this for her. It's one way I can help without pressuring her. I know she thinks she has to protect us all from her life, but I need to be a part of this. I'm trying to back off and give her some room, but if she won't let me be there, at least I can provide some more protection. She may be stubborn, but she should understand that we have to know she's safe and that she feels safe."

"I'll try; but you know her, Joe."

"I know her better than she thinks I do. I wish she understood me enough to realize I'm not going away because some things about her aren't convenient." He changed the subject. "Does she need someone to be around wherever she's off riding?"

"Probably, but the freedom factor may be even more important as long as the risks aren't too high. She's staying where she can see around her for literally miles both on the road and on the horse. And she checks in with me every so often to let me know she's okay and the coast is clear. For right now, while she's so uptight about everything, let's try to give her all the room she needs. Otherwise, she's going to do something incredibly foolish, thinking she's being unselfish."

The look he gave Joe didn't need much of an explanation. This time Joe did swear as he headed back across to his house.

****

Kristin hadn't ridden enough lately to ride this many hours straight without becoming painfully sore. Every spring she'd had to ease into riding long hours, but this year she had a need to be out and free that overrode the discomfort. The second afternoon of riding though, even the need to feel free didn't camouflage the ache in her left thigh and hip. In a week or two she'd be conditioned, but right now the injuries from the propane blast had flared past an ache into outright pain.

When her horse threw a shoe she was almost relieved and got off to walk even though Jet wasn't lame. She smiled a little to herself. The horse wasn't lame, but she certainly was. She'd ridden close to twenty miles in the last day and a half. It wasn't all that much for an old time cowboy, but her body was still in ski season mode and she was tired. She walked the mile or two back to the trailer, loaded up and turned for home.

Murdock met her as she came in and gave her a bouquet of flowers from the boys. She thanked him and smelled them with a sad smile.

Both days she'd spent praying and pondering about what to do with her feelings for her neighbor, and she hadn't come to any concrete conclusion other than to admit begrudgingly that she missed him terribly. So much for some quiet solitude so she could listen for personal inspiration. She'd been trying to listen. She honestly had, but even giving it her best shot, she wasn't hearing what God was trying to tell her.

Somehow, when she thought of Joe, her feelings sidetracked her spiritual funnel. She would get off on a tangent of thinking about him and she was actually falling in love deeper because of the focus of her thoughts. Thinking about him and how he treated her and how she felt when he was around left her with a sweet, peaceful warmth in her heart that belied the fact that her head knew she should get away from him as soon as she could make herself.

Dragging her tired body into the house to shower after caring for her horse, she told herself she would get her inspiration to shut him out on another day. Tonight she wanted to see him too much to battle heart, mind and body. Stepping under the soothing hot water, she smiled to herself. Joe would laugh at her "unresponsibleness".

He didn't laugh, but he smiled when he looked up from his paperwork that night after dinner when she walked into his office, with Teal at her heels. She had gotten high fives or fist bumps from all three of the boys as they sat at the kitchen table doing homework when she went through. As she passed them, they all started loudly humming Here Comes the Bride. Seeing Joe bent over his work with the same dark hair of the other three made him all the more attractive. He had done a good job of passing on his good habits.

He stood up and came around the desk to her. Before he touched her or even said anything, he looked at her for a minute. She wondered if he could read her mind, because that's what it seemed like he was trying to do. Finally, he wrapped her in a close hug and she let out a long sigh as she returned it. Oh, but this felt like coming home.

She didn't know what to say. He apparently didn't either, but the intimate silence was perfect, and when he pulled back far enough to look at her again, the kiss they shared was as natural as breathing. In the back of her mind, she'd thought maybe the inspiration would come through when she saw him, but all she felt was warm and happy and loved inside. It was going to take a lot more praying to get past the fact that he had that effect on her. He took her hand and led her into the TV room where they wouldn't bother the boys' studies.

Once there he turned and hugged her again. He didn't act like he wanted to let go anytime soon and she was good with that. He finally sat down on the sofa and she sat next to him. He put an arm around her and she automatically turned and leaned against him. She wasn't planning to act this friendly to him, but their friendship had always come easy and the trust she had for him was automatic. He pulled her against him and she literally heard him sigh as he leaned his head against her hair.

"How are you?" It wasn't a rhetorical question, and she knew it.

"I don't know. Just now, I'm perfect. In an hour I'll feel guilty about being here. I'm still as mixed up as I was the other night." She looked up at him and knew that wasn't what he'd been hoping to hear. "Sorry. You asked."

He shook his head. "Don't be sorry for being honest with me. I did ask. How have you been sleeping?"

"Two nights, all the way through. Thanks, and thanks for asking. Have you been able to sleep or do you wake up and worry about me?"

He eyed her and then looked away. "I'm going to plead the fifth on that one. I saw you limping. Were you hurt or just sore from riding?"

"Just ridiculously sore from riding. I took it a little too hard, too soon. Some ibuprofen and a swim will help."

He hesitated and then said, "I'm assuming the scar is from the blast. Does it ever bother you when you overdo?"

She wondered again if he could read her mind. "Days like today it does. In a week or two, I'll be back in riding shape and it'll be fine."

"Do you know that when we're resurrected all the things like that will be made whole? Just like your daughters' bodies will be back to perfection."

She looked up at him sharply. "What?"

He gently touched her thigh. "The scar. In the hereafter, it will be gone and that leg will be as strong and healthy as the rest of you."

Her face clouded. "No. What did you say about the girls?"

Meeting her look, he said, "That their bodies will be perfect. They'll be whole and beautiful just like they used to be. Actually, even better because they will have been resurrected and will no longer feel pain or hunger or any of those mortal things. In a way, you should actually be comforted by knowing they were such perfect spirits that they only needed to come to earth to gain a body and didn't have to pass the test here."

Her eyes narrowed questioning. "What do you mean, they didn't have to pass the test? How can they be back to perfection after being hurt so badly?"

Joe looked at her and his face fell. "Kristin, are you telling me that in all this time, none of us have helped you understand that when little children die before they're eight years old it's because they were such strong and obedient spirits in the pre-existence that they didn't need to be tested?

That Heavenly Father already knew how good they were and they only needed to come to gain their bodies? And that their bodies will be perfect just like before they were killed?"

She just looked at him, trying to understand what it was he was telling her. She could see the guilt wash over him. "Oh, Kristin. Please forgive me. I had no idea you didn't understand that. I thought both Gabriel and the missionaries had told you that. I'm so sorry."

He went to wrap her back in a hug, but she pushed him away. "Whoa. One more time. What are you saying?"

With a sigh, he gently pulled her back into his arms. "I'm saying the two things that we all should have made sure you understood almost before anything else. Your girls must have been the most superlative of spirits because they didn't need to be tested. The fact that they died before they were eight is proof of that. Their bodies will be perfected in the resurrection. The prophet Joseph revealed that not one hair will be lost. Oh, Kris, I'm so sorry I didn't help you understand that right off."

She just sat there in shock. Her girls' bodies would be healed. How had she missed that in all of her studies? She'd understood they would be resurrected, but had assumed that that just meant they would be alive again. She'd thought they would still have the grievous wounds and assumed it would work out because we would all be Christlike enough that ugly scars and wounds wouldn't matter. But the girls would be made whole again! It was hard to even comprehend.

The idea overwhelmed her as it took hold, and she found herself crying uncontrollably in his arms. Her beautiful little girls. The terrible, nightmare-spawning wounds would be gone. She cried for her daughters, but this time the tears were an overpowering emotion of hope and gratitude. The girls whole again was an image she'd had to force herself to deny for all these months and years because she hadn't ever known.

She'd wondered time and again why an all powerful and loving God would take that beauty and physical perfection from such innocence. Deep inside she must have known He wouldn't. Why else would she have had such a hard time trying to make herself give up the vision of them beautiful again? How many nights and days had she fought the images both good and bad? She cried against him until her tired body lay on his damp chest in exhaustion. How she wished she could have known this all along.

At length, he urged her to let him get up and take her home. "You need to rest, Kristin. Let me take you home so you can go to bed. I'd love to keep you, but we can't." He gently pulled her up off the couch and with an arm around her, escorted her safely home. At the door to her room he held her for the longest time and apologized again. After one gentle kiss, he turned and walked away, leaving her to lie down to rest with a concept so overwhelming that she could hardly wrap her tired head around it. Her girls would be made whole.

# Chapter 25

This time, he heard her scream inside his house with the windows all closed. It wasn't just a scream, but was drawn out and only let up long enough for her to catch her breath. He threw on his robe and went down the open stairway and out the back door at a run, the continuing sound making the hair on the back of his neck bristle. The Murdocks were just headed toward her wing and opened the door at his knock as they rushed past, pulling robes on as they went. She was still asleep, screaming in horror, the strain on her body intense. He had to literally shake her and shout to get through the images that gripped her mind and body.

The sound stopped so abruptly that the relative silence was strangely empty as she came awake. Her breath came in ragged gasps and he could feel her heart racing through both her pajamas and his—and his robe.

When she was awake enough to realize he was there with her, she looked up at him and then at the Murdocks and then turned away and wrapped her arms around herself protectively. She buried her head against her drawn up knees and shrugged off his attempt to rub her back. The Murdocks left the room and he instinctively pulled back to let her have the space that her actions demanded, shaken to the core at what he had just seen. Her demons were ghastly when witnessed in action. His heart went out to her more than ever over what she was still having to endure after that horrible, horrible disaster.

He sat on the edge of her bed, praying silently, and waited to see what she was going to do. For several minutes, all she did was breathe deeply without raising her head, and then abruptly she lifted her head and looked at him. The way she squared her shoulders and the deep sadness in her eyes made him dread what he knew she was going to say to him.

"Go home, Joe. Go home and stay home. I'll get this stalker thing taken care of and sell this house and move away so you won't have to hear me anymore. It's never going to work. Forgive me for leading you on."

He was appalled at her words, but knew this wasn't a good time to try to discuss anything. He got up and pulled her head against him for a second or two and went out, feeling like he'd left his heart behind on her bed. He loved her character strength, but for once he wished she wasn't so strong. She honestly thought this was for his good, and making her understand was going to be the hardest thing he'd ever done.

****

When she woke up with Joe and the Murdocks all three in her room, she knew it must have been bad. Joe wasn't dressed like he'd been in the hot tub. He must have heard her clear inside his house. It took her several minutes to calm herself enough to breathe evenly and get her thoughts even slightly under control, and in those several minutes she made her decision.

She knew what she had to do. She'd known it all along, but just hadn't wanted to do it because she liked him so much. The like had grown to love, which was good. She loved him enough to do what she needed to do for him and his family.

After he left, she went to the pool. Overcoming the nightmare seemed like nothing this morning compared to overcoming the heartache from knowing it was over. She should have walked away long ago before he ever had the chance to mean this much to her. Swimming for close to two hours still hadn't helped the ache in her heart and she gave up and went to the cabin to paint.

Maybe she'd been going about this all wrong from the start. Maybe instead of trying to control the images and what was in her head, she should have been trying to just become strong enough to handle the images and dreams without letting them get to her. She didn't know. All she knew was that the hopelessness she had felt before coming to know the Facianos was back and her black mood made the very air feel thick around her.

Pulling her easel around, she retrieved her pallet and began to paint, mindlessly, focused on the thoughts and feelings instead of what she was putting on the canvas. The brush strokes were simply her subconscious working while her conscious mind went around and around with her train of thought and her discouragement.

As the wee hours stretched out, she got to the bottom of a few things. She knew she had to sell the house. Even if she could have found a way to sound proof it enough to know that no matter how the nightmares went she wouldn't disturb the neighbors, she knew in her heart that she couldn't survive having to face the rest of however long, knowing Joe was just across the yard. Just trying to face today knowing he was there, was hard enough.

She knew she needed to own up to the truth that someday in the not too distant future, she needed to let the Murdocks move on with their lives, too. She loved them, and she knew they loved her, but she had to release them to have a life of their own that didn't include her specters at all hours of the night. They had retired once for a reason, and she was sure when they agreed to come work for her they had never dreamed it would be this bad, this long. She knew she hadn't.

She had to just face the fact that even though she might have better days off and on, it was always going to be like this and she needed to come to grips with that. This time she would buy acreage and build in the very center of it so she wouldn't ever bother anyone again. Then she'd put up a fence that was secure enough that she would feel safe behind it and she'd let the Murdocks go. That thought hurt almost as much as the thought of losing Joe and she had to wipe at her tears just so she could see what she was doing on the canvas.

When her attention came back to her painting, she realized she had painted a landscape of a stream bank with two little girls with long, dark hair wading with their jeans rolled up around their knees. The image was painterly, but felt familiar and she had to think about where she had ever seen them before. She didn't know them that she was aware of. She did recognize the stream as the one that wound at the bottom of the ridge in the woods behind her house. She continued to paint, trying to figure out who the little girls were and finally gave it up when the sun came up over the mountains in the east enough to brighten the blinds on the cabin.

She took a bagel and went out and loaded up her white horse Knight and left a note for Murdock and drove away. This time she didn't even have an inkling where she was headed and just drove west, hoping she'd find a likely place to ride where she'd be safe.

When she pulled back around her house that evening at dark, she had accomplished one thing. She was tired and hungry enough that the physical sphere had overcome the mental struggle and she'd finally gotten a handle on her sadness. She was half tempted to go to bed hungry in hopes the hunger pangs would take center stage and her mind would behave. She noticed the camp trailer in the pasture as she unloaded and cared for her horse and figured Murdock and Joe had succeeded in whatever it was they had planned to do for her security.

She decided she was simply going to check the stalker off of her mental list. At this point, what happened to her almost seemed a non-issue. Her emphasis had slowly migrated throughout the long day of trying to exercise the Facianos and Murdocks from her heart, from hopes and plans for the future to committing to just getting through the future with as little impact on others as possible.

In a way, life stretched out there like a long and dismal sentence. When she faced up to how negative her thoughts were, she did opt to forego dinner and simply showered and went to bed.

Whether it was skipping dinner or not, she didn't know, but she didn't dream that night. At least she didn't have nightmares. She woke up in the first light of day, remembering bits and pieces of a good dream. She had seen her daughters. She knew it was them even though they were much older than they had been when they had died. They must have been in their late teens or early twenties and Joe had been right. Physically, they were perfect and exquisitely beautiful. In the dream, their faces had fairly glowed with a happiness that felt like a literal light.

Jaclyn M. Hawkes

They hadn't said anything. At least not that she could remember and she couldn't remember what they had been doing in the dream either, but she knew she had seen them and spent time with them. It was the most incredible emotion she could remember feeling, and lightened her mood enough that she was much less negative about facing this day and all the ones ahead.

This morning, she was so hungry she felt shaky and took the time to make a real breakfast before heading out to load up Jet. On the table was another bouquet of flowers from Joe's sons. They made her smile and feel guilty at the same time.

On the way to the stable, she met one of the new security guys and stopped to talk to him for a minute, and then went to their trailer to meet the other two. Dressed in fatigues, they were all three in good enough shape that the brawn was obvious even fully clothed, and she wondered if they had hired a trio of Rambo wannabees. She decided it didn't matter either way as long as they helped catch whoever it was that was stifling her freedom.

She had absolute faith in Murdock and Joe's judgment and loaded the horse in the trailer feeling like it was only going to be a matter of time before she felt secure again. The thought lightened her mood even more until she reminded herself that as soon as the stalker issue was settled, she would be listing her house and moving. It was a sobering thought that stayed with her throughout the long day in the saddle.

She loved riding horses in the outdoors. She always had and hoped she always would, but this spring wasn't going as smoothly as planned. She knew she was over-doing, but kept telling herself that within a few days her body would get used to it. In the mean time, the aches and pains helped

284

keep her mind occupied. She just hoped the distress from her old injuries wasn't a hint of what old age was going to be like. Her left leg and hip were killing her, and she dragged in that afternoon feeling ancient.

Even though it was only six-thirty, she ate, swallowed some ibuprofen, showered and went to bed. If she had nightmares early, she would deal with them then.

She did have nightmares earlier than usual and was up and trying to deal with them when Murdock and the Rambos went into gear. She understood that whoever it was who was watching her must have been prowling, but she made a purposeful decision to let the guys handle the worry and she tried to occupy her mind with something else. She swam, jogged the treadmill, and worked out on the universal and then went up to the cabin. Physically, she was thoroughly exhausted to the point she wasn't even sure she could hold a paintbrush, so she sat down on the couch, and picked up her scriptures to try to read instead.

She had determined the other day, after talking to Joe about superlative spirits and perfected bodies, to study everything she could on the subjects, but so far she had spent more time trying to get her mind off of walking away from Joe than studying. She had no idea even where to start and just turned to the Index and Topical Guide and dug in. From the first few minutes, she began to yawn and for once she honestly thought she could go back to sleep. She sat on the couch where Gabriel had talked to her that first night in hopes she could get some of the peace from that night to come back and let her relax.

With her legs crossed Indian style, she read and cross referenced and studied and then leaned her head back against the couch and closed her eyes to ponder what she was reading. She thought back to her dreams of the night before and tried to call back the images of her grown daughters. She'd been taught that she would be able to finish raising them, but they had looked like they'd turned out such nice, happy, beautiful girls she was almost tempted to wish she could just get to know them as adults. It was going to be nice to enjoy them all grown up when she got to the other side.

She lay down on the couch and pulled the throw over her achy thigh and wondered about the life after this one. She wondered why in all these years of nightmares, she almost never had dreams about Ryan. She'd always assumed it was because she never saw him after the propane tank exploded. He'd been buried and gone before she was ever able to leave the hospital. She wondered how she would feel when she saw him again.

There was no deep, sweet emotion like she felt when she thought about seeing the girls again and that troubled her. She felt guilty for not having missed him more over the last years. She slipped her rings off and looked at them. It was long past time, but they had been convenient occasionally. There was no longer an emotion associated with them and she felt bad about that. There should have been. She set them on the table next to her tubes of paint with a sigh.

She wondered how the whole judgment day thing was going for him. He had been a good person, and had been good to her and the girls; she just worried about his apathy about God. She prayed as she lay there, that he would accept the gospel and that whatever was supposed to happen between them in the next estate, would. She wondered how her feelings for Joe would factor into that. She didn't feel guilty about being in love with Joe, as far as Ryan went, but she did feel guilty for not being more in love with Ryan.

Somewhere along there, she fell asleep again which would have been wonderful, except for the fact that it resulted in her having nightmares two times in one night. When she understood what was happening as she woke up in the clear light of morning in a full blown bad dream, she had never felt more discouraged. Discouraged and tired. She didn't want to face that pool house, but didn't know what else to do.

The appearance of Howard Cummings at her house made the morning almost more than she was up to. She spoke to him briefly and then very forthrightly told him she had plans for the morning and had to get ready to leave. As she dressed to go riding, she wished she had just told him right out that she didn't want to see him again, especially not at her own house.

****

Joe knew the prowler had been around in the night because he had been awake again, the same as he was every night, wondering if she was okay. He'd seen her come limping in earlier than she had for the last several days. She must have gone down earlier than usual, too, because he knew she'd been up long before Murdock and the men he had come to think of as her soldiers were up and investigating. He caught himself looking over there for what seemed like the thousandth time and tried to tell himself he was watching her far too closely and to go back to sleep.

He'd felt a little better when he'd seen the camp trailer pull in and set up, until he saw the three young men walking around over there. They didn't necessarily swagger, but their military bearing and confidence were obvious. He gave himself a stiff lecture about doing whatever it took to help Kristin, even if that meant paying for three dashing young men to hang out with her. If she decided to be with one of them instead of him, it would devastate him, but it would still be better for her than planning to basically go into exile again. As awful as it would be, if it came down to it, he loved her enough to even lose her if he had to for her safety and happiness.

It had been two days since she had sent him away this time. She hadn't said the boys had to stay away as well, but she had made herself conspicuously unavailable, and he had no more ideas now about how to get her to change her mind than he had that morning. He had thought about it almost continually and had finally come to the conclusion that he had to give this one over to God.

Even though he knew without a doubt that marrying her was the right thing to do, and what he was supposed to be doing, he had no clue how to help Kristin to decide to let him in on a permanent basis. He could keep working on her, but even when he'd made headway in the past, she always had second thoughts. He knew they needed more help than he and Kristin could come up with on their own. Moreover, though he'd prayed about it and felt good about it, he was still realistic enough to know that in the end it might not all work out. The thought was devastating, but he had to admit that right now that was the direction they were heading.

He went into his office and closed the door and knelt down. Pouring out his heart, he asked for some help to do what he felt he was unable to do alone. He told God that he truly wanted what was best for Kristin, and he would do whatever he needed to do to help her, and finally asked that God's will be done. When he finished, he stayed on his knees to listen for a few minutes, and then got to his feet and purposefully sat down at his desk and switched his computer on. He was determined to get something constructive done while he waited to find something he could do to help her.

****

Finally, on that morning's ride, she felt like her body was beginning to get used to the long hours in the saddle. She took Jet up into the hills behind her own house for the first time in weeks and even though she was a little nervous about it, it was great to be back out on her own turf. The security guys, Kurt, Brent, and Rodie, had felt like it was okay for her to ride nearby in the broad daylight as long as she kept in touch with her cell phone, so she hadn't hesitated to set out. She was able to stay out until dusk without her leg aching so badly, and she came home still tired enough that she was able to rest without thinking too much.

On waking refreshed and nightmareless in the morning, she wished she could find a rhyme or reason for why some nights were horrible and then some nights she was fine. At any rate, she was grateful and lay in her bed for a few minutes, enjoying waking up. She had dreamed of her daughters again. The good dreams were still harder to remember, but the good feelings weren't. She tried to recall what the dream was about, but it was vague and intermittent.

Somehow the three of them were watching and pointing, and she had the impression they were looking down on her from wherever they were. They had someone with them, and she did her best to remember, wondering if Ryan was there with them somehow. She didn't remember dreaming about Ryan, but there was someone, children maybe. She closed her eyes to concentrate, but couldn't tell who it was. Her dream had somehow gotten mixed up with her painting from the other night of the little girls she had thought were familiar.

Giving up on her disjointed impressions, she got out of bed, still trying to remember where she'd seen the little girls. They didn't belong anywhere in her memory that she could think of, but they were familiar. She walked out of her house at the same time the boys were pulling out for school and they all waved and smiled as Robby honked. She tried not to dwell on how much she missed them and their serenading and teasing, but waving to them broke her heart into pieces.

It took every bit of self-control she had not to look up at Joe's house. She knew without even having to look that he was watching for her and rubbed at what had suddenly gotten in her eyes as she walked to the stable.

She needed to move as soon as possible. As hard as all of this was on her, she knew it wasn't any easier for him. At least she was able to have a say in what happened. A heart-wrenching say, but a say nevertheless. She took Knight out of the yard at a trot, trying to ease the guilt she felt at knowing she was deserting Joe.

**** 

When he saw her leave for the day, he went across and asked Murdock for permission to go into her studio. He'd decided to frame the painting of her girls with the dolls. Maybe having it hanging where she could see it would help her nights. It wasn't much, but it was something.

He dug through the pile of canvases stacked against the wall, appreciating her talent as he did. She was good. It was a shame that she didn't ever sell anything she did. He pulled a painting free of the pile. It wasn't the one he was looking for, but there was something about it. He took it over to the light from the window to study it.

It was two little dark haired girls wading in a stream. He wasn't sure who they were but they were familiar and the painting was incredibly evocative. The expressions on the little faces were dreamy and peaceful. He almost pulled it out to frame it too, but decided that was too fanciful and continued to look for the one he had come for. He found it, but before leaving he turned back to the other painting. It was a fascinating work. Maybe Kristin would sell it to him.

On the way back out with the painting, Murdock stopped him to tell him the prowler had been around every night for four nights, sometimes two and three times. "He's apparently figured out how to avoid the wires and cameras so we still don't have good photos. And he gets in and out before we can get to where he is. It's a different place every time. But we're going to get him, which is a good thing, because he's certainly ratcheted up his visits."

"Does Kristin know all of this?"

"Some. Not all."

Joe trusted Murdock's judgment, but this was a little frustrating. "If he's cranking up his obsession, why is she out there riding horses practically in his lap?"

"She's about as tightly wound as she can get, Joe. She has to be able to live, and trailering her horse away presents two problems. First off, she's completely out of our reach to help her, and two, she's killing herself. She's been putting in fourteen hour rides, and then limps home and falls into bed half dead. She's lost probably fifteen pounds and she didn't have any to spare as it was.

"I'm hoping she'll just come on home when she needs to. The physical stuff helps her, but only to the point that it doesn't trash her in the process. And as far as riding here, two of the guys left ahead of her and are hidden up there on points with high powered binoculars, glassing for any sign of him. These rides may be a good thing. He might come right out into the open and let us take him easy."

"How are these guys? Are they as good as you hoped?"

Murdock nodded. "They're good. Very good. We're going to get him, and as much as he's begun sneaking around, it's going to be soon. We just need to keep her happy and here long enough to catch him."

"Why here? Wouldn't it be better if she was away when it happened?"

"No, Joe. I mean here in this house. I don't know if she's ever mentioned it to you, but I think she has every intention of selling this house and moving away from you and firing me. She has it in her head that she has to get away to protect everyone from her demons."

Joe sighed. "She has told me. That last night when she screamed. I know she plans to, but I don't know how to stop her, Murdock. She knows I want to marry her, and I think she'd like to take me up on it, but she still feels like she has to protect me."

Murdock shrugged. "Now she even thinks she has to protect me. She's never felt that way before. I don't know what to do either, except pray and get some of the other pressure off. Maybe when we get this guy, things will get better. I hope and pray they do."

"They will. They have to. Keep me in the loop." He turned and headed for home and repeated to himself. "They have to."

Joe took the painting in to be framed that very morning, pushed by a feeling of urgency. Something had to break loose fast. The thought of losing her to a self-imposed life of seclusion made him heartsick. He prayed again as he drove and then talked the guy in the frame shop into working on the painting while he waited. He put it in a frame that would match her bedroom hoping it would help keep the dragons at bay, took it home and hung it right across from her bed, praying again as he did so.

He flew out the next morning for a fast trip to Phoenix to tie up some loose ends he had to be there in person for. He was coming back in one day this time. It was going to end up a twenty hour day for him, but he felt like he had to. Even though she wasn't letting him anywhere near her, for some reason he felt like he needed to be there. As he boarded his plane, he wondered if she had liked the painting, and if it had helped her rest like he hoped.

It wasn't fifteen minutes after he walked into his office that Cindy Kunz walked in. Joe was so brusque with her that Max was flabbergasted after she left and it made him feel guilty when Max asked, "What's going on to make you this edgy? You almost took that poor woman's head off."

"Oh, Max. Women's heads are more firmly attached than you think. I just want to be done with her once and for all. It's kinder that way. It's like having to amputate something, but just doing it in one clean, fast slice."

"If you call that kinder, I'd hate to see you on a mean day! Whew! Talk about your clean, fast slice using a machete."

"Was I really that bad?"

"Yes."

"Bad enough that I have to invite her back in here to apologize?"

Rolling her eyes, she said, "No. That would be two clean, fast slices with a machete."

"Oh good. Now, can we please get back to business? I really need to catch a plane this evening."

Paul showed up mid-morning and poked his head in. "I need to come in here and give my boss a whole hearted apology for hitting on his woman, but rumor has it that it's not even safe to step onto this floor. As my friend and confidant, Joe, what do you think would be the wisest course of action?"

Joe finally laughed and it felt good. "Get in here! Did she really come down there and tell someone that I'm on the warpath up here?"

Paul came in smiling. "Cindy didn't, but a couple of the others who heard you did. Did you really smash a woman's heart to pieces in front of spectators?"

Joe sighed. "Max, I thought you said I didn't need to apologize. Now it sounds like I need to make a public apology."

Max raised a hand at him. "Don't blame this on me. I'm the innocent bystander here. Did he just say he needs to apologize for hitting on your woman?"

This time, Paul sighed. Joe laughed and Paul said, "At least you're laughing now. I thought you were going to hit me at your house. So, are you engaged? How is that going?"

Joe laughed again. "Why do you want to know? You're not going to ask her out again if I say we're not engaged yet, are you?" Max was looking from one to the other of them in interest.

Grinning, Paul assured him, "Considering the reality that you sign my paychecks, absolutely not! But does she have anything to do with the fact that you're miserably irritable?"

"Probably. And no, we're not engaged. Yet. But don't you dare tell anyone else in this entire metro area I said that or I'll quit signing your paycheck."

Paul chuckled. "That bad, huh? Why do we do this, Max? Why do perfectly intelligent men let women give us heartburn?"

Max was still looking at the two of them, obviously wondering whether to worry or laugh, and said, "It's just their way of getting back at you for making them go through labor occasionally. You haven't given him a whole hearted apology. I'd really like to see that."

Paul laughed as he extended his hand to Joe. "I'm sure you would. You've always enjoyed watching me stumble on my way to the top." To Joe, he said, "Sorry, man. I had no idea you were together. It will never happen again."

Joe shook his hand, wondering what was happening at home. Right now, Paul had about as much chance of marrying her as he did. Not much.

He was still wondering what was going on at home that night when he pulled in at a few minutes after one a.m. Her house should have been dark and quiet, because even on a bad night, she usually slept until at least two, but there were several lights on. None of them were Kristin's or the pool or cabin.

Joe hesitated for several minutes and then went next door, hoping that whatever was up, she'd been able to sleep through it. Murdock and a man he introduced to Joe as Kurt met him at the door and took him straight back through to the computer terminal that ran the security system. The stalker had been back tonight and although he had come in and realized he set off the alarm and gone straight back out, they finally had decent film of him.

Murdock showed Joe the footage hoping he could identify who it was. The man was remotely familiar, but try as he might, Joe couldn't place him. At least it wasn't Howard Cummings. At the back of his mind, Joe had wondered if it was him for now. This was a younger, scruffier slender man with medium brown hair pulled back into a pony tail. They all three looked at each other with the unspoken question of whether to wake her up or not. Joe turned to Kurt. "Will knowing who it is before morning help us catch him?"

"Probably not. I doubt he'll go straight back home. We may have him caught before morning if he tries to come back. Brent and Rodie are out there now hoping he does."

"Then let her sleep when she can. Heaven knows it's hard enough for her. Are the two of you staying here with her in case he would somehow get inside?"

Murdock said, "I'm going to go back to bed so I can watch over her tomorrow when these guys sleep. But, we're all within shouting distance. Can you help us tomorrow if we need you?"

"Tomorrow or tonight. Just call my cell. I can do whatever you need. Do you think she'll talk to me yet?"

Kurt looked from one to the other of them as Murdock said, "Probably not, but who knows. She won't order you out at any rate when you're here to protect her. Maybe that would be the key. Come over when the boys leave and take a turn watching. Maybe you can catch her before she leaves to ride."

Joe gave a concerned look. "Is it wise to let her ride when he's this persistent?"

"So far, he's never been here in the day that we know of."

Joe's brow furrowed. "So far. Has she been taking Teal with her when she rides up here?"

"She's been leaving Teal the last few days because she's getting so big with her puppies that the long rides are too much for her."

"See if she'll take Teal with her. Or Hershey. Or both. Maybe having Teal will serve two purposes. Another set of eyes and ears, but also maybe she won't overdo so much if she has to think about the dog. I'm going to head home, but the insomnia is worse than ever, so I'll be up. Call me if you need me."

Jaclyn M. Hawkes

# Chapter 26

Kristin woke up at a little before two, but she hadn't been screaming. She wasn't even having a bad dream; in fact, the dream had been wonderful. She hated to even wake up because she wished she could go on sleeping and not lose that feeling. She'd been dreaming she had a new baby and it brought back that little bit of heaven she had felt on the days her daughters were born. As hard as the c-sections had been on her, those first days with a new baby were the sweetest times she had ever known.

Then she realized that it wasn't that she was reliving those days. It had been different. Joe had been with her instead of Ryan and this baby had dark, almost black hair. She sat straight up in bed and put her hand to her heart. She thought about the face of the baby in her dream and her breath caught in her throat. She knew this child. She had painted this face before, only a little older. This was one of the little girls with the long dark hair, wading in the stream.

In that instant she understood that the other children who had been with her grown daughters in her last dream were the same little girls, and the dream came back to her. Her daughters had been pointing. Guiding the way for the younger girls to go. The images in her head were fleeting and elusive, but she wondered if they were her older daughters showing her younger daughters the way to go to reach her. It was the most enlightening, and yet intimidating thing she had ever felt. She got up and quickly dressed and hurried out to her studio being careful not to wake the Murdocks.

Digging through the canvases, she pulled out the one with the little wading girls, and studied it at length, realizing now why they had seemed so familiar. The faces were very much like that of Gabriel. She covered the long hair with her hands and marveled at the likenesses. She backed up and sat down at her easel and looked at the painting from a distance. They looked like Gabriel, but there was something else that so reminded her of her own girls.

She put both hands to her cheeks. What was going on here? Was this all really just her dreams? She shut off the lights and walked to the window to pull up the blinds. Joe's house sat across the way there, dark and silent. She didn't understand. She had been sure she should get away from Joe and protect him from her demons, but if that was so, then what was going on? She pulled the blind again and turned back on the lights and sat at her easel to paint.

The image of the new baby came easily from her head to the canvas, and there was no doubt it was the same child that waded in the stream when it was a couple of years older. She stopped painting with her brush poised, and prayed for inspiration, "Father, what is it I'm supposed to be doing here? Please help me to understand." She thought back on these last days of riding until her body ached, all the while praying and searching her soul to know what to do about Joe. Then it came to her. Those four simple words he had asked her from the first. "How did you feel?"

She'd been listening for God in the wind, not seeking the still small voice that came after the wind.

She had been so sure she was supposed to be hearing a loud no, that she hadn't even listened for a quiet yes. She knew how she felt. She felt warm and peaceful. She'd thought it was just that she was in love with Joe and thinking about him made her feel like that, but now she wasn't so sure. She wished she'd known God longer. She was terrible at this personal inspiration thing. She continued to paint, trying to ponder and listen, and then she had a sobering thought. Was the baby in the dreams a new baby? Or had Joe and Nicole lost a baby, too, and it was past this earth life and with her daughters in the next estate? Maybe that was what was going on.

As the oils on the canvas continued to become the image of her dream, she tried to figure out if all of this was just a simple dream. A figment of the mixed up impressions from her mind, or was there something to all of this. She hadn't had any dreams like this until she had understood her daughters' bodies would be made whole again.

She had suffered from nightmares since coming to that understanding, but somehow that knowledge had healed something in her soul that had been so scarred by her daughters' wounds. The last few days had made her see that. She was afraid of this stalker, and she missed Joe beyond belief, but she had to wonder if those things hadn't been more troubling to her than the nightmares just now. Or at least had made them so much more frightening.

She had decided after that last worst nightmare that she needed to sell the house and get away from everyone, but she had been uncomfortable with that decision ever since. Was that the still small voice telling her it was the wrong one? Her head was so at odds with her heart over all of these things and she struggled between logic and feeling to know what to do.

Last night's dream had made a huge difference in that aspect. The peace she had woken up to had come with no confusing addendums. This was God's peace. That one fact she knew without question and she clung to it with a surety. Now, she just had to figure out the rest of her feelings.

As she painted, she wished she could have asked Joe to come visit her tonight. She was beginning to think that getting away from him wasn't what her Father in Heaven had in mind for her at all. If not, how was she ever going to ask his forgiveness for jerking him around emotionally the way she had? Had she ruined the best thing that had ever happened to her?

****

Joe went home after checking with Murdock and Kurt and surprisingly was able to go right to sleep, but he was up again, wide awake at two-thirty. He laid there for a minute before he got up, trying to figure out what he'd been dreaming about that made him wake up in such a mellow, happy mood. The anxiety of last night had completely disappeared in less than two hours.

The dream was elusive and it took him a minute to figure out that he had dreamed about having more children. This time, two little girls and they looked just like the two little dark haired girls in Kristin's painting. He'd known the painting was evocative, but it must have affected him even more than he realized. The dream had left him with a serene sense of sweet peace.

Thinking of Kristin, he got up to look out and check on her. There were lights on in her studio. He wished he could go to her, but he couldn't. He knew he wasn't welcome.

Actually, he knew she loved him, but just wanted to protect him from the dragons. After thinking about that for awhile, he followed a prompting to get up and go to her, hoping as he dressed that he truly was feeling like he should go over there and that this feeling wasn't just his wishes speaking.

He called her cell phone from the porch of the little cabin so she wouldn't be afraid when he knocked. She answered with a tentative, "Hello."

Just hearing that one word from her made him realize again what she meant to him and he said, "Kristin, it's Joe. I'm at your door. Is there any way I could talk to you for a little while tonight?"

Instead of answering him on the phone, she walked over and unlocked the door and pulled it open for him. "Hi, Joe. Come on in. How did you know I was thinking about you?" She pulled him inside and shut the door.

He looked at her, trying to figure out how she was feeling about him and wondering if Murdock had had a chance to show her the photographs they'd gotten. She didn't look like she usually did after a bad dream and he didn't ask as he said, "I didn't know. I just knew I wanted to see you and know for myself that you're okay." He hesitated and then added, "You look happier than you usually do at this time of night. How have you been doing?"

She gave him a mellow smile. "That's a good question."

When she didn't go on, he said, "It is a good question. Are you going to answer it, or are you dodging it?"

She let out a long breath. "Come in and sit down, Joe. Yes, I'm dodging your question, but it's okay. Somehow, this is all going to be okay."

He followed her in and sat down on the couch beside her easel. It was turned around and he couldn't see what she was painting. Hesitantly, he asked, "What is the 'this all' that's going to be okay?"

Looking up at him, she said, "That's another good question. One I truly don't have an answer to. How have *you* been doing?"

He didn't smile as he asked, "Should I be honest or polite?"

After a tentative second she said, "My, but you are full of good questions tonight. You and I have been through enough together, Joe, that you can always be honest with me, no matter how impolite it is."

"Okay, then I've been miserably lonely without you."

"That's pretty honest. Why?"

"Why what?"

"Why have you been miserable?"

Still not smiling, he said, "That's another good question, Kristin. Now it's your turn. You tell me."

She met his eyes. "I deserved that. Does it help at all to know that I'm miserable, too?"

He changed the subject. "Let's don't talk about this, Kris. It can't do any good, and I want to enjoy you for a little while before you tell me to go away. Not that it's going to work all that well for until we catch this guy. I've already arranged to help Murdock keep an eye on things when the others are sleeping."

She continued to paint without looking up at him as she said, "All right. Then what would you like to talk about?"

More gently, he asked, "Did you like the painting I hung?"

She nodded. "Yes. I loved it. Thank you. I think it has helped me."

"Did you mind that I did it without asking?"

"No. It made me feel loved."

There was a long silence and then he quietly said, "You are loved."

This time she raised her head. After a long look, she said, "I know, and it's incredibly nice. You are, too." She held his eyes and he began to wonder what was up.

He asked her almost warily, "What's going on, Kristin? Why can you tell me that now?"

She tipped her head. "Another good question. Do I have to answer that one right now? Or can I think about things for and then answer?"

"Is this one of those I'm mixed up things? Or are you going to change your mind again about letting me be your friend?"

"I deserved that, too. I'm mixed up, but what else is new? No, I'm not going to change my mind about letting you be my friend."

He continued to hold her gaze. "You sound pretty sure of that."

"I am." This time she changed the subject. "How was your trip?"

"Fast. I wanted to get back home. How did you know I went on a trip?"

With the hint of a smile, she said, "Murdock told me. He's definitely on your side. He tells me everyday how wonderful you are."

"Really?" She nodded, and he grinned and said, "I hope you believe him. He's a very reliable source."

Returning the smile, she said, "I know. I trust him implicitly. But I already knew you were wonderful before he started reminding me."

He got up and came to stand next to her. "Why are you saying these things to me tonight, Kristin? What's going on?"

She glanced up. "I'm honestly not sure, Joe. I don't understand either. That's why I asked if I could think about things and answer you later."

He thought to himself, *And she thinks she's mixed up.* To her, he said, "Can I ask you a personal question? And then I'll go home and let you paint."

"That depends on how personal, I guess."

He put a hand on her shoulder. "Have you prayed about whether you should marry me?"

"Yes."

"Can I ask you another personal question?" She nodded. "How did you feel?"

"Now you're getting too personal."

Dropping his hand, he let out a tired breath. "I'm sorry. I'll go. I just wanted to know you were okay." He started toward the door.

"Joe, wait." He stopped and looked back at her as she asked, "Can I ask you a personal question?"

Hoping not to sound bitter, he said, "That depends on how personal? What do you want to know?"

"Did you and Nicole ever lose a baby? A little girl?"

He looked at her, trying to figure out what she was asking him. He had no idea what was going on. He shook his head. "No."

She swallowed hard. "Oh."

Questioning, he studied her. "Why?"

Setting her brush down, she shook her head. "I just wondered." She got up and walked to him at the door. "Thank you for coming tonight, Joe. I appreciate it. I'd just

306

been wishing I had the right to call and ask you to come." His eyes narrowed as he tried to figure her out. She reached a bare left hand up to cup his cheek. "Go back home and get some sleep and don't worry about me. I'm going to be fine."

He shook his head and left, locking the door behind him. What in the world had gotten into her tonight? She'd been so mellow and peaceful that she almost scared him. And why had she finally taken her rings off? At this point, he was afraid to even let his thoughts go there.

He went home and went back to bed, but just laid there wondering what was up with her. She'd been so comfortable with him that he almost dared to think everything was going to work out. Almost. Then he remembered how she had been after that last nightmare when he had rushed into her bedroom while she was still screaming, and his hope crumbled.

No, God was still the only one who could get her to believe she could lean on him without having doubts again and again. He got back up and knelt beside his bed to ask for divine intervention one more time. He still knew he had to turn this one over to his Father in Heaven. Back in bed again, he willed himself to have faith and be patient, but sleep was a long time coming.

****

The next morning, Joe was dragging as he got up and got the boys' breakfast and sent them off to school. His long day and short night were coming back to haunt him. He had lain awake trying to know what to do with Kristin and still wasn't sure, but decided he had to go with his gut on this one and headed back over to see her before she left with her horse this morning. He took Hershey with him, hoping to talk her into taking him with her on her sojourn into the hills.

He stopped to ask Murdock if she had known who the stalker on the film was and he nodded. "She did. It's a guy who ran one of the snow cats up at the resort last winter. She was surprised. She said he had only spoken to her a handful of times all year. He's ex-military. That's why he could slip through so easily. He's also a convicted sex offender and a possible suspect in the murder of a young woman but they never got enough evidence to take the murder to trial." That news made all the blood rush to Joe's heart and Murdock added, "I'm leaving in just a minute to meet with the sheriff to go pick him up."

Joe shook his head and breathed a sigh of relief. "Maybe this will all be over then. I'll be here waiting to hear back from you. How is she this morning?"

Murdock shrugged, but he grinned. "I don't know what has happened. Maybe it was finally finding out who this guy is, although she was different before we even showed her the pictures. At any rate, something is different this morning. The weight of the world is off her shoulders. She looks and acts better than she has in—actually, she's different than I've ever seen her since I've known her. I don't know what's going on with her, but it's the answer to our prayers. I'd almost venture to say she's going to be okay. Go talk to her yourself and see what you think."

Joe caught up with her as she was headed outside, and Murdock was right. Something was definitely different. She still had that sense of serenity, almost wonder, he had noticed last night, and she still wasn't wearing her rings. He didn't understand it, but he wasn't going to question it either. He was just unbelievably grateful for whatever had happened to help her.

She wouldn't agree to take his dog, but she was taking hers. Coming up to him, she laid a gentle hand on his arm, thanked him for his offer and looked at him with a concern in her eyes that reached all the way to his heart, as she asked, "Short night?"

He nodded, wishing he could voice his concerns and talk her out of leaving the safety of her house today. She reached up to softly touch his forehead where his brow was creased. "It's all going to be okay, Joe. I know that now. You need to quit worrying and trust more. We're going to be all right."

She turned and walked into the stable and came out leading her white horse, and Joe went into the tack room, brought her saddle and blankets out for her and followed her to the hitch rack. He set the saddle over it and when she had finished tying her horse, he took her hand and pulled her away toward him. For a minute, he studied her, trying to figure her out, but finally gave that up. He had no clue what was up with her. This soul-deep serenity he was seeing baffled him.

Finally, he simply said, "Kristin, I don't understand what's going on with you, but whatever it is, I'm glad for you. Have a good day out there, and please be careful. Don't take any chances, okay?"

"I'll be careful. You need to be more careful than I do. If there's trouble, I think it will be down here, not up there." She inclined her head toward the hills that were just beginning to show the first greens of spring as the trees began to leaf out.

Still concerned, Joe asked, "Have you got your gun?"

She patted her side. "Right here. Just under my jacket, but I don't think I could shoot a person, Joe."

"Do you have your phone?"

"I have my phone. Will you stop worrying? I'm going to be fine."

"Do you have plenty of battery?"

She laughed and the sound of it was like music. It was the laugh he had first been fascinated by almost two years ago when they rode horses together. She said, "Joe, enough already. Go home and get some more sleep. I'll come and check on *you* this time when I get back."

He must have looked at her strangely because she laughed again and hugged him before stepping onto her horse. "Good bye, Joe. Have a good day." She left the yard at a lope with Teal struggling to keep up with her and he turned and headed back to his house for breakfast, noticing Kurt watching him from the step of his trailer.

Joe had noticed him last night, too, as he had returned from visiting her at her studio. Kurt's presence was reassuring. Joe didn't feel like they missed much. Maybe he should keep these guys around even after they caught this creep. A full time security team might not be a bad thing.

After watching Murdock pull out to go meet the sheriff, Joe puttered, checking out the windows every few minutes, while Gram did stuff around the house. She didn't say anything about his nerves, although he knew she had noticed he was uptight. He didn't know why he was so keyed up this morning, but he was ridiculously anxious about Kristin's safety.

He tried to go into the office to see to some paperwork, but gave that up as hopeless and went outside to walk around and take stock of what needed to be done to overcome the ravages of winter on his relatively new yard. Lunch time rolled around, but the thought of food was impossible. He went over and walked around Kristin's yard as well, wondering where Kurt and the others were. There was no sign of them anywhere. Even Elena had gone shopping earlier. He hoped they were somewhere that they could help Kristin in time if she needed it.

He scanned the hills above them time after time, almost wishing spring hadn't come because the visibility had been so much better with the trees bare. He went back into his house and pulled the spotting scope closer to the window and spent a long half hour studying the entire range of hills, focusing on each gully and ravine. He didn't see so much as a glimpse of anything living. The sense of urgency continued to grip him and he tried to reason with himself that his worry was over the top.

Then, he saw her horse.

At first he was relieved that she was coming home so soon, but where the trail opened up wider he realized the horse was riderless, the stirrups flopping as it jogged toward home. His gut wrenched in fear and he left his house on the run, praying and punching her number on his cell phone as he crossed into her yard. Kurt was outside, heading across to the trail with a backpack as Joe rounded the back of the house. He saw Kurt shut his phone in disgust at the same time he did after realizing that hers went straight to voicemail. Kurt turned back to talk to him as Joe caught up the horse and began to adjust the stirrups to fit his longer legs. Joe asked him, "Where are your guys?"

"They're up there. They've been keeping her in sight all morning, but they lost her about ten minutes ago in some trees. The horse came out of the other end of the trees riderless about two minutes later. They're headed that way right now."

"Have they seen anyone else up there?"

"First thing after lunch, they spotted another hiker across the valley from where she was."

"Was it him?"

Kurt met his gaze fully. "We believe it was. Brent and Rodie had gone after him, but now Brent pulled off of him to go and see about Kristin."

"Have you called Murdock? Where are he and the sheriff?"

"Supposedly they're on their way here. They're out of cell service. I'm heading up there."

Joe had finished with the stirrups and turned to head back to his house when Kurt asked him. "Where are you going to be?"

Joe answered him with conviction, "I'm going back home to get my gun, and then I'm going up there, too."

Kurt shook his head vehemently. "No! You'll only be in the way and then we'll have to watch out for you, too. You need to stay here. We need someone to be here in case she comes back. She shouldn't be alone."

Toning down his intensity, he went on, "We're gonna need someone to handle things between us and law enforcement. And we certainly don't need someone else out there with a gun that we'd just have to worry about. Inside the trailer on the table there's a radio to touch base with the three of us. Keep trying to get Kristin on her phone, and radio me as soon as you hear from her. She's afoot now so watch for her coming straight down instead of on the trails."

He must have seen Joe's distaste at sitting and wondering if she was okay or not, because he said, "Look, man. She's gonna be okay. They've probably already found her and are on the way back. We're good at what we do.

Trust us. Just stay here and hold down the fort. We need someone here to handle things and you're it." He gave Joe a grin. "Don't mess up."

He turned and jogged up the trail toward the gate and Joe did indeed go back to his house and get his gun, and brought the spotting scope and Hershey back with him while he was at it. He got the radio as instructed and took everything into the house to where the security terminal was. Stringing the cords out long enough that he could put the terminal in front of the glass wall near the pool house, he set up the scope to scan the hills above. Next, he opened the door so he could hear anything that was going on anywhere near outside.

He had the radio on and knew that Kurt and his guys hadn't located her yet. Kristin still wasn't answering and when he couldn't even reach Murdock on his phone, his frustration level was through the roof. When he finally got hold of her, he was going to give her a talking to that she'd never forget! They weren't going to live like this anymore! Life and time were too precious.

Unable to reach Murdock, he called the county dispatch and explained what was going on and they promised to reach the sheriff for him.

The longer he went without word, the more he thought about how foolish they had been to let things go for so long. The thought of something happening to her turned his stomach, but his mind wouldn't stop running through every possible scenario from a simple fall from her horse to being at the mercy of a crazed stalker gone over the edge. He paced the pool deck as he watched, and listened, and tried to reach her and Murdock from time to time.

At length, he heard a truck coming, but it was just the boys returning from school. He called home and told Robby a bare bones version of what was going on and told them all to stay inside and even keep the doors locked. Hanging up, he went back to his pacing. He was still tempted to go up there, but Kurt had been right. The last thing they needed was an over zealous business man up there with a gun. He needed to trust them and willed himself to stay calm and continue to pray and wait.

Finally, after what felt like an eternity, his phone toned and he looked down to realize she had sent him a text message. He pushed okay to view it and had never felt such relief at her first two words. *"Im okay hes here coming down hes not far behind me be ready I love you"*

He breathed a prayer of relief as he keyed the radio to contact her soldiers. He told them exactly what she'd texted and they assured him they were right behind them and would be back down within half an hour. He texted her back to relay information, hoping her phone didn't make enough sound to give her location away.

He tried to reach Murdock again but it was twenty more minutes before he called Joe back telling him he'd been out of cell service. He started to tell Joe that they had been unsuccessful in picking the guy up when Joe broke in to tell him what was going on. Joe could hear the engine of Murdock's truck begin to race even over the phone, and he prayed once again—this time that Murdock would reach home safely.

After doing all he could do to facilitate getting her home safely and her stalker finally apprehended, he let his mind acknowledge the fact that she had said she loved him as he paced the pool deck. He wasn't sure if this was the worst time to tell him something like that or the perfect time to say it. Either way, it was a good sign that she could finally come right out and admit it to him. Now he just hoped and prayed that when all of this was over she didn't regret it.

Even if she did, he was going to do better at talking some sense into her. This was past the point of nuts! He was sick and tired of this roller coaster! He had to make her see that they needed to get married, for both of their sakes. For everyone involved.

It wasn't just him and her who needed this. The boys and Gram and the Murdocks. All of them needed them to be married at this stage. Even their future children needed it, or there wouldn't be any future children. After his dreams of last night, he knew he wanted that with her. He knew it. Now he just had to figure out a way to get her to agree to it.

His thoughts were interrupted by the sound of a gun shot. It was one single shot and it made his heart shudder as the echoes of it died away into silence. He went out onto the deck and looked up into the hills, not even able to face the thought of what had just happened. The sound of his phone telling him he'd received a message made him jump and he clawed it out to view it.

*"Im okay"* Those two simple words helped him to breathe again. What in the world was going on up there? Who had shot? Where was she? Where were any of them?

He relayed her message to her soldiers and then turned at the sound of a truck to see Murdock come flying in, spraying gravel, followed closely by two county sheriff trucks. He told them all he knew and then watched the three of them head up into the woods behind the houses. Again, he relayed messages to the security guys and then texted Kristin, hoping she would be able to retrieve it to know they were trying to help her.

The wait was interminable and he began to feel like the strain was overwhelming. He heard something behind him and looked up at his house to realize that all three of his sons and Gram were glued to the windows watching him and the mountain beyond. He'd been right. He wasn't the only one who desperately needed her to come home safely. He called Robby and encouraged them to stay back from the windows, at least a little bit, and went back to his pacing and praying.

Even though the radios remained silent most of the time, he knew the guys were closing in on the stalker and Kristin. The closer they got, the less came across on the radio, and finally it remained completely silent. Several minutes of absolutely no communication from the hills above him had his nerves stretched to the breaking point.

It was actually Hershey who alerted him to the fact that they were getting closer. The dog that had been lying near the security computer suddenly sat up and cocked his head to the side listening. After several seconds of this he got up and went out to stand at attention on the deck, and then went down onto the grass and began to walk slowly toward the gate, sniffing and turning his head this way and that.

Joe picked up the radio, his phone and his gun and followed the dog through the yard and out the gate and pulled up next to the trunk of one of the first trees in the direction Hershey was focusing. He made Hershey stop and stay with him, a fact the dog wasn't very happy about, but Joe needed his senses and didn't want him in the middle of whatever was going on up on that slope.

It was still several minutes before he heard or saw anything, and when he finally did he was shocked. There was the smallest hint of sound and Joe turned toward it to realize that Kurt was standing within just a few feet of him. In his camo and now face paint, the only thing that even gave him away was the whites of his eyes.

Kurt gave Joe the slightest flicker of his head to indicate he wanted him to go back to the house. Joe only hesitated for a second, and then silently took the dog and did as he was asked. Hershey whined quietly when Joe insisted he come with, but even he seemed to know they needed to get out of the way. Just inside the gate, Hershey hesitated momentarily and looked back up the hill. Joe followed the dog's gaze and far up the hillside he could see a spot of black moving soundlessly through the thick trees.

He knew Kristin had to be with Teal, but it was minutes before he finally caught a glimpse of her sneaking through the undergrowth with the dog at her side. Joe glanced at Kurt and knew Kurt wanted him to go further, but he couldn't make himself. He went a few steps and ducked down behind the water trough against the big corner post with the dog at his feet.

Kristin continued to sneak down the hillside and then suddenly looked up and turned to run down the hill at reckless full speed. Teal was beside her in the thick undergrowth and when they were about sixty yards up the hill from where Joe was, they both tripped and fell headlong at almost the same second. Behind her a man emerged from the trees and before she could regain her feet he was at her side, jerking her upright. Time slowed down to a pace that made every detail stand out sickeningly clear to Joe as he watched the man drag her brutally down the hill beside him at a run.

Joe looked around frantically for Kurt and the others. There was no sign of anyone else but Kurt, although Joe could hear movement somewhere nearby. Kurt had his gun drawn and was ready to shoot, motionless and all but invisible. Joe's fear factor ratcheted up with the new worry that Kristin would be accidentally shot in the fray.

Her captor continued their careening flight down the steep hillside and then brought up short when he almost ran into one of the other guys just up from where Kurt was concealed. Realizing he was about to be apprehended, before the soldiers could take him down, he instantly jerked Kristin in front of him and put his right hand to her head.

Up to then, Joe hadn't even realized the guy was carrying a gun. In an instant that almost stood still, her soldier dropped his gun and put his hands into the air, while at the same moment Teal tore into the stalker's leg with a vengeance that startled him into letting go of Kristin to flinch away from the dog's snarling fangs. Hershey hit the guy from the other side a split second later and Kristin literally dove down the hill to get out of the way. Her captor looked up from the dogs and jerked his gun up toward the surrendering guard. In that second there were the sounds of three gunshots one on top of the other, the reports almost sounding as one.

At that point, the whole hill erupted into movement and sound but Joe was only conscious of the fact that Kristin had landed from her headlong dive, regained her feet and plunged into the bushes in front of her to run frantically down the hill toward him. She ducked in the gate with both dogs flying at her heels and turned to hide behind the same thick post he was crouched beside.

She obviously didn't know he was there and for a split second her eyes widened in fear as he stood up, and then in grateful comprehension, she buried her head against his chest and held onto him. Wrapping both arms around her to protect her, he spun back to see what was happening up the hill, preparing to take her and run again. In those couple of seconds, the chaos on the hill had subsided into absolute silent stillness. The stalker was down and Murdock, both deputy sheriffs and all three of the security team had drawn weapons trained on him.

For a full thirty seconds, all seven of them were motionless. Six of them waiting to see if the seventh would turn on them again. He didn't. He would never turn on anyone again.

Kristin began to stir in his arms and he looked down at her and put himself directly between her line of sight and the scene behind him up the hill. When she went to glance over his shoulder he pulled her back in close. "Don't, Kristin. There's nothing back there you want to see."

They heard whining at their feet and looked down to find Teal and Hershey both crouched almost on top of their shoes. Kristin bent to see to them and for the second time in less than a minute Joe was incredibly grateful for those two dogs. He was even grateful they were both injured because he could notice their bleeding and insist they take them back to the house to see to their wounds. Teal had two pretty good gashes across the point of one hip, and Hershey was bleeding from the gums on the side of his mouth.

With one arm firmly around Kristin, Joe led her across the pasture and into the side door of her house, taking both dogs right into the kitchen in spite of their dripping blood. She bustled around trying to clean up after them and doctor them at the same time and it worked wonders to divert her attention for a few minutes from what she had just been through. He kept her busy in the kitchen for as long as he could, and by the time she was finished, there were two more police vehicles in the pasture.

Finally, she locked both dogs in the mudroom and came back into the kitchen to where Joe was still putting away her first aid box. She came to stand beside him and glanced out the window to the pasture and woods beyond. He put a hand on her shoulder and gave it a squeeze and she turned away from the window and came into his arms with a sigh. Neither one of them wanted to talk about any of it, so he just held her close and thanked God that she was safe and okay and back in his arms.

# Chapter 27

It was almost seven o'clock that night before the last law enforcement personnel left and her soldiers went back to their trailer. Murdock and Kristin had answered innumerable questions from one officer after another. Joe had wondered about the one shot that had been fired first and it turned out the stalker had tried to shoot Teal to get her out of the way.

Finally, after an excessive number of questions, Joe had put his foot down and insisted they get the information they needed from someone who had already questioned Kristin, and he helped her to escape to her studio.

Gram and the boys had come over with dinner, and when Robby had gone to let the dogs out of the mudroom, he had discovered Teal was the proud mother of seven puppies. Joe left the others to take care of things and took two plates of the chicken pot pie Gram had made during all the commotion, and went back and knocked on the door of the cabin.

When Kristin opened the door, he wasn't sure, but she seemed to be a little wary of him as he came in. It was not the reaction he wanted to see right now. He knew she was traumatized, although she was better this evening. She'd been shell-shocked all day and he'd hoped she would relax when it was just him.

She led him to his usual seat on the couch and he handed her a plate, but she set it down on the end table and went back to sit on her chair at the easel. He gave her a concerned look and asked, "Not hungry?"

"No, I'm sorry." She shook her head. "I don't mean to be ungrateful. It looks wonderful, but I'm not sure I could eat anything right now."

He took a bite of his and watched her, wondering what was going to happen here tonight. "Did you have any lunch up there today?"

"I had lunch with me, but never got it eaten before everything started."

"But you aren't hungry? You've lost so much weight in the last few weeks. Skipping meals probably isn't that great of an idea, is it?"

She shook her head again. "No, but I'm too nervous to eat."

He could understand that. It had been an awful day. "What did you do when you were a little girl to help you when you were nervous?"

She thought about that and then smiled at him. "My brother used to brush my hair for me before every dance recital. It helped a lot."

"Do you have a hair brush out here?" She shook her head no.

He put his plate beside hers and got up and went to the door. "I'll go get it. Where is it?"

"On my bathroom counter."

When he brought it back, she seemed even more nervous, and he wished he could help her find the peace she'd had late last night and this morning. She came and sat on the couch beside him and he pulled the pony tail holder off the thick braid that hung down her back and began to brush her hair.

He'd dreamed about getting his hands into her hair. It had fascinated him from the start. He'd had no sisters, and both his mother and his wife had had really short dark hair. Once he got started, he decided it was better than he'd ever imagined. It was like soft, spun corn silk and smelled like some kind of fruit. Within minutes, he was fairly hypnotized by it.

He was definitely relaxed, but he wasn't sure it was helping her. Finally, he pushed her hair aside to squeeze the muscles at the top of her shoulders. She was miserably tense and he leaned around to look at her. "Brushing didn't help much. What else can we try?"

She hesitated. "I don't know. Maybe I'll just go in and shower and get ready for bed."

"I was kind of hoping to talk to you for before you went in tonight."

She bent her head and began to fidget with her hairbrush. "I know. Honestly, I think that's why I'm nervous."

He leaned around to look into her face again. "What's that supposed to mean? Why should talking with me make you nervous?"

She shook her head and wouldn't look at him. "Well, for one thing, I'm expecting somewhat of a talking to from you, and for another, I need to talk to you about some things and I'm not sure how to go about it."

He chuckled at her. "Why do you need somewhat of a talking to from me? What have you done that you're feeling so guilty about?"

His question got a smile, but then she said, "You know, on second thought, maybe I'll beg off on this talk and go take that shower."

He put his arms around her and pulled her back against his chest. "Lighten up, Kris. I won't tease you, but don't go yet. We'll change the subject. What happened to make you so much more at peace last night and this morning?"

"I know you don't realize it, but that's not changing the subject at all."

"If it brought you peace last night and this morning, why would it make you nervous now?"

She shook her head. "*It* doesn't make me nervous. Talking to you about it makes me nervous."

This wasn't making much sense. "Okay, we'll change the subject again. To something that isn't very scary. When you told me this morning that we are going to be all right, did that mean you'll finally agree to marry me?"

Pulling out of his arms, she scooted up to turn and look back at him with wide eyes. "You call that not very scary?"

He drew her back. "Well, okay, it's scary, but it's easier for you. You're not the one who has to get up the guts to ask."

"I know." She sounded truly regretful. "I'm sorry for jerking you around."

With a voice as mild as he could make it, he said, "You sound honestly penitent. How come you're not getting ready to argue with me this time?"

"I am penitent. Honestly. And I'm not going to argue with you."

At that, he sat up and turned around so he was looking straight at her. "What?"

She couldn't even look at him and leaned back against him again and murmured, "I said I'm not going to argue."

A minute or two passed before he pushed her away and bent around to look her in the face. "You're not?" She shook her head. "Are we talking about the same thing here? Are we talking about you marrying me?" She nodded this time, and he suddenly stood up and pulled her up to stand by him. He still had to tip her chin to make her look at him.

For another long minute, he studied her, and then he gently asked, "Why are you not arguing this time?"

"Can we sit down and let me lean on you again? It was much easier to have this conversation that way."

"I don't know. I can't tell what you're thinking when your back is to me. Can't you just tell me why you're not going to argue this time?"

"I'm not going to argue with you because you were right."

"Right about what?"

She glanced away. "Right that this is what we're supposed to be doing."

"Why do you say that? How do you know?"

"Uhm. A still, small voice told me."

He paused to study her. "You don't look very happy about it. Don't you want to marry me?"

Her eyes flew to his. "I want very much to marry you. I always have."

Pulling her into a tight hug, he asked her gently, "Then what's the problem, Kristin?"

"There are two problems. I still feel terrible about the nightmares. I wish I could marry you without doing that to you and your family."

He released her to take her hands and look into her eyes and earnestly ask, "Kristin, don't you realize that with you and me in the same bed every night they're going to get a lot better?"

"I hope so. With all my heart, I hope so."

Pulling her back tight, he asked, "What's the second problem?"

She shook her head against him. "It's not a problem, but I don't even want to talk to you about it. You're going to think I'm a nut."

He rested his cheek on her hair. "I'm never going to think you're a nut, but if it's that hard for you, let's don't talk about it right now. Tell me when you're comfortable telling me." He sat back down and pulled her back again. "You never did tell me what brought you peace."

She gave a sigh. "Oh, Joe. We're going around in circles here."

"What? What did I say?"

"What brought me peace is the second thing you're going to think I'm a nut over."

"Oh." He grimaced behind her head where she couldn't see. "Sorry. What else would you like to talk about?"

She turned in his arms to face into his neck. "I don't know. You choose."

He put a hand on her silky hair. "I've been trying, honey, but so far I'm not doing so hot."

"You're doing fine. It's me who's got issues. Try one more time."

"Okay . . . " He paused for a minute. "There is something I've been meaning to ask you. Why did you ask me last night if Nicole and I ever lost a baby?" She sat up to look at him with the strangest look and he grimaced again as he asked, "Bad question?"

She got up and sat back at her easel and picked up her brush. "No, it's not a bad question. I just don't know if I dare tell you the answer. Have you ever had dreams that mean things? Important things? Things that really affect the way you think about stuff?"

This time, he was the one who hesitated. "Yeah. I had one just last night. Why?"

"I've been having the most amazing dreams the last few nights. Good dreams. Peace giving, happy dreams. It has something to do with finding out my daughters won't always have the terrible injuries they had. A couple of times since then, I've almost wondered if they were visiting me." She looked at him and her eyes shown. "They were grown up, beautiful young ladies with the sweetest faces."

"That sounds wonderful. Why would I think you were a nut because of a dream as nice as that?"

She hesitated and then instead of answering his question, she asked one of her own, "What did you dream about last night?"

"Uhm. I don't know if I can answer that without embarrassing us both. You'll think I'm the nut."

She looked up at him, a little lost. "Why would I think you're a nut?"

He looked at her steadily. "Because my dream involved having children with you. Beautiful, little girls who look like Gabriel with long, dark hair." Her eyes widened. "Sorry, but you asked. It was a great dream. I didn't want to wake up from it." She just kept looking at him and then leaned down next to her easel and picked up a canvas and handed it to him.

"Did they look anything like that?" He looked at the painting she handed him and then back at her, stunned. It was the same one that had so intrigued him before, that he thought had sparked his dream. "My grown daughters were sending those two to me in my dreams. They've been back to visit me several times."

Surprised, he looked back at her and asked, "Your daughters, or these two?"

"Both. I've been unbelievably confused. I've spent days riding, trying to figure out what to do about you. I loved you, but I didn't want to harm you with my dragons, but I wasn't sure I could walk away from you.

"After that last bad dream, I knew I had to leave, but it was killing me. I kept asking God to help me know how to walk away, but all that was happening was I wanted to be with you more. I was waiting for Him to answer me in the wind, with the answer my head came up with."

She nodded at the painting. "Then these two showed up. With the most amazing peace. You want to talk about confused! So, I went back to God and asked again, and last night, finally, I knew for sure what I was supposed to be doing about you. I finally recognized the still, small voice for what it was. It was a feeling, not a logical decision."

She gave him a shy smile. "Then I had to figure out how to talk to you about it. Have I ever told you how grateful I am that you're so patient with me?"

He got up and came over to her. "Do you think you could ever face having more children of your own again?"

She nudged the easel with her foot so it turned toward him. She'd been creating a painting of Gabriel with a tiny, new baby with dark hair and a miniature mouth that looked exactly like her own. "Somehow, I get the impression I'm supposed to face that idea." She couldn't look at him again and whispered, "I've been so worried about how I was going to tell you."

Quietly, he turned to her. "Can I ask you a personal question?" She nodded. "How did you feel when this baby came to visit you?"

Shyly, she admitted, "Like I didn't want to wake up and lose that sweet feeling."

He took both of her hands and pulled her up and into his arms. He searched her eyes and then bent to give her the most gentle of kisses. "Will you marry me, Kristin?"

She didn't hesitate for a second. "Yes, I will."

"How soon?"

Still looking into his eyes, she asked, "Would this evening be too soon?"

"Probably. We have to have a license and an official."

"How about tomorrow, then?"

He wrapped her in a hug. "Perfect." He held her tightly for a few minutes.

Finally, he asked, "Do you think you can eat now?"

**The End**

# About the author

Jaclyn M. Hawkes grew up with 6 sisters, 4 brothers and any number of pets. (It was never boring!) She got a bachelor's degree, had a career and traveled extensively before settling down to her life's work of being the mother of four magnificent and sometimes challenging children. She loves shellfish, Meat Lover's pizza, the out-of-doors, the youth, and hearing her children laugh. She and her adorable husband, their younger children, and their happy dog, now live in a mountain valley in northern Utah, where it smells like heaven and kids still move sprinkler pipe.

To learn more about Jaclyn, visit
www.jaclynmhawkes.com.